BLINDFELL

By T. L. ASHTON JR

Order this book online at www.trafford.com
or email orders@trafford.com

Most Trafford titles are also available at major online book retailers.

Note for Librarians: A cataloguing record for this book is available from Library
and Archives Canada at www.collectionscanada.ca/amicus/index-e.html

Printed in Victoria, BC, Canada.

ISBN: 9781-4269-1199-6 (soft cover)
ISBN: 9781-4269-1200-9 (hard cover)
ISBN: 9781-4269-1201-6 (eBook)

*Our mission is to efficiently provide the world's finest, most comprehensive
book publishing service, enabling every author to experience success.
To find out how to publish your book, your way, and have it available
worldwide, visit us online at www.trafford.com*

Trafford rev. 09/21/09

 www.trafford.com

North America & international
toll-free: 1 888 232 4444 (USA & Canada)
phone: 250 383 6864 ♦ fax: 812 355 4082

To my loving family and friends who were there during the crisis my mother Arnita, my father Tommy Sr.

My siblings Leeneen, Ronald, & Tina

My children Tommy III, Michael, Tyrek

My wife Le

Lubirder (Granny)

My dear friend Paul Perrow

PFFCU

Bobby & Kim

And most of all My God

Thank you

Psalm 19:14 Let *the words of my mouth, and the meditation of my heart, be acceptable in thy sight, O LORD, my strength, and my redeemer.*

Contents

"In the beginning we cherish the encouragement of our family and friends and are fueled by the dissuasion of our foes."- T. L. Ashton Jr.

".... in the end, we will remember not the words of our enemies but rather the silence of our friends."- M. L. King Jr.

Introduction

I incurred many different motivating factors before writing this novel; a fear of God being foremost to all and success being another. There were others also love, truth, obedience and faith but my God remained the greatest of them all. I wrote out of love because of two reasons. First being the love of all who may have suffered some ordeal similar to my own and secondly, for the love of a woman who inspired me even though she was not there physically during the rudiment stages of its conception. I am grateful for her sporadic calls of concern which made me think of her all the more. She moved to Memphis and I knew without any doubt that she would succeed in whatever endeavor she desired. She motivated me to press on and to attain that which I wanted.

Truth inspired me because in a world of deceptive, insensitive relationships, truth was all I had to base my encounters on and like love it is the one thing that remains untainted if given and received with a pure heart. The two are alike in many ways; they are always appropriate no matter what circumstances you are faced with. Just as the truth sets things straight, love also makes our path straight. To seek truth is to find love and to find love is to have sought for truth which no one can do without.

Often I would have to place pen and paper aside because embellishment would sometimes seem more appealing to write, but truth and my love for God would not allow me to just conjure up any fictional thoughts and insert them at will. I wanted it to be what God wanted it to be and self reliance would make it impossible to do. Writing when He had inspired me to write and ceasing when He had commanded me to cease assured me of the things He wanted revealed.

Everything that you are about to read could have possibly happened to anyone.

Or could it? Not a fabricated paradox of fictitious true lies, but a deliberate meaningful reflection of what is the truth. I can only declare that in all my doing that God remains true. History has proven that procrastination has abated many endeavors of the human spirit. After contemplating the idea for some years now, I feel compelled to write this. Not to receive glory and praise from man, but to give glory and praise to the Son of Man. "Glory to God."

Relationships are not productive unless they become personal. It was not until I surrendered completely to Christ that I was able to see growth in my personal and spiritual life. Before then every choice I made, every step that I took was a reproachable stumble from the truth; a spiraling descent into an abyss of darkness and consuming death which seemed to have no end. During the times I was out of communion with God my creative writing skills reflected just that, a dark and gloomy outlook on life.

No desire to carry on, no hope in what tomorrow would bring; a psychological bombardment of lingering doom and despair. Least I should boast, in my current profession I have witnessed the results first hand, time and time again the calculated and premeditated suicides of people who felt that they could not handle the circumstances they were faced with, and that was just it they couldn't, not alone. The love ones so near to us in their overburdened lives of their own sometimes fail to notice the pain until it is too late. Thanks be to God in all of His infinite wisdom for loving and caring parents; a mother who raised me to fear God and a father who instilled a social fear for authority.

My purpose for writing this book is simple: One to help someone who may have no hope, or at times may feel dissuaded to persevere; and to give encouragement to you and proclaim that Jesus Christ, a friend that sticks closer than a brother can and will see you through. If you would do as He told Jarius, a ruler in the synagogue, in the fifth chapter of the book of Mark, "Do not be afraid; only believe."

ONE

Finding Joy in Paradise

Unlike the majority of my relationships when I entered into the union of the body of Christ I knew this one thing that He is consistent just as the Father which is in heaven is consistent. He proclaims this very truth in the third chapter of the book of Malachi.

"For I am the Lord, I do not change;
Therefore you are not consumed, O sons of Jacob.
Yet from the days of your father you have gone away from My
  ordinance
And have not kept them. Return to Me, and I will return to you,"
Says the Lord of host. (Malachi 3:6 & 7).

I have to admit I would have never received this revelation about God in the world. I had to surrender to Jesus in order to find such hope, and I thank the Lord for not hiding Himself from me. Nevertheless, this is not the joy of which I speak; this joy was found one night after the wedding of my oldest sibling Leeneen, March 17, 1992 to be exact. She had found joy in a man she had met while in junior high school, and I am proud to say after some sixteen plus years they are still happily married today; living productive Christian lives with one offspring which they have instructed and trained to be fearful of God.

That night some sixteen years ago God had not entered my mind not to mention my heart, and the lifestyle that followed was evident; one of chasing short skirts and pretty faces. The more gullible the prey the less exertion I had to invoke in order to carry out my sinister plot. In all of his ingenious schemes to get me to walk contrary to the Spirit of God, Satan allowed me to view that which is immoral as moral and that which is moral as immoral. A tactic he employed even in the beginning to cause Adam and Eve the serenity that they had in the Garden of Eden. A tactic that is evident even today as he goes to and fro upon the earth seeking, searching, and looking for whom he may destroy. All Satan needs is the opportunity to interject or plant the seed of discord the flesh then takes it from there; the bible tells us that there is nothing good in me that is in my flesh. So basically what happened was that the seed of corruption was planted and the flesh nourished it and sin took flight.

Recalling that night I can vividly remember during the wedding reception making the statement during a toast that I proposed to the newly wedded couple, "To Leeneen and Larry I wish you all the best in life and may you be happy and prosper, but as for me I'm never getting married," or something to that effect. Everyone in the assembly erupted with laughter. Two hours later a lifelong friend of mine named Derek accompanied me to a local club called Paradise. I was still arrayed in that evening attire a white tuxedo with a tail; my present wife and a cousin of mine Felicia tagged along. Le La, my girlfriend at the present, had been my prey a time or two, but tonight she was not on the menu. Although she was a very pretty girl I was not in the mood for the same entry. There was fresh meat to be hunted and I was hungry. I strolled into the club and all eyes were on me. Clean is not a word I would choose to define my appearance. I was in a word immaculate and I knew it; it exuded from the fifty dollar bottle of cologne I had just sprayed on, it dripped from my pores and my speech which conveyed a sense of conceit and arrogance. Satan had led me to believe that I had it going on; another tactic he uses in his arsenal of weapons to bring about the destruction of mankind. Needless to say I didn't know then as I know now that no weapon formed against me would prosper.

Some two hours or so into my dance of delight I saw her; she was stunning absolutely breathtaking. She was a possible victim whom I wanted to clinch my talons into and simply ravage for my evening consumption. To my dismay it didn't happen that way and like an inexperienced prowler returning to his den after an unsuccessful hunt, I returned to the bar for replenishment of more liquid courage. At this point I am not looking to get inebriated, but to just achieving that edge that would settle me and give me that confidence I thought I needed to approach this beauty. Little did I know that Proverbs chapter 20 and verse one says to us that *wine is a mocker, intoxicating drink which arouses brawling, and whoever is led astray by it is not wise.* Well no fighting broke out that night, and being intoxicated was not an issue at this point I was only interested in having a good time and getting what I had come for. After visiting the bar a couple of times with my friend Derek and settling at a nearby table, I obtained a glimpse of Joy.

My present wife, (then girl friend) and my cousin had joined us at the table, but I was not at all distracted by their conversation or their presence. I had found Joy and nothing else in the club mattered. At that point I wanted nothing more than to have Joy. The place could have been set a blaze; I was not taking my eyes off of this newly found jewel.

Drinking was no longer a necessity because I wanted all of my wits about me. Not to mention the scenery was intoxicating enough as I watched her sitting with her girlfriends smoking on what I now know was a Benson & Hedges menthol cigarette. She was a mythical goddess, a rare Asian artifact, a porcelain geisha, the objet d'art. "How could something so beautiful not be married?" I asked myself. "Tommy Tommy! Dude what the hell is you looking at?" Derek asked. "Man I think I just found my wife," I replied. The scene was broken by the boyish laughter of my now severely smashed friend. "Man you're crazy," he slurred. "Man I'm serious that's my wife," I insisted. "You gonna try and hook up with her?" he asked. "Hell yeah," I replied.

"Now all I have to do is maneuver my way over and not make a fool of myself," I said to myself. "Don't trip, watch your step, get yourself together," I said nervously coaching myself. "What if she just straight dis me or laugh at me, what then," I thought.

"Yeah you've had a few drinks, but you can do this "T" just relax," I said. "Hhhh Hhh breath check, it's okay." "Here we go she sees me coming can't turn back now." The music was deafening as I strolled up to her fretfully. "HEY!" I shouted. "HEY!" she replied. "I was wondering could I give you a dollar for one of your cigarettes," I asked. "You don't have to buy it I'll give you one," she replied. "Thanks," I yelled. She nodded with approval. As I stood there I could sense her friends checking me out. Not in an arrogant or conceited way, but they looked on with acceptance as to say to their girlfriend go for it girl. I felt esteemed in their presence and higher than any alcohol could have ever made me feel. "What's your name?" I asked. "Joy," she replied. "That's pretty," I yelled. "Thank you what's yours?" she asked. "Tommy," I replied.

I finally put together enough courage of my own to ask her to dance. "Would you do me the pleasure of dancing with me?" I asked. "Sure but let's wait until a full song comes on," she replied.

"Oh my God she's gonna allow me to be with her for a full song," I said to myself.

Guys you know the ordeal when a lady is not really interested in you she short changes you. She'd give you that last few seconds of the song as not to be rude, but in her mind she is thinking when this song is over I'll tell him I've got to go to the restroom, and I'll just disappear in the crowd. The ones who are really smooth in the club have got this down to a fine art; I called it the old "DF" maneuver the dash and fade tactic, she dashes off to the restroom and fades into the crowd. I could have sworn while in the club on one occasion I had a Shelia pull the old "DF" on me; she must have had a change of clothes in her purse. I'm walking around looking for her in a white blouse and she had changed her whole wardrobe I was like damn girl. Needless to say pursuing a woman of such evasive strategies was not my intent; remember the easier they were the less work I had to do.

We stayed on the floor which seemed like forever; I implored the DJ to maintain what he was doing because it gave me more time to make a better assessment of what I was surely about to put my arms around just as soon as he slowed the music down. Her hair smelled almost tropical, a curly autumn color; you could tell by her countenance that she was of Asian descent. Her body structure indicated that one of her parents was Afro-American. She had the dimensions of a sister, she was fine. A smile like a well pampered queen and her eye although contacts complimented her completely. "Finally a slow song," I thought to myself. A lot of women don't care to slow dance for whatever reason. Without saying a word, without any persuasion at all she stood quickly as to bestow the very thing I had come there to receive. "Would you care to slow dance?" I asked. "Sure," she replied. The name of the song was one I would never forget ("Let me come inside"). I stepped to her, grabbed her around her waist and drew her close to me. With no resistance she melted into my arms; not knowing her thoughts I was very content with my own. Damn she felt good

I thought to myself. Her skin was that of a soft rose petal; Clichéd I know, but true.

As the night grew on I found myself thinking of nothing else. The final stage of sealing this evening was to get her phone number; yet I didn't want to come off as being too aggressive. So I did the one thing I knew would prove as such I gave her my number on a bar napkin. With this suave move I allotted for only two outcomes; one she would not call me and I would feel I had lost nothing, two she would call me and I could convince her that we were meant for each other. So the ball was in her court. The napkin simply stated Tommy 631-****call me.

At home that night in my recently acquired bachelor pad I could not bring myself to slumber. I had found Joy and it was hard to sleep. Visions of brighter days were all I could imagine. Meeting her somehow inspired me to write:

A Rose Petal's Confession

A rose has many petals that embrace a treasure inside;
Time and the elements coaxed them to unwind.
But a fool the petals are not as they reveal the world her
    treasure;
A gift from her that signifies I am worthy of your pleasure.
I would gaze at your modest beauty and savor your imbuing
    scent,
And share the thought with someone else the joy that you
    present.
And the thorns are not to discourage you from touching or
    lavishing her petals;
They are just a reminder that they protect a precious
    treasure.

If given the chance in my vineyard I would embrace your
     treasure inside;
Neither time nor would the elements coax me to unwind.
And a fool I would not be; yet I would know of your
     treasure;
A gift from you to signify I am worthy of your pleasure.
To gaze, to savor, to share your lovely scent;
To share you with the entire world and what a rose presents.

That next day was Sunday and I went to church not because I
wanted to but because my mom had admonished me several times
since I had left the confines of her house. "Give the Lord some of
your time," she would say. I think King Solomon said it best in
the book of Ecclesiastes eleventh chapter ninth verse: *Rejoice, O
young man, in your youth, and let your heart cheer you in the days of
your youth; Walk in the ways of your heart, And in the sight of your
eyes; But know that for all these God will bring you to judgment.* So
now I warn you reader as King Solomon also warned his readers
in the following chapter and the first verse: *Remember now your
creator in the days of your youth, before the difficult days come, and
the years draw near when you say, "I have no pleasure in them."*
     I did not expect to hear from Joy that day although it would
have been great. I thought that she was playing the same game I
would have played if she would have given me her phone number;
the old waiting game, not wanting too seem to eager or desperate.
We've all been there at one point and time in our lives. I went
on to work and dropped by the tuxedo rental shop to return my
tux. The day at the fire station was not one of particular interest
sort of mediocre.
     Twenty four hours to spend in this joint and the only thing
that could possibly prolong it was the thoughts of her not calling.
One of the things I used to do was give females my mother's
phone number that way my baby sister Tina would answer the
phone which sort of threw them off; if they would call back that
showed that they were not afraid of a little opposition. The shift
was finally over I had gotten off at 3:20 or so Monday afternoon

and ventured over to my mom's house where she broke the news. "A young lady name Joy called for you," my mother announced. "She called you three times," Tina added. I let out a scream like a little school girl. "The first time was at 6:00 Sunday evening, she called at about 11:00 last night and once again this morning," my mom instructed. My mom had given her the run down of why I could not be reached. Seems she had inquired about the timeframe in which I was working; mom took the liberty of telling her that I was a fireman and I would not be getting home until later Monday afternoon. With that being said, Joy felt inclined to leave her phone number. "Where did you meet her?" my sister asked. "At Club Paradise Saturday night," I explained. "She sounds real nice," my mother said. "Momma she is the most attractive thing I've ever seen in my life," I confessed. "Momma she's the kind of woman that I would burn my little black book for," I added. "Mmmmm," Tina commented. "She must look good for you to give that up," added Tina. "Yeah she does," I replied. "Looks aren't everything," my mom implied. "Beauty can only be skin deep," she went on to say. To hear her say that made me not at all reluctant in my pursuit; if nothing else it drove me even harder to make this woman mine. I knew with every being in my now nasal flared body that if my mother got a chance to meet her that she too would be captivated by her beauty. So it happened, I finally decided to call this mysterious mythical Mona Lisa. As I dialed her number a feeling of doubt came over me. I questioned in my mind if she was actually sober when I gave her my number and would she even remember me at all. "It's ringing," I squealed. "Hello!" the voice cried from the other end with a very strong oriental accent. "Awe yes may I speak with Joy please?" "Oke you hold on I get her;" the few seconds that passed felt like hours. "Hello!" the voice called. "Hi is this Joy?" "This is she." "This is Tommy I gave you my number the other night at the club." "I remember you." My God she sounds so good. "Why were you in that tuxedo that night? I and my girlfriends were talking about you all night." Beads of sweat accumulated and the biggest lump

I could have ever swallowed clogged my throat. "Excuse me," I asked.

"Oh it wasn't anything bad we thought you were performing or something we were wondering who you were," she explained. "Oh!" I said with a bit of relief. "I was in my sister's wedding and rather than go home and change me and my homeboy came as we were," I enlightened her. "You are a hard person to reach; I called you three times," she declared. "What do you do?" she asked. "I worked for the fire department," I boasted. Now I know every man who has the privilege of donning a uniform has at some point and time in their career used the fact that they were aware that a woman loves a man in uniform; not all women but the majority would agree. We continued with some small talk as to what brought her out that night, where was her man and things of that nature. Then she asked "Do you stay with your mom?" No, I stated defensively. "So why did you give me her phone number?" she asked as if to catch me in a lie. "Well I have my own place, but my phone is not on yet," I explained. "When I get my number will you call me?" "Yeah if you give it to me," she said. "Say those last four words you just said to me again three times," I asked. "What four words?" "Think about the last four words you just said and say them to me again," I teased. "What give it to me?" she asked. "That's five I just want to hear four," I taunted. "Give it to me! Give it to me! Give it to me!" she said. "Oooo yeah that's the four I was looking for." "Oh my god you are so silly!" she laughed. Her laughter was a delight like the music we had slow danced to nights before, she actually had a sense of humor. She liked that I could make her laugh. That was our first of many shared laughs, and to have heard her was to have loved her. "So where do you stay?" she asked. "On Prentiss street right off of Midway," I answered. "I know where that is." "So when are you coming to see me?" I blurted out in disbelief. "That's up to you," she said to my surprise. "Well they are delivering my furniture tomorrow I should be finished painting by that time and maybe we could go out to see a movie and get something to eat," I suggested. "That sounds good, what time so I don't have you waiting?" she asked. "Whenever it's convenient for you I'll most definitely wait for you I'm off this week," I replied. "Is seven-thirty okay?" she asked. "That's fine with me," I said. "Okay well I'll see you tomorrow." "Okay bye," I said with regret. "Bye-bye," she replied. When I had placed the receiver down I had a radiance about me that was very evident; both my mom and my sister seemed to be as elated as I was over the news that I had found Joy. Tomorrow was an immense day nothing could damper the feelings I was experiencing; for I was on cloud nine and the heavens would be my playground as I prepared for a night of blissful dreams.

Tuesday morning I was awakened with Joyful thoughts. I had slept like a pacified infant and I awaited the opportunity to see this Asian queen. The entire day I walked with an heir of confidence and assurance that everything would go as planned. Contrary to Murphy's Law it did; the paint was dry, my errands were complete, the furniture movers had come and gone as scheduled, the only thing undone was my attire for the evening's festivities. Contrary to popular belief men do agonize over such things as making an excellent first impression. In the course of everything happening that day, my friend Derek happened to come by at about six o'clock or so with inquiries of my plans for the evening, in all of my excitement I had forgotten to inform him of the news. To say he was enthused was an understatement. He marveled at the thought that I had talked to her since our meeting at the club. Like gossiping hens the two of us rekindled the events that followed after Joy and I met. "So what are you two going to do?" "Well I invited her to come over to see my place and then we discussed going to the movies and getting something to eat," I stated. "Straight dog," he grinned. "Man I remember you talking to that girl, but I was so messed up that night I can't remember what she looks like," he added. "You wanna see her?" I asked. "Hell yeah I know she was cute but I don't remember the details," he went on to say. Don't get cynical; women you do it all the time when you meet a new guy. They promenade him before their girlfriends to get the four-one-one on his "ass-sets" or any blemishes he may have as to get a second opinion, but nevertheless that was the plan for the moment.

At the time I was driving an eighty-eight, four door, gray Cutlass Cierra Brougham, chromed out, low profile tires, screaming sound system it was clean and I knew it. For no apparent reason I rode with Derek rather than driving my own car. He was sporting an eighty- eight, two door, black, Mazda hatch back, kicking sounds but in need of a washing terribly. Not leaving anything to chance the two of us got on the way not detouring for any last minute errands and the likes. We arrived at her home at exactly seven-twenty nine, and when I rang the doorbell it was exactly seven-thirty. And like a good girl should she was promptly awaiting my arrival. As she exited her mom's home I was greeted with the warmest smile and hug I could have ever received, and it was given and received enthusiastically. "My goodness you're stunning," I complimented. "Thank you, you look nice yourself." "Thank you I need to change though," I replied. "Your hair is beautiful," I added. "Why thank you," she smiled. "I thought it was like an auburn color though," I inquired. "It was until yesterday." "I wanted a change do you like it?" "Yes it's great," I interjected. "Oooo look at your eyes!" "They're contacts," she added "I know but they look so mysterious; what color are they originally?" I asked. "A dark brown." "You must let me look into them one day," I requested. "Okay," she smiled. She was adorned with a pair of stonewashed jeans and a matching blouse; as for her physical build she fit in her denim well, nice round thick rear I thought as I tried not to undress her with my eyes. I could not believe how beautiful this woman was. Her hair was jet black and pulled up in a wrap with the long pin or rod that the geisha girls wear in their hair to keep it in place. We journeyed to our awaiting chariot and the look I received when she saw the third wheel sitting in the driver's seat was one I would not forget. "Joy this is Derek my best friend, Derek this is Joy the young lady I met at the club Saturday night." "Hey, how you doing Joy?" "Fine how are you?" she asked. "I'm fine, damn Tommy she is fine," he injected. "So ya'll have been talking about me huh?" "Well I just explained to him how you looked and as words were not enough he had to see you for himself," I explained. "Naw we ain't like that but after he told me about you just like he said I had to see," he implied. "Liar," she smirked. We all laughed. "So Tommy you don't have a car?" " No I don't have one Derek is gonna take us to the movies, then come get us and take us to dinner and pick us up and take us home at the end of the date."

The look of humiliation on her face was astounding and the caper would have been a success, but to my dismay Derek could not keep his composure. "Man you so crazy! That's wrong man," he laughed. "What?" Joy asked. "You have a car?" "Yeah I'm just messing with "D." "Oh because I was about to say take me back home," she snickered. "I was just sitting here thinking this man done came and picked me up and doesn't have a car, that ain't funny Tommy." "So why are you laughing?" I asked. "Because you're so silly I was starting to feel sorry for you," she giggled. "Hell," she continued in her laughter. "Boy you're crazy as hell," Derek chuckled. That was another one of many comical moments.

A sense of humor is very essential in a relationship; without it bonding is weakened. Laughter may sometimes be the remedy for a multitude of problems encountered in a union of such. It lessens sorrow and has the power of making grievous situation merry. Humor is a bitter sweet remedy; when used correctly it has the ability of creating unforgettable memories or causing irreparable damage. That was one of the things I loved about finding Joy she made me laugh; not that it doesn't exist today there is a lot of laughter in my days now. The scurrying of little feet running about, the things my young boys sometime say in their innocence are all I can sometime manage. Not to mention those times when I am with friends they are memories I'm delighted to be a part of.

Derek dropped the two of us off at my place and he jetted, and the two of us were now left alone for the first time. There was a sense of anxiety in the atmosphere. You could cut the apprehension with a knife; yet I was inclined to make her feel comfortable in my humble abode. We had entered through the upstairs entrance and reached the living room. "Well this is it not much, but this is home for me right now," I explained. "So the bedroom is downstairs?" she asked. "Yeah," I replied. So I gave her the extensive but brief tour of my bachelor pad and she was pleased with the modest but well adorned appearance of my place and complimented me on my taste. "Did you do all of this yourself"? She asked. "Yeah my mom helped some, but the majority of it was all my idea." "Well make yourself at home, I'm going to take a shower and get dressed I'll be done in a few minutes okay," I added. "Okay take your time," she replied. During the time I was in the shower the only thing I could think was I can't believe she is here. "Man she looks so good," I thought to myself. I'll get cleaned up and make this awkward but necessary trip past her to the downstairs bedroom. So being the gentleman I was I prepared my underclothes so that when I left the bathroom I would not be exposed to her as to insinuate any sexual connotations that I may have felt for her. Regardless of my past relationships I was going to resist any sexual confrontation for the moment. So I got dressed downstairs while she was upstairs watching television, sprayed on my most intoxicating cologne and proceeded upstairs. "You clean up nicely," she said. "Well thank you that's sweet of you," I responded. "So where are we going first?" she asked. "Well I thought we'd go and check out a movie," I suggested, "That's fine," she added. The night was indeed a delightful one; we seemed to agree on everything.

Now I would be lying if I said I remembered what we went to see that night, and for some time I had even thought of calling her to discuss the details of our most enchanting evening. But in life I have come to realize that there are some things better left uncharted, some things better left unsaid. This I do remember

I did not want the night to end. I wish that I could remember so that I might have it in my mental memoirs as a testament of times that I once held so near to my heart. Not to mention that I feel obligated to enlighten you of that event but the truth of the matter is my thoughts of it are deleted. My only logic for this basis is that I was totally unavailable, entirely consumed by her and to a sickening degree I worshiped her. This is also the reason I feel obliged to write this manuscript. I feel that in sharing that which God has allowed me to experience, that which He has brought me through and delivered me from may benefit someone and inhibit them from making the same mistakes that I made; due to walking in the flesh and not in the Spirit of God. Once again I give God all the glory and praise for allowing me to share with you.

The times were good and I learned through our frequent conversations that she had a little boy; we'll call him Corey. And when she had allowed me to meet him he took to me like a young duckling in water. He was a very sweet kid and the time spent with him was just as pleasant as being with his mother. He was four when the two of us started spending days on end with each other. One of the most memorable things I can recall about young Corey was that he had a hard time pronouncing things that started with the letter "W". On one occasion when I had told him that we were not able to go to the park that day he inquired "Yhy?" Sort of like the way my smallest son today has a hard time with the word yellow; for some reason it comes out as lellow. And when he says it I'm often reminded of young Corey. I had often wondered why his father had not been around, the boy was never a troubling child; just in need of some fatherly attention. The two of them made me so happy when we were all together; I cared for him as he was my own. I helped him with little things such as learning to tie his shoes, his speech, writing and such. So the bond that we had was of a father and son; in a word I loved him.

There was a time when I had felt so sure of the Joy that I had found that I sought nothing more than to introduce her to the other woman in my life my mother. She had heard about her on several occasions, and the truth is it seemed almost conceited to mention her so much. "You need to slow down," my mother would warn. What did she know she and my father had been separated for some twenty years or so. To this day I wished I had taken note of those words of advice from my prudent parent. But like so many of the children of this generation I knew everything; I knew what was best for me or did I? Apparently not or I would not be writing this manuscript as a testament of those things suffered. Knowing what I know now, children are to obey their parents in the Lord, for this is well pleasing to the Lord. I could not grasp this concept because I mentioned earlier that I had not yet surrendered to Christ.

Looking back on those times we seemed to have it all; I remember telling my family and friends that I found Joy in paradise and have been catching hell every since. I can honestly say that the two of us had never prayed with one another. Neither had we gone to church together. Come to think of it we eloped and were married eleven months after we had met, but more importantly we did not have a personal relationship with the person that mattered the most to sustain us and complete our union and that person was Christ Jesus.

Before one of our outings we stopped by my mother's house and this was the first time she had seen Joy. "Mom, Tina this is Joy," I announced with great pride. "Joy this is my mom and my lil'sister Tina. "Well I've heard a lot about you Joy," my mom stated. "All good I hope," Joy said as she looked at me with a smile of total embarrassment. "Oh nothing but good things," my mom explained. "So how did y'all meet?" my sister asked although I know I had told her a while ago. I think they were just feeling her out to see what type of person she really was. "He didn't tell you," Joy exclaimed. "Child I was sitting with my girlfriends at the club minding my own business and I saw Tommy come in; we thought he was performing or something. My girlfriends all asked who he was; I said, "Child I don't know." And a little later on he came over and offered me a dollar for a cigarette and we've been talking every since." "I wasn't gonna call him at first, but the way he gave me his phone number and told me to call him I thought we could just be friends." she continued.

She wasn't really shy at all around them, she talked with my mom as though she had known her all her life and in some way that was true. As my mom continued in her investigation she said "You know you sho' do look familiar, what's your last name?" my mom asked. "Johnes," Joy replied. "Isn't your father's name Jo?" "Yes mam," she replied. "Because your mom isn't from here is she?" my mom asked. "No Mam," Joy answered. "She's from Korea." "For the life of me I can't remember her name I know your mom," my mom exclaimed. "Her name is Duangrat (du- an- grat) but everybody call her Dang." Joy explained. "Yeah y'all stayed on Harper St; it use to be a little Asian woman with two pretty little girls in a green house. I would see her and the girls almost every day." "That was us," Joy answered. "Are you serious?" my mom asked. "Yes mam, my grandparents still lives over there." "No they don't," my mom expressed in disbelief "What is your grandparent's name?" "Willie and Johnetta Holms." "Girl no it isn't!" "Yes mam we use to stay over there when my mom would go to work," Joy added. "Where's your sister?" my mother asked. By now I'm sitting there stunned in disbelief while my mother and future wife are going down memory lane. I was tripping at all the information that my mom had gotten in just under twenty minutes or less. Women are like that I guess (no disrespect intended) they love to talk, and the two of them had much to say.

Now Joy had an older sister named Mahlisa and one of the unique things about these two sisters was that they had the same middle name Suwattanee (su-wat-ta-nee); it means "good woman" I later learned. "She stays here in town I see her everyday," Joy explained. "I see you still have that long black pretty hair," my mom complimented. "Thank you I wanna cut it but Tommy don't want me to," Joy said. "Why?" my mom asked. "It's getting too long and too hot?" Joy added. "What are you two doing today?"

my sister inquired. "You know my friend Eric I was in the Guard
with, well he invited us to a barbeque so we'll go hang out over
there for a while." "That sounds nice," Tina added. "Well y'all
have a nice time and Joy it was great to meet you," both my now
zealous family members acknowledged.

At this point Joy and I had been seeing each other for two
months and everything was peachy we wanted nothing more
than to spend every moment of the day together. And we did.
Whenever the two of us were not at work we were at my place:
cuddling, kissing and just enjoying the day with each other. Now
don't get me wrong the conversation of sex did come up but I
truly and honestly wanted it to be something mutual. Yeah right,
I know some of my readers may attest, but the truth of the matter
was I didn't want her to feel pressured, nor did I want to dissuade
her. I felt when she was ready she would initiate the affair and I
would wait with horny anticipation and all.

Now this barbeque that the two of us attended convened at
four o'clock or so. We arrived at this nice apartment where we
all assembled on a beautiful picnic area with a volleyball court,
swimming area, and a great view of the lake. The scene was very
memorable; so much in fact that I later moved to the area, but I'll
tell you that story shortly. Let me conclude with the present. As
soon as we walked in I could feel the eyes of everyone, especially
all the males piercing me in my back and I knew it was because of
the jewel that came in holding my hand. We acquainted ourselves
with the other guests there and then we strolled over to the
beverage table to get my lady and me a drink "E what's going on
baby?" I said in greeting my buddy Eric. "Nothing what's up with
you cuz, boy how the hell have you been I missed you kid"? Eric
replied. "Damn who the hell is this?" he asked in his candid and
embarrassing tone. Eric was cool we were roomies during Desert
Storm; we looked out for each other and if no one in this place had
my back including Joy I knew he would. "What's your name?"
Eric asked Joy. "What are you Japanese, Chinese or something?"
he continued. His frankness was amusing to Joy she could only

laugh at his antics, and just before she opened her mouth to respond to his interrogation I pulled a joke of my own. "Wait!" I calmly said to Joy. "You may speak." During the laughter of Eric's interrogation and the sum of my punchline we all erupted in this explosion of laughter that could hardly be contained. "Boy you're crazy as hell," Eric said as he/we continued in our laugh. "I'm just playing baby," I said trying to allow the laugh to subside. "Eric this is Joy, Joy Eric." "Boy you're sick," Eric added. "Man let me introduce y'all to a couple of my people; this is Tasha my lady." "Hi!" Tasha said. "Hey," we both replied. We were then introduced to the host of the affair a guy named Randall and that's when the drama began. This guy was convinced that he was going to take my girl it was evident in the way he introduced himself. "Hey Randall this is my homeboy Tommy and his lady friend Joy," Eric explained.

Now I would have recognized and respected the relationship of any couple at this event, but this guy was relentless. His boldness and inquiries were aggressive and rude; he would direct his questions to my Joy as though I was not even standing there. "So this is your man?" he asked Joy. Yes! She replied confidently. "Are you happy?" he continued. Yes! She reaffirmed to him. "Hey! Hey! Hey! Man," Eric interrupted before I could even open my mouth. "Didn't I tell you that this was his lady," "My bad dog you can't blame a nigga for trying," he replied half- heartedly. "Respect my boy's shit," Eric added. Although this was not his last attempt my Joy stood steadfast and declined his every advancement. Now I know it's not in good character to gloat but she made me feel that way when we were together; she made me feel like the conqueror of great spoils and everyone was after my treasure, one I was willing to stand for and defend. In my own chivalrous way I did just that and I think it incorporated a sense of alpha distinction between those there. Nevertheless, I became very irritated while playing volleyball when he was allegedly trying to assist her with her serve. Joy had never seen me that infuriated. After telling him that I would kick his ass all of his advancement ceased and we continued with our game and the evening was a blast with plenty of laughter and fun.

Later that evening at my place I became upset with Joy for being so damn attractive and engaging and I even confronted her about it. But there was nothing she could apologize for she was just being herself and I could not fault her at all. After pondering the thoughts of that guy with his hands on her I became jealous; sad thing was my jealousy was not warranted. She informed me that I didn't have anything to worry about, she also conveyed to me how much she cared for me. She not only told me; she showed me and without any persuasion from me she instructed me to go take a shower and to go downstairs and relax. I did just as my princess had commanded me to do. While lying down there in my dungeon I was comforted by her words she had just spoken. When suddenly I heard the shower running and I thought to myself, no way. She had a small black bag that she had managed to conceal which contained all the things a young lady would need in order to spend the night. I laid there with the lights dimmed thinking this is not about to happen; the shower stopped running; she dressed upstairs and she slowly and gracefully appeared before me. I watched as her still moist feet landed on the steps below, her legs glistening from the freshly applied oil on her skin and her torso adorned with a black lace see through negligee left no mistaking of what her body looked like. Her hair now down; I had never seen it so sinuous or wet. She was everything I had imagined she would be and more. "I can't see I don't have my contacts in," she said. "Why did you take them out?" I asked. "Because you told me that you wanted to look into my eyes someday," she added. "My God you are so beautiful," I commented. "Don't," she said "You're making me blush I don't like my body." "Don't be ridiculous come here," I instructed her. When she laid next to me her scent was magnificent; her body just the right warmth. All the passion that I had in me she was about to experience for the first of many times. "Go slow it's been awhile since I've made love," she instructed me. And I had every intention of doing just as she had commanded. I had patiently waited for this moment I wanted it to be pleasurable for her; something she would enjoy and long for when we were apart. As the night went on we were both satisfied with each other's performance; passion, love, and desires were fulfilled and in the rapture of it all she nestled even closer to me and in the most angelic voice I had ever heard she said to me, "I love you Tommy no matter what." It didn't sound rehearsed it didn't feel awkward; it felt right, perfect.

From the deepest part of me I replied, "I love you to Suwattanee" [good woman]. She looked up at me with her beautiful brown eyes and smiled. We spent the entire night entangled in each other's arms. I did not sleep at all that night I laid there relishing every moment of that day. Every once and a while she would squeeze me as to assure me she had not left and I would answer back with a gentle squeeze of my own. We would also periodically share an intimate kiss and the soft little sighs she would sporadically release assured me that she was in a place that she felt comfortable, and it pleased me to know that I had given her comfort among other things.

It was difficult for me to just watch her. I had experienced a part of her that created an insatiable desire for her and once her passion to be satisfied again was awakened, I was all to eager to give her the loving she wanted. She finally fell asleep and I, finding so much delight in her beauty, I watched her as she slept. That night was so memorable and complete that she inspired me to write the following lines of a poem I called Reminiscence:

> As we lay here now, together, we have time to reflect.
> On the things we have done and the things we may regret.
> The silence of the night and the warmth of its air;
> Makes me think of holding you and the fragrance of your
>   hair.
> To kiss, to touch, to comfort one another;

To fill the room with all our passion as we kick away the
    covers.
The elements of the weather show themselves on the window.
Crying glass wet with tears shields us from the wind though.
Love and passion are here and I will remember this night
    forever.
Not only because of the love that we made but dreams we
    shared together.
Together growing old embracing each other's soul, no
    convictions no regret;
Just you and I at last for a night we won't forget.

TWO

Riding with Joy

I mentioned to you some paragraphs prior that I wanted to move to the place where the festivities took place because it was so beautiful. Now the way in which it happened was quite amusing; at least now it is, the night which it happened was terrifying. Joy and I had spent the day together; she had to be at work early so I dropped her off a little early and I and my buddy Derek went out to the club. This was not to pick up other chicks but just hang out with my homeboy. After a night of drinking and loud music I phoned my Joy to check in. I got to the house at about 2: 45a.m. or so, talked with her for about ten minutes, watched T.V. until about 3:30, took a shower and got ready for bed. I lay there in bed and thought of Joy. During my dozing off I felt something run across my chest; swatting as hard as could I thought that I had eliminated the problem. Then suddenly it ran across my face I jumped up out of my bed and walked around to the lamp at the side of the night stand; I turned on the light and there prostrated from the ceiling to the floor was the largest spider web I had seen in my life with a gargantuan spider scurrying for cover. I didn't even put my pants on I grabbed my keys from the nightstand, jumped into my car and drove around the block to my mommy's house. I stood there on her porch with nothing on but my underwear and my keys in my hand and knocked as if it had chased me to her door. "Oh my God are you alright where are your clothes?" my mom asked. "Yeah I'm fine," I replied. "Where

22

are your clothes?" she asked again. "At home," "What happened tell me what happened?" she shouted. "A spider built a web over my bed and I need somewhere to sleep tonight. About that time Tina walked in wiping away the sleep from her eyes. "What's wrong, what happened?" she asked. "He woke up and a large spider had made a web over his bed," my mom explained. "Oh my goodness you okay?" "Yeah I just need a place to sleep tonight," I replied. So that night I slept at my moms. The next day I called the apartment complex which I had my eyes on.

Unfortunately they did not have a two bedroom unit available when my friend Derek and I had decided to become roommates. We found a very nice townhouse southwest of town and the two of us settled there where we were roomies for a year. The times we had there compared to none of my former experiences in the past; we were two single guys living a life that single guys live. I recall this one time when Joy and I had decided to call it quits for a while and I had met this young woman named Connie. She wasn't my Joy but this chic was very well endowed in the manner of being top heavy and bottom proportioned need I say more?

Well it happened one night that Derek and I were sitting around bored with nothing to do and he blurted out in a rather frustrated voice, "Man I wish I knew some chicks we could call over to hang out." "Really," I replied. "Well I just happen to have one I could call for just such an occasion. "Man you're lying," he said. "No I'm serious I'll give her a call." So I proceeded to go through my address book to find someone I knew he would enjoy kicking it with. "Angela, nope every time we hook up she wants something," I thought to myself. "Michelle, damn every time I hook up with her I have to pay her sister to watch her kids nope." "Patricia, yeah Patricia but damn if I tell her to bring a friend she'll bring Kim she's too difficult and I really do want to mess with her tonight." I reasoned with myself. So with no other options I decided to give old Patricia a call. Now I've never slept with Patricia I just knew her through Kim and Patricia just happened to give me her number one day. If she was interested or not I never ventured to see, besides I had already slept with Kim and to do so with her would have been taboo. "Hey girl," I said in starting my plot with her. "Hey Tommy," she replied. "How did you know this was me?" "Because you're the only guy I know that sounds like a white guy when you call." "Where's Kim?" I asked. "She's out of town she went to see her sister." "When is she coming back?" "I think Sunday." "You sound as though you were sleep," I stated. "Yeah but I was about to get up," she replied. "What's up?" she asked. "Well my friend and I were sitting around bored as hell and we were looking for someone I mean something to do," I hinted. She found it funny and laughed. "You so crazy," she replied. "So you want to see me huh." "My friend does." "Oh he does huh"? "No I'm for real I have a friend name Derek that wants to meet you." "What she say, what she say"! Derek asked in his boyish excitement. "Shhhh, shut up you're going to fuck it up," I said. "Oh I thought that you wanted to see me, what does he look like"? "About my color, just a little taller than me, hair cut like mine hell everybody thinks we're brothers." "Sounds handsome." she replied. "When does he want to hook up"? "Now," I replied. "Damn y'all are bored," she added. "Oh one other thing do you have a nice friend?" I asked. "Yeah I think I can work something out," "Hey, is she cute don't be bring no hyenas to my house." "Connie, she's real cute," she added. "Little baby monkey cute or cute like you?" I asked. She laughed "Boy you're so damn silly." "Let me put it this way if I was a man I'd do her." Slot machine bells and chimes went off in my head that was the first time I had ever heard a girl speak in that manner. As they say it was on. "Where do you stay?" she asked. So I proceeded to give her directions to the apartment and told her that we would be waiting; I also asked her what they wanted to drink and that I would go pick something up. We finished ironing out the details for the evening and ended the phone call with a hearty good bye. As for my overly enthused roommate and lifelong comrade he could hardly contain himself. "Man it's on," he implied. "What does she look like?" "You mean Patricia?" "Oh she's real pretty you don't have anything to worry about." I'm the one that needs to be worried." "Why?" Derek asked. "Because I don't know what this chick looks like that Patricia is bringing with her." "Hey let's go to the liquor store and pick up some stuff," I said. In all of his excitement he even agreed to pay for tonight's beverages. Hey that's what friends are for. Nevertheless, I was not really that hyped about the ordeal because after the whole plot had been laid out I still found myself thinking about having Joy.

The girls got to the apartment at about 10:00. Derek and I were about three sheets to the wind when we saw the headlights of an approaching car flicker through the mini- blinds. "That's them, that's them," Derek shouted with excitement. "Don't open the blinds they'll see you, just act normal," I shouted; using one of the most ridiculous oxymorons to describe our present state, anything but normal. Suddenly there was a knock at the door. "Who is it?" as if I didn't know. "Trisha," the voice replied on the other side. "Hey girl long time no see. This is Derek, Derek this is Patricia." "Hey, how ya doing?" Derek asked. "Fine and you," Trisha asked. "I'm good now," Derek replied. "Tommy this is my friend Connie, Connie this is Tommy." "Hi, nice to meet you," "Same here," she stated. "So do y'all want anything to drink?" I asked "Yeah what'cha got?" Trisha asked. "Malibu rum, beer, E & J, cokes, 7-up, and orange juice, but if you will allow me to make a suggestion you've gotta try the rum it's great." So I mixed the ladies drinks and we sat down at the dining room table for a chat. After a couple of drinks the games started, first dominoes, then spades and for the finale, quarters. Trisha lost the most of the games of quarters and was the most inebriated by now. Then I came up with the craziest idea. "Hey let's all go for a swim," I insisted. By this time it was well past pool hours, I didn't care. I figured we pay rent here we should be able to swim any time we wanted to for these prices. The skepticism was prevalent and it took a while for me to convince everyone to go along with my plan. "We don't have anything to swim in," Patricia stated. "That's not a problem," I assured her. "Connie do you trust me?" "Yeah I guess so, why?" "Because I have a pair of shorts and a t- shirt for you if you're interested in going." "What do you wanna do Trisha?" she asked. "I'm going if Derek will," she stated. "I'm in," Derek replied. "So how about it Connie come on don't be a prude," I teased. "Mmmm okay but I can't swim." "That's why I asked you if you trusted me. I won't let anything happen to you we want be horsing around or trying to get anybody hurt because I want to see you again," I added. "Okay, where can I change?" So I accompanied her upstairs where I went through my things to find her something suitable to wear. A tight shirt and loose shorts, "Will this do?" I asked. "That's fine," she replied. "I'll be down stairs just come down when you're finished." "Okay," she replied

Once at the pool the scene was so erotic she would cling on to me for dear life pressing her huge breasts against my chest and with her legs she wrapped them around my waist tight. "Relax and whatever you do don't fight me; I will not let you go you're weightless in water just relax," I assured her. At the other end of the pool Derek and Trisha were warming up to each other splashing in the water and laughing and carrying on as though they had known each other for years. The two of them together enjoying each other laughing and such made me think of Joy, and I knew right then that I wasn't going to make any advancement toward Connie it just didn't feel right. I slowly, but surely, gained the confidence of my pool pal within minutes; before long she began to ask me to tread out deeper into the pool. She would lie on her back and without much effort at all I would support her remarkable body with one hand as I watched the water caress her tempting frame. Then she wrapped her legs around me and gave me her hands and I'd spin her around as fast as I could drenching her and she screamed. Suddenly several lights in the complex came on, so we dashed for the darkness and when the trouble had subsided we ventured back to our play area.

By now my pool pal was becoming a lot more frisky toward me she would do things like put her back to me and put my hands around her as to give me the pleasure of stroking her nearly exposed breast, and when it seemed like my hands would stray from their mark she seemed only more than eager for them to return to where she had placed them. During one of our voyages to the shallow end she intentionally spread her legs giving me a view I didn't really expect. I'd blush now if I could; it was as if she was begging me to advance, but I stood fast. (I know guys not quite the reaction you were expecting). Although she was becoming more and more aroused hinted by the perkiness of her nipples I just couldn't do it. When she emerged from the pool her t-shirt pressed against her entirely wet body. "Come over here," she commanded. As she slithered back into the shallow water, she sat with her legs opened and motioned for me to sit between them. I did as I was instructed and in a shy like girlish voice she asked. "What are they doing down there?" By now Derek and Trisha were kissing and fondling I mean they were having the time of their lives. "Hey what are y'all doing down there?" I asked as my voice alerted them that we were watching them. "Can y'all see us?" Trisha asked. "Why hell yeah we can see y'all," I responded. "Y'all need to take that back to the house," Connie said. Taking her advice as though it was warranted the two of them enthusiastically left us alone and retired to Derek's room; he later told me the details as to what took place but that's his business and this is my manuscript. (Sorry)! As for Connie and me it was quite evident that we wanted to have sex but I could not bring myself to do it. I confessed to her some weeks later that under different circumstances I would have. My heart wasn't in it because it belonged to someone else.

The two of us got back to the apartment where she showered, got dressed and borrowed a ball cap. Sometime later Trisha emerged from Derek's quarters dressed and ready to go.

I walked Connie out to the car where we exchanged numbers and a brief kiss; Trisha followed she gave me a big hug and the two ladies expressed what a good time they had. They left at 5:00 a.m.; it was a very erotic experience and I'm delighted that it ended the way it did. No one's emotions damaged just consenting adults having a good time.

This experience left me so determined to be with the Joy I was missing that I called her early that morning to express to her how I felt. She could tell in my voice that I was missing her like crazy. We decided to see each other on a totally monogamous basis. I was ready to commit to the relationship. She came over that day and we made love and discussed our future. After being with her for ten months I thought I knew everything there was to know about Joy. I made up my mind that day that I would marry her but, how to propose to her I was still formulating that one.

There were still some I's to dot and some T's to cross; not to mention I had to inform Derek of my intentions. Single life for me was to be no more after I had made up my mind to pop the big question.

The two of us lay in bed talking and consoling one another. One of the things we had discussed was getting our own place; I was determined to reside where we had visited for the barbecue, so first thing in the morning I was going apartment shopping. Another thing we talked about was prior relationships and with a bit of guilt I retrieved my little black book from the night stand. I didn't feel guilty because of it; I felt guilty because of the number of entries in it. We had discussed everything from the number of intimate relationships we had to unusual places we had had sex nothing was left unspoken so I thought. "Here, I want be needing this anymore" I said. "What's this?" she asked. "What we just talked about," I added. "Every female that I know I want you to do whatever you want to do with it, burn it, bury it whatever you want; I want to prove to you that I want to be with only you." "Tommy I don't want this I never said I didn't trust you," she stated. "I know but I don't want any doubt in your mind when it comes to how much I love you. "Better yet give it here, pass me the phone," I pleaded. I was determined to prove my unwavering devotion to her. I began with the A's and called to let everyone know that I had found Joy and was about to get married. "Tommy you don't have to do this," she urged. "I know I don't baby but I want to," I replied.

The responses that I received varied from blessings to cursing, from conformity to denial, from congratulations to commiseration. On some instances the unbelieving party demanded that they speak to my Joy and I complied. I had absolutely nothing to hide I had told my beloved all. Being somewhat reluctant she spoke to all those who were eager to speak with her; never once did she become intimidated, argumentative or hostile to them. And when finished with their conversation she humbly ended it with, "It was nice talking to you too." Damn what a lady. I felt that this was a major obstacle for us and when all was said and done I fell even more in love with Joy and for a second time that evening we consummated our love.

Derek was the first and only person who knew about the nuptial that was about to take place. "So when is the wedding?" he asked "We haven't set a date yet but we know it will be soon," I replied. "Where are y'all going to stay?" he asked. "Well that's the thing, we were going to look at apartments tomorrow," I said. "That's cool." "Will that put you in a bind if I was to move out within the month?" I asked. "Man no as a matter of fact I was about to suggest we get the hell up out 'a here because this motherfucker keeps flooding," he stated. "Man are you sure because I don't want you to be out of a place to stay." "Tommy for real it's cool, y'all are going to need your privacy and I'm gonna have my chicken heads coming over we need our own places," he added. "Hey man thanks for being so cool with this if I can help you with anything let me know."

Not many days later I was on my days off; Joy and I had made some plans for the week. Little did she know that one of those days would include a wedding. I had picked up her ring earlier that week and put it away; my recently formulated plan was now ready. We talked on Friday night and I asked her could she get someone to watch Corey on the following day. "Why, what are you up to?" she asked. "Oh nothing I just wanted to hang out with you." "Yeah right!" she added. "It's a surprise," I explained to her. "Come on Tommy tell me," she pleaded. "All I can tell you is that you're going to do it or not that's all I'm saying until in the morning." "That's messed up Tommy," she giggled. "I think you're going to love it," I added. We talked for a few minutes more then I let my bride to be get some rest for our long day ahead.

Early that Saturday morning my Joy was promptly prepared for our outing just as she was the first time I picked her up for our first date. She emerged from her mom's house and the scene played out slowly as she walked down the driveway. She looked breathtaking as her jet black, straight hair cascaded down her shoulders while momentarily being lifted by a gentle breeze. The scene still gives me an awe-inspiring phenomenon that I just can't erase from my memory rolodex. Envisioning this image of beauty as my wife, the one I would wake to every morning elated me like nothing else and sent a tingle down my spine. "Good morning gorgeous," I greeted her. "Good morning," she replied following up with the exchange of a blissful kiss. "Well are you ready?" I asked, as I started driving off. "Ready for what?" she asked with excitement. "I thought we'd go get a nice breakfast, drive north toward the lake, do a little sightseeing, get married and do a little shopping." "Are you serious?" she asked in a giggling girlish manner. "I've never been more serious," I replied. "I'm for real let's go right now; we will return home as husband and wife." "Oh my God you are serious!" "Yes I am will you marry me?" I asked with butterflies in my stomach and a lump in my throat. "Yes, but." "But what," I interrupted. "But nothing I'm just surprised," she added. "Why?" I asked. "I was not expecting this," she replied. "But I don't have a ring," she stated. "You mean like this?" I grinned. She screamed with delight "Oh it's beautiful," she added. "Ooooo Tommy I

30

love it, so this was your surprise?" she asked. "Yeah it is." "Who
did you tell?" "Nobody," I replied. "Oh my God oh my god!" she
screamed as she began to cry. "What's wrong baby?" "Nothing I'm
just excited," she replied. "Do you really wanna do this and are
you happy?" I asked. "Yes!" she replied. Then she did something
that melted my heart totally she reached for my hand and held
it firmly as to insinuate that she would never let me go. During
the remainder of our voyage northward she would occasionally
look at me and smile (what a beautiful smile) and clutch my hand
with affirmation. Then she spoke those words to me that made me
beam, "I love you Tommy." "I love you too."

She could hardly contain herself she had to tell someone so
she called her best friend Teresa and gave her the spill of our trip
northward. The place in which we were married was a three hour
drive from where we lived; there was plenty to say and plenty
enough time to say it. Teresa conveyed how happy she was for
the two of us and Joy urged her not to tell anyone; we wanted to
do it ourselves. If Joy was afraid of the response that she would
receive she never showed it; she looked totally confident in the
decision that we had made. She ended her phone call and warned
her friend once again not to tell a soul.

When we arrived at our destination we did those things that
we had discussed breakfast, sightseeing, got married and went
shopping. It's strange but I don't remember a thing that we bought
nor where we went to eat; neither do I remember what we saw on
our tour of this place, but I remember the ceremony. We got to
the small courthouse at about 11:00 or so where I proceeded to
ask one of the clerks their policy and procedure for performing
a wedding. After a brief clarification we were solicited for fifty
bucks, a price that would be multiplied twenty times for the
separation of an irreconcilable divorce. We were then introduced
to the arbitrator who was about to perform the holy union. He
was an old gent who was full of wisdom, and appeared eager to
share it with us at no additional cost. He warned us of both the
blessings and woes of marriage. We could tell that he had done

this plenty of times throughout his judicial career; his point of reference, forty-six plus years of marriage to the same woman. His knowledge of matrimony was given to us in both a comical and surreal manner yet rightly dividing the truth of the matter.

He started with a series of questions that were directed to us as individuals then collectively to us both to answer; "Are you perfect Mr. Ashley?" "No Sir I'm not," I replied. "Then don't expect her to be." "What about you little lady are you perfect?" "No Sir," Joy replied. "Then don't expect him to be." "Did you get her pregnant and now decided to try and make things right?" "No Sir," I replied. "Good because that is a horrible reason to get married," he stated. "Do y'all have any children?" he asked. "I have a little boy," Joy answered. "What about you Sir?" "No Sir, I don't have any right now." "Now do you hear what he is saying young lady, what you think he means by that?" he asked Joy in a condescending tone. "That he does not have any children," she replied. "No mam you heard what he said, but you are not hearing what he is saying he wants to have children; am I right Mr. Ashley?" "Yes Sir," I answered in a perplexed tone. "That's why me and the little Mrs. have been together so long I understand her; it's gotten to the point now she doesn't have to ask me anymore. I can pretty much anticipate what she wants, and guess what Mr. Ashley I get it for her." "Now don't get me wrong I'm not her slave I just know how to keep the little Mrs. happy and likewise with her she pretty much anticipate my needs." This went on for about thirty minutes or so as the elderly clerk sat at a table near by with a grin on her face ready to record the event for public records. From money, to sex, to household chores we really got our fifty bucks worth as he continued to enlighten us with his years of experience. "I'll tell you what, y'all are a handsome couple," he added. "Let's get started so the two of you can get your lives on the way." The ceremony was not spiritual in the manner of reading scriptures and all. He performed a simple customary ritual of basic vows and asked the traditional questions which the both of us had to answer, I do. "By the powers vested in me by this great state of Arkansas I now pronounce you husband and wife," He announced to us and the only witness available. It was official the woman I had met only sixteen months ago was now my wife. I couldn't believe it. I didn't have any suspicions it was just an overwhelming feeling of completion for me.

To have wanted something this much and have it come to fruition gave me a sense of joy, an eager steadfastness to commitment, a tangible possession, Joy. I was always writing down my thoughts and feelings as it pertained to life's events this one was no exception. During our visit to one of the area lakes I retrieved a pencil and note pad that I had in the car, and as we sat on a bench at the lake I started to write:

How Much

Do as you wish with my heart, but don't break nor forsake it.
And do as you please with my love,
I ask that you only weigh it and not betray it.
Speak to me with kind words, Never ever lie to me or deceive
  me.
And comfort me with your hands, Use them to console me
  not control me.
And all these things that I ask of you I shall gladly do in
  return.
Because I've yearned for you, now I live for you and I'll love
  you unselfishly.
Your heart I won't forsake, your love I won't betray, And
  kind words I'll have everyday.
I'll comfort you and console you; I'll control you in no way.

I love you today, I'll love you tomorrow, and I'll love you in
  joy and even more in sorrow.
I'll love you in sickness, and I'll love you in health. I'll love
  you forever; because I love you to death.

"What are you writing?" she asked. "My feelings and thoughts,"
I replied. "About?" she asked. "You and I," I answered. To this
day she has never read it I only hope that she understood how
much she had inspired me. After I had finished fine-tuning my
thoughts on paper we took a walk, holding hands and occasionally
exchanging intimate kisses. Before long the afternoon hour began
to creep upon us, so we journeyed back to the car and started
our trip back home. The trip home was basically like the journey
there we had some small talk and discussed getting our own place.
We chatted about the response we would receive once we told
everyone of our marriage. We were as happy as two people could
be and we expressed it openly and without regret.

Back home no one had any idea of what we had done with the
exception of Teresa, and she had kept her word on the matter. The
first place we went was to my mother's house. Evening had caught
us as we pulled into the driveway. We emerged from the car and
were greeted by my sister who was saying good-bye to one of her
little friends. "Hey Bop Bop Is momma here," I asked. "Hey how
y'all doing, yeah she's in her room." I entered the house and my wife
followed close behind. "Momma!" I called out. "I'm coming!" she
cried from the other room. "Hey how y'all doing?" she asked. "Fine,"
we both replied in unison. "I wanna introduce you to somebody," I
stated sarcastically. "I know Joy we've met before." "I know but she
wasn't my wife then," I replied with a tone of arrogance. "Oh my
God are you serious?" my mom asked. "Well all I can say is welcome
to the family and it's great to have you as a daughter-in-law." "What
did your mom and the others have to say about it?" mom asked.
"We haven't told them yet," Joy replied. "So when are y'all gonna
tell them?" she asked. "I guess when I get home," Joy answered.
"What do you think they are going to say?" mom inquired. "I'm

not real sure but they love Tommy," she insisted. We visited for a while longer then made the trip to my in-law's house.

We arrived at her parent's place and as always her mom was standing over a wok in the kitchen preparing a meal for her family, which reminds me of a funny story. One day while at her place her mom had just finished cooking one of her traditional Asian meals. I was so hungry that day I could have eaten the rear end of a moose. She greeted me as always in her strong vernacular, "Hi Tommie you hungry, you sit, you eat." "Yeah sure," I replied. "What's this?" I asked. "You like?" "Yeah, it's pretty good," I commented. "Noodles and squid tentacle," my host replied. What had appeared to be chicken flavored Ramen noodle soup was far from it. I kept my composure and finished my meal due to the warm invitation to sit at her table and dine. When she left the room Joy warned me, "Tommy you don't have to eat that because I seldom do, if I can't identify it I don't eat it," she stated. Her mom returned to the kitchen and asked, "You want, here eat," she urged. "Okay what's this?" I asked. "Assorted fish eyes with gravy," she replied. "Noooo, I think I'll pass on fish eyes with gravy." She laughed so until she cried. "I will take one of those peppers though." "Tommy don't eat that," Joy urged. "Awe baby it's just a pepper it can't be that hot," I insisted. "Okay!" she warned. I took a fairly good size bite of what I can now only describe as a continually consuming flame. Suddenly I couldn't breath, my tongue and gums began to burn it felt as though my teeth were desensitized and they burned; my lips burned I started to panic, I pushed away from the table and looked for something to quench the volcano in my mouth. Needless to say to no avail. I would have cried but I didn't want to seem weak in the presence of my in-laws. "I told you not to eat that damn pepper," Joy went on to say. "Damn it, how long is my mouth going to burn like this?" I asked. "Here you drink," my tickled host urged. "What is it?" I asked warily. "Sweet milk you drink," she added. I gulped it down and it soothed the unrelenting flame that consumed even my thoughts. From that day forward I investigated everything I ate at my in-laws. As I began to say earlier we arrived at her mom's house with the news of our recent elope; it was received well no one shouted and there was no arguing about the fate we had decided for ourselves All and all the reception was as genuine as the one Joy had received from my family. The only question that was raised was where we were going to live. I quickly assured my in-laws that an apartment would be ready for us before the week was over. My answer was satisfying for them and I kept my word. The next morning I signed a lease in the apartment complex that we had visited for the barbeque and prepared to move my new family in and start our own life together.

THREE

Living with Joy

After moving all of my furniture from my one bedroom bachelor pad to our freshly adorned two bedroom, two bath apartment, things were looking good for us; we had gone to a local appliance store and started a line of credit together and bought our first washer and dryer. We later ventured out and I traded in my car that I took so much pride in for a more suitable family sedan, a ninety model Dynasty in which I gladly gave her keys to and took her old clunker that her mom had given her. That was fine with me I wanted her to have everything I was able to give her which was very evident. I felt so fortunate to have her as my wife and I wanted to preserve every thought, every feeling and every desire for her. During our intimate time together the times of sharing and bonding Joy became sick one morning; the inevitable had happened she was pregnant I was elated. During her entire pregnancy she began to blossom into an even more beautiful woman. Every feature about her seemed to be magnified. Her hair looked and smelled more enchanting, her skin felt softer, her hips more desirable. She thought she looked fat; I thought she'd never looked sexier and I conveyed it to her every chance I got.

Soon after we found out that she was pregnant we discussed buying a house; renting seemed to be ridiculous since we could get more for our money. So we began looking in areas we could afford somewhere nice, and while going to her mother's house one day

I found a beautiful house; three bedrooms, one and a half bath, two carport drive with a huge backyard. I was so sure that she would love it. I later picked her up from work and we went and took pictures of it. As we toured the grounds I could see in her eyes how much she loved the house. To see her that excited drove me to secure the house we had wanted so much and within days of our discovery I did just that. As the time rolled along we settled into our home having family and friends over in celebration of different holidays. We enjoyed entertaining family and friends. I remember this one time when we had about thirty- five or forty something people over and we all barbequed, played volleyball, dominoes and water games. Again we were enjoying our life together and we made the most of every moment.

Joy was still pregnant at this time and everyone thought that she looked absolutely stunning. I would have to agree she did, but with the extra weight that she had gained I guess she didn't feel the same. One of the things I enjoyed the most about those times was making her feel adored, belly rubs, feet massages etc… I knew that it relaxed her and pleased her to have someone pampering her and I, for a better phrase, got off on it. I am a pleaser by nature and if I knew she was enjoying it I loved it.

Several months had passed and we were expecting the arrival of our child. The event was one I had not experienced before. To be in the delivery room opened my eyes to all I had to look forward to. I had scheduled my vacation around the due date of her delivery and was prepared at a moment's notice for the call to go; her bag was ready by the door, I made sure my pager had fresh batteries in it just in case I was away from the house. She was eager for the day to come and I, like a newly expecting father, stood vigilant. It didn't happen the way I had expected it to. I was actually at home the day she calmly walked into the living room and announced, "Its time." "Are you sure, where is your bag, do we have everything, do I need to call your mother, where are my keys"? I asked in great distress. She remained ever so calm as she coached me to the hospital. "Tommy you need to slow down we have plenty of time," she stated. She sat in the passenger's seat repeating her Lamaze breathing technique as I coached from the driver's seat. We arrived safely at the hospital and at 12:55 p.m. we welcomed our son into the world. We celebrated at the hospital with a steak dinner and a bottle of grape juice, complements of the hospital. Of course the entire family was there to welcome our bundle of joy. And once again things were looking pretty good in the Ashley household.

Several months after the birth of our first and only son together things started to change, drastically. I didn't know if it was because I was working three jobs and was seldom home or what but I could sense a change in our Eden. She returned to her job as an insurance adjuster and I continued at the fire station working 24 hour shifts, leaving there and working as a security guard at night to make ends meet, not to mention the lawn cutting service I had started. I was taxed; dog tired at the end of the day. Sometimes I would have to come home and sit up with Treyon while she either worked late or hung out with her friend Teresa. I felt that she was due that leisure time since she had put in nine months of burden. Nevertheless, her outings became more frequent and the length of time in which she stayed away gradually progressed.

Then one day my father-in-law left an urgent message that he needed to speak with me. What was this about I thought; what was so important that he had to speak with me face to face. I remained confused about the matter for some weeks until he was able to reach me. I could not phantom what he was about to convey to me. Was it a bombshell or just a bit of fatherly advice for his new son-in-law. What transpired afterward disturbed me but I really didn't know how to respond. Toshiro greeted me as always with a firm handshake

"How you do Tommie?" "Fine, Mr. Toshiro how are you?" I asked. "I want to talk to you bout Joy something wrong with her." "What do you mean?" I interrupted. "She not right she give her mother hard time she keep wrong company I worry for her. She not right," he repeated. All I could get from our brief exchange was she is not right. Okay I thought what am I suppose to do with this bit of useless info? Whether he did not have the words to explain his intent or whether he had no idea of what he was saying I couldn't decipher. "You keep eye on her," he said with an ominous warning.

I returned home and as I waited for my Joy to come home I was constantly pondering the words of Mr. Toshiro in my head as though they were forever being played back on a damaged phonograph; I was dazed as Treyon and I just sat in the dining room. He was of no age to comprehend all that had been said; not to mention he had been sitting in the car the whole time. For the most part I would not have allowed anything contrary to be said about his mother in his presence. As she entered the house the feeling of someone dragging a needle across an old vinyl record interrupted my consuming thoughts. "Hey baby," she said greeting me with a kiss. "Oh hey baby," I replied. "What's wrong?" she asked. "Oh nothing how was your day?" I asked. "It was okay I got two new clients today," she stated. "That's good," I replied with a look of perplexity. Do I tell her of my recent foreshadowing revelations from her step-father or do I keep quiet and let destiny unfold? I've often thought that I should have spoken up and confronted her, but accusations are often more damaging to people than words unspoken. And suddenly all was not so good with me in the Ashley household.

There comes a time in relationships when the couple feels that they need some time for themselves whether it's to go shopping or maybe to work on a hobby you've had since you were a kid; regardless this time is crucial for the individual and must be respected. By the same token time must be allotted to spend it with each other. These concepts I was very aware of but the one that matters the most is the time you set aside to spend with your Heavenly Father. King David said it best when he penned Psalm 27:4-5

> *One thing I have desired of the Lord,*
> *That will I seek:*
> *That I may dwell in the house of the Lord*
> *All the days of my life,*
> *To behold the beauty of the Lord,*
> *And inquire in His temple.*
> *For in the time of trouble*
> *He shall hide me in His pavilion;*
> *In the secret place of His tabernacle*
> *He shall hide me;*
> *He shall set me high upon a rock.*

I had not grasped of this theological truth yet, due to my infantile spirit. And it was apparent that I did not have a grip on it because I thought it was something that I could fix. I thought if we could just get away for a while and spend some quality time together things would definitely get better.

Luck would have it that my brother Ronald, a Navy veteran was stationed in Okaloosa, Florida at Ft. Walton Beach Air Force Base right on the Gulf of Mexico. He had called to invite us down for the summer and I was only too eager to go and see him and his family. They had just returned from Italy and it had been two and a half years since I had seen them. I ran the idea by Joy and likewise she was eager to go. Neither of us had ever been to Florida and I figured it would be just the thing we needed to keep the flame burning in our marriage; evening walks on the beach, dining in places we had never been and taking photos to remind us of the times we would share with each other.

We packed for our trip and headed out for our ten hour drive south Joy, Corey, Treyon, my sister Tina and myself. The drive was exhausting we left at 4:00 that afternoon and arrived at the base gates at approximately 2:30 the next morning. We all got settled in at my brother's place after a warm welcome from his wife and kids. My crew that traveled with me bunked down for the morning. My brother, on the other hand, had plans for the two of us to go sight- seeing at 2:30 on an early Friday morning, and in all of the excitement what started out as a tour of Okaloosa ended up as a 73 hour excursion. My wife and his must have thought we had abandoned them; from the time I arrived we were gone just the two of us from early morning breakfast at one of Florida's finest establishments, to basketball at a near by gym, to the demolition range to watch some of his co-workers blow up discarded equipment, back to the house to take the kids to the amusement park, out to dinner with the wives and to the club later on that night. The ladies were tired after the club so we decided to drop them off at the house and me and my brother painted the town again.

My brother and I watched the sun come up Saturday morning we had breakfast again and once again we went to the gym to play ball. We finally got home after driving for hours to places like Valparaiso, Niceville and Crestview where we played who knows how many hands of dominoes with some Sea-bee friends of his. We got in that afternoon and took the family out to the beach where we stayed until dark. Once at the house we stayed up until morning talking with the Mrs. and reminiscing about our childhood memories once again watching the sun rise. We all got the children dressed that Sunday morning and went out for breakfast then to the mall for a little shopping and finally back to the beach where we watched the sun set. My brother and I went back to the damn club. When I finally got to sleep that Monday morning I was beat. I didn't wake up until Tuesday evening at about six o'clock. My internal clock was thrown off something terrible.

Afterwards Joy and I got to spend some needed personal time together we went to a secluded place on the beach and walked hand and hand occasionally stopping to share intimate kisses and provocative thoughts. We ended our evening with a beautiful candlelight dinner and topped the night off yet again with a passionate love session. I was so into her, so deeply in love and thus inspired by her touch I again picked up my pen and wrote down what I had experienced that evening.

The Kiss

Lips of silk touched mine tonight extremely soft and sweet;
And the thought of it occurring again seemed to be a treat.
Perfect are their contours, quenching like cool milk,
Soothing like satin, comforting like fine silk.
As I inhaled your breath it was all I could contain,
Ecstasy is the only word that I could use to explain, the way
I feel when we kiss, delightful a heavenly bliss.
Kiss me again and this time do it even slower,
Let me experience the fullness as our tongues start to explore.
Permit me to inhale you concealing you inside,
Kiss me beloved and never let me be denied;
The pleasure of your warmth, the dept of your abyss;
And the emotions of love that I feel when ever we share a kiss.

We spent the remainder of our time in Florida with our family and frequently stealing away to be alone. Our conversations were stimulating and thought provoking and words she had spoken to me once before she declared them to me once again, "I'll always love you no matter what." I took them for what they were worth I didn't question her implication it was just nice to hear them again.

They made me feel that we honestly had a chance to make things work. A sense of confidence had been restored to our relationship and I was sure it would work.

When we returned home from our trip things remained passionate for sometime. We would plan to spend time with each other and nothing would hinder the appointed rendezvous. As I reflect back on our relationship now it was very evident who I adored. The one I had proclaimed as my love was she actually not my love? I desired a love so profound that I over-looked the One true love of my life. God loves us so much until He gave the ultimate His only begotten Son. It took nearly ten years for me to understand its true meaning. The one thing I had desired was not Him, the place I wanted to dwell was not in His presence, and the beauty that I longed for was not of the Lord. I could not be hidden in my time of trouble in His pavilion because I did not know Him. How could I find refuge in someone I did not know?

How could someone in the midst of a storm find shelter unless they had foreknowledge of that place? Behind the shroud of what appeared to be a firm relationship was a backdrop riddled with holes; voids that could only be filled by Christ Jesus. Yet in the name of love I was determined to make it work.

The Thanksgiving holidays were slowly approaching and we had agreed that we would share the day with our family and friends it was fine with my wife; we started at her mother's house then we would go to my mother's house. The day was filled with so much joy and laughter as we visited from house to house eating, drinking and reminiscing over moments in all of our lives. Tradition would have it that each member of the Ashley house would stand before everyone at the dinner table and give an expression of the things we were most thankful for in our life.

My mom would normally go first as if to set the stage for all of her blessings that God had bestowed upon her. "Well I would like to thank God for allowing me to see another Thanksgiving and allowing me to spend it with the ones so near and dear to my heart." To some it may have sounded like Blah! Blah! Blah! Blah! Blah! But in my ears it was a reassuring testimonial for what she was truly thankful for in her life.

My mom and dad separated sometime during my senior year of high school simply because my mom could not and would not tolerate being my father's verbal and physical abuse bag any longer. And when the holidays rolled around, for the most part he would instinctively show up, but if he had been drinking my mom would tell him, "sober up first before you come over here;" this would insure us all of a happy holiday. On the Christmas holidays it was funny because my father would say the same thing each year and the older we got we could paraphrase his little speech word for word. It went like this "I would like to wish all of my family love, peace and happiness." Wittingly my younger brother Ronald would whisper ain't that's an old Al Green song and during my father's most sincere moment of the year it would be overshadowed by my brother's quick wit which made the holidays much more enjoyable.

This particular Thanksgiving we (that is Joy and I) went to see some of my folks who resided in Manville which is about a thirty minute drive from where we lived. Upon our arrival we were greeted by my aunt and all of my cousins; as always, they made us feel welcome and there was plenty of food remaining when we arrived. This particular aunt was my father's sister and as little kids we would spend a great deal of the summer with her; not to mention the seven kids of her own that she would care for on a daily basis. She would cook for us and do all of the motherly things for us, and before we left to return to the city she would go school shopping for us in the efforts to help our parents out for the school year. She was and still is a very loving Christian woman and I love her for contributing to make me the person I am today.

As we entered her home I introduced my wife to everyone, "Aunt Mae this is my wife Joy, Joy this is my aunt Mae." "Oooo she is a beautiful girl how you are doing honey?" my aunt asked. "Fine nice to meet you," Joy replied. "Y'all want something to eat?" my aunt asked. "No mam," I replied. "Baby you want something to eat," I asked Joy. "No I'm fine," she replied. Now rather than name all of her seven children I will simply say that she had two sons and five daughters and Joy was able to meet them all except Lacy. Lacy was a pure tomboy with one of the most wicked cross-over's I had ever seen a girl attempt. She could always be found where the guys were shooting hoops, riding bikes through the rural streets of Manville and wrestling with any young boy willing to take the occasional low blow to the groin. She was a tough cookie.

Lacy was not at the house when we arrived; this was not a strange thing she would often go off and hang out with the guys for hours and return home right at dusk. And when I asked where she was a look of nervous perplexity could be seen on my wife's face. I paid it no mind because she could have possibly looked that way for several reasons and I didn't push the issue of why. Lacy came in some hours later and had a chance to meet my wife they spoke to one another as though all was normal. "Hey how y'all doing?" Lacy asked as she greeted me with a huge hug. "Lacy this is Joy my wife, Joy this is Lacy." "Hey," Lacy replied. "Hey," Joy whispered. And even though I thought the introduction was peculiar I could not put my finger on why it seemed so odd at the time. Nothing was ever said about the strange gathering and I for one had no suspicions about anything that had been done or said; as far as I was concerned everything was in a word just unusual.

We returned home that evening and got back to the norm if it could be called normal. I was yet confused over two matters now the baffling introduction of my wife to my cousin Lacy and the perturbing conversation that her step-father had with me before.

What was I to formulate from all of this? How do I pretend that nothing had happen or nothing was said, how could things go back to the way they were; well they couldn't and they didn't. Things started to spiral downward fast. They started one day when Joy was at work and the notion came over me to investigate the things that started to bother me. I started in the bedroom going through personal items searching old purses in the closet. My eyes became fixated on old shoe boxes and to my surprise I found a well endowed sex toy in a shoe box on the top shelf. I have to admit I was shocked initially then I started to wonder what other secrets had my wife kept back from me. Then I became outraged, disappointed, insulted and deprived of a logical reason for her need of such a device. I said to myself there has to be an explanation for her recent behavior and for her new interest that had been tucked away in secret.

I decided to confront Joy when she came home I was determined to get to the bottom of my recent discovery. I left her package as I found it and when she walked in I announced, "We need to talk." "Okay what about?" she said with an intolerable attitude. "What's wrong with you?" I asked. "Well you didn't say hey cat, rat, dog or anything and you expect me to just talk to you," she stated. "What's with the attitude you've been acting strange every since you and Teresa have been going out," I added. "We seldom make love and you're hanging out regularly, I don't know what I've done but whatever it is I'm sorry." "Who said it was something you did I've just been feeling different since Treyon." "Okay then what's the deal with this?" I asked as I opened the box that concealed her secret. "Oh that belongs to Teresa and why are you going through my stuff?" she replied. "Because something isn't right," I added, "Why in the hell can't she keep it at her house and why are you hiding it, is there something you need to tell me?" "Like what?" she asked. "Like what the hell is going on with you two, do I not satisfy you in bed?" "What are you talking about?" she asked. "Is this what you two are doing when I'm at work?" The argument continued this way for some time and I was reluctant to accept the answer that she had given me. Yet it was an answer but was it the truth? Teresa was her best friend and she would come over and spend the night sometimes when I was at the station I didn't suspect anything, but I was now in a position whereas everything and everyone looked suspicious. This was one of the few arguments that I experienced with Joy and after coming to a mutual conclusion that it was all a substantial miscommunication we reconciled and made love and things went back to the way they were.

We continued to work long hours away from each other but we would make time to spend with each other and often we would spend it making passionate love for hours at a time, and in my mind I had conceived that everything was fine.

One night after we had gotten the kids to bed she went into the bathroom and drew herself a hot bath there she sat for about twenty or thirty minutes relaxing from the day. She proceeded to the bedroom to lie down; I was an hour behind her. I was finishing up my call list for my lawn clients. I later went into the bathroom and took me a hot shower. The day had been long and I was aching from cutting grass all day. Nevertheless, I was in the mood to give and receive affection. I finished with my shower and entered the bedroom I noticed that she had turned her back to me when I entered the room. "You okay?" I asked. "Yes," she replied in a callous tone. Being somewhat apprehensive I got into the bed and to my dismay when I put my arms around her she let out a disturbing shout, "Don't touch me!" "What's wrong with you?" I asked. "Nothing I just don't want you to touch me," she replied. "Why what did I do?" "Nothing I just don't want to be touched. "Why what's the matter with you?" I asked astonished in disbelief. "You can talk to me," I stated as I tried again to console her. "Didn't I tell you not to touch me." I was flabbergasted I didn't know what to do. So I did what countless men have done for years after being denied affection from their significant other. I snatched my pillow from the bed and headed for the sofa. As I lay there alone I contemplated everything that I had done. I knew I had not cheated on her; I had not wronged her in any way. My heart was devastated as I lay there trying to make sense of what had just happened.

The next morning I awoke from what I thought was a bad dream but to my disappointment it had happened; she was gone. The kids were still asleep she had left without any explanation or any reconciliation and I stood there in the living room crying in uncertainty. I didn't hear from her all day she didn't call to tell me what had happened the night before; she didn't call to say where she was or when she would be coming back. I felt a sense of detachment she was no longer in love with me and it was evident. She no longer told me when and where she was going; at times she would decide to go somewhere and just leave.

She no longer showed me the attention and affection she once did. After months of her nonchalant activities I became more and more deprived of the things I needed to sustain me in the marriage if it could hardly be called one. We no longer shared the same bed we didn't say two words to each other some days. And after I was denied an explanation and attention I felt I was entitled to my interest was given to someone else.

The young lady that won my affection was named Angela; she, at the present time is a respiratory therapist very independent, smart, and very much into pleasing me. I met her through a mutual friend while at the station one evening. She had inquired about me and asked if I was married. Our mutual friend came in from the parking lot with the news of her wanting to meet me, so being the deprived and lonely guy I was I met her in the parking lot where we exchanged numbers and commenced our two year sex affair.

Christmas of 1995 was the year it could be said that the bottom fell out of the relationship that Joy and I had. Three days before Christmas I put the tree up while Treyon watched. His brother was at her mom's house and the holiday season just didn't feel the same with all we had just experienced. Joy came into the house after shopping for Christmas gifts and asked if I had any money. I told her that I had a few hundred dollars. She had been gone all morning and I was at home with our son until about 4:30 that afternoon. There were things I needed to do but whatever she was up to seemed to be more important. I told her that she could take our checkbook just don't over do it. Then I asked the question of the day, "Hey are we going to talk about what happened with us?" I asked. "Can we talk later?" she asked. "Yeah that's cool," I replied. "But we've got to talk." "Okay," she replied.

To keep my mind at ease I invited my father and brother over to the house and the three of us played dominoes and drank a little beer. I was by no means drunk, but I did have a nice buzz by the time Joy returned from her outing. She came in and I can't recall if she even spoke to anyone; by this time it was late that evening. I proceeded to confront her. "Where have you been all day?" I asked in an irritated tone. "Shopping," she replied in a snobbish tone. "Where is the checkbook?" I asked. My actions afterwards were brought on by something that I could not accept. She had already put my gift under the tree and I had spied during her absence and found that she had bought me a pair of twelve dollar gloves, but the shot that got me was the amount that she had spent on a male co-worker of hers, sixty-seven dollars for a cologne set which was the making of a terrible situation for the evening. I snatched her purse from her and searched madly through the contents to find more evidence for her madness. "What the hell are you doing?" she asked. "What does it look like I'm doing I'm trying to see where the hell you've been all day." I came upon the checkbook and inquired about her spending. "Who in the hell do you know so well that you would spend this kind of money on?" When her answer did not appease me I tossed her purse and its contents down the hall against the wall. By this time my father and brother hearing the commotion came to intervene, but by that time Joy and I had already exchanged insults. "Why can't you tell me who he is?" I asked. "Somebody I work with," she replied. "That's bullshit you've been walking around here for the past few months like you've got a damn chip on your shoulder. If you weren't happy why didn't you just say so," I added. "Because I wasn't ready to talk about it" she replied. "Are you sleeping with him?" I asked as she started to walk away. I grabbed her arm. "Are you sleeping with him"? "That ain't any of your damn business," she replied. "You bitch get the hell out!" "What did you call me?" "You heard me bitch get the hell out!" Without a word she drilled me to the head. Now I don't concur with violence but rage had taken over and I certainly don't condone my action but I grabbed her and started to choke her; by now we were on our bed the bed that we had made love on a number of times and now it seemed it would be the place it all ended.

My father and brother came to her rescue pulling me from her sparing what might have possibly been her life. The two of them shoved me toward the kitchen where my brother proceeded to calm me down. I could hear my father and Joy talking in the bedroom and he was trying his best to comfort her. She had picked up the phone and dialed 911. Whether she did it out of fear or not, I do not know, but I could hear my father saying, "Don't say that, that's not true you're going to get someone hurt." By then she had come to the kitchen with her warning; "I called the police and they're going to take your ass to jail."

The police had shown up within minutes of the call. I was outside to greet them as they arrived. Seven of them responded and when they leaped from their cars the one officer commanded me to get on the ground. "Officer its cold as hell out here I am not a threat to you." "Sir we had a call from a young lady that stated that a black male at this address had a gun." "What!" "No sir my gun is in the bathroom closet locked up in a lock box; no one has a gun here," I explained. "Where is the person who made the call?" the officer asked. "Inside," I replied. "Would you take me to the gun?" "Yes sir," I replied. A Female officer questioned Joy while I proceeded to show the male officer my gun. He questioned me of the events that had taken place. "What is this all about Mr. Ashley?" "I don't know she won't talk to me," I answered. "Well my partner will talk with her while I take your statement and secure the fire- arm." "Would you retrieve your firearm for me Mr. Ashley?" "No, but what I will do is show you where it is because I don't want to become a statistic of an accidental shooting." The officer retrieved my firearm and finished his line of questioning. After the two of them had collaborated the two stories I found out that Joy had told the officers that she had struck me first and that there was no gun involved. The male officer came and asked me if I wanted to press assault charges against her. I could not find it in my heart to do such a thing to a woman I still was in love with. I just wanted her to leave since she could not provide an answer that would appease me. The condition that would follow would be a bitter sweet one. I gave her one month to vacate the house and allowed her to keep the family car under one condition, she allowed me to take our infant child with me. But how could she agree to something as vindictive as this? It was as if she had found someone to share her deepest thoughts and most intimate desires with and we were being discarded like yesterday's trash. She agreed to the terms of the separation and I, along with Treyon, my father and my brother left our house. My tomorrow seemed uncertain, my past was painstaking and my present unpleasantly predetermined. That night as I sat afraid of what would become of us I again grabbed my pen and paper and wrote:

"Certain as the Sun"

Certain as the sun I was there when you needed me to
    comfort you.
Your tears I saw fall from your eyes during times of sorrow
    and I was there certain as the sun
The world showed no concern to your despair yet during
    those times I was there certain as the sun.
As we rejoiced to the news of a new beginning I helped you
    in your delight;
And I was there certain as the sun.
During times of change and discomfort I was there certain
    as the sun.
But now as the sun starts to fall from the skies so have the
    tears from crying eyes.
The sun will rise yet it will not shine and tears will fall but
    not those of joy.
Times will change our eyes will open and become dry to all
    that we have done
And will you not cry? And the only thing you will have are
    the memories and the thought of me being there certain
    as the sun.

FOUR

A Plot to Kill Joy

The night we left the house was one of the saddest I've ever experienced in any relationship. There were so many questions that were left unanswered and so many allegations made to me once we had separated; I didn't know how to separate the fact from fiction. Like the relationship she had with my cousin Lacy it was later confirmed that they were actually in a relationship, and most recently who was this guy driving our car?

While at my mom's house that night the questions were plaguing me from everyone, but I had no response that would placate them. "Is she seeing anybody?" my mom asked. "I don't know." "What did y'all get into it about?" she asked with trouble inclination. "Junior didn't do anything to her she had a funky attitude when we came over," my dad explained. "We were just hanging out at the house when she came in; she looked like she had something on her mind when I spoke to her, but hell it wasn't any reason to ruin everyone's holiday," my old man continued. "Did she say anything?" my mom asked. "Well I asked her if she was sleeping with anyone and she told me that that was none of my damn business." "Do you think she is?" "I don't know momma I just want to get to the bottom of this and go home." What I was not prepared for was that there would be no Joy for me when I returned home. In all of my desperate attempts to hold on to what I had loved so much I found it slipping away with no conceivable means of grasping the real truth; it was over. She had found something or someone that would embrace her far better than I could and understand her skirmishes far greater than I would. Christmas had never seemed so cold and the harsh reality of it all was it was about to get even colder. What a horrible way to spend Christmas without Joy, not to mention I was extremely homesick. My son and I were staying with my mother until Joy moved her things out of the house. Living out of boxes really becomes tedious and constantly reminds you that you are in the process of starting over. The starting over was not that hard to do it was the existing and the uncertainties that had me in such a dilemma. I would be lying if I told you that I was glad it was over because that, my friend, was far from the truth. Nevertheless, it was a situation I was now confronted with.

For whatever reason people have a tendency of becoming very insensitive during breakups. The numbness is almost to the point of becoming inhumane to each other. They do and say things in the heat of the moment that they often regret. But somehow I'm convinced you were already aware of that. Malicious, spiteful, hurtful things that are buried so deep in their psyche erupt and you hardly recognize that person once the madness is released. The childish parading of their present relationship before your face seems obvious that they are trying to make you jealous. The most disturbing thing is how they use their children as pawns to get the other person to relent to ultimatums that were made during heated exchanges.

When Joy finally moved out, Treyon and I hightailed it back to our home about three weeks later where we were met with the sight of the Christmas tree fully decorated in the corner where we had placed it some weeks earlier. The smell of pine and holiday candles saturated the entire house. I inhaled and released a deep sigh of regret as I reminisced on the day of our Eden going south. I placed my son in his bed to finish his nap and I sat in the living room overwhelmed with the feelings of loneliness, sadness and heartache; so flooded with these emotions I hung my head and cried myself to sleep.

The next morning I was awakened to the sound of my now twenty month old son calling for me "Da- Da I want bah bah." Once I got him settled for the morning I tried to continue the best I could as if nothing had gone wrong; cleaning, rearranging to try and make the place look different from the weeks before. But no matter what I did around every corner, behind every door there was something there to remind me of Joy. I would catch myself just standing there and daydreaming about the things that had taken place in that very spot. Things like the first time I saw our home and how excited I was to show it to her; the day we closed on it and the day we moved in were all re-emerging. She was pregnant during the time we moved in and for a brief moment I could see her sitting there watching as I sketched cartoon characters on the wall of our son's bedroom in order to turn his room into the nursery we had planned to welcome him home from the hospital; and for a brief minute I could smile, yet the smile only camouflaged what my soul was really feeling.

My mother would come by along with my sister and they would help me organize a few things and console me in my times of need. And from time to time Joy would drive by the house on her way to her mom's where I assumed she was staying. In the beginning she would just drive by and one day she stopped. An unexpected knock on the side door startled me as I sat at the kitchen table. I rose from my chair and pulled open the curtains and standing beneath the carport was Joy. My heart began to race, my palms became like a wet dish rag and I was at a total loss for words as I pushed open the kitchen door to let her in. "Hey," she called out to me. "Hey," I replied. "How are you doing?" she asked. I wanted to say, "damn I miss you, I love you, can't we fix this, I want you to come home your son needs you, I need you, please lets work this out," but instead I answered with a heartbreaking "I'm okay." "How's work?" she asked. "Oh about the same; nothing new I get to the station and wait for someone to call me," I hinted.

"Where is Treyon?" "He's at day care I had some errands to run so I took him there." "What day care is he in?" "You know the one we discussed before the holidays," I added. "They finally had an opening so I jumped on it to kind' a give him a change from his old routine." "That's good does he like?" she asked. "Well not at first he cried all day the owner said, not to mention it nearly tore me up to leave him there," I explained. "Well you know I'm off in the evenings. He can stay with me when you're at work and when I go to work in the morning I'll take him and you can pick him up after you leave the station," she suggested. "That's fine," I answered.

This pattern went on for several weeks and one day she called the house to inform me that she had to bring our son home and when I questioned why she became very irritated. "I've got plans," she stated. Not an inconvenience nonetheless because I wasn't doing anything so the option for him to return home was not a problem. She had been coming by throughout the week and I figured I would have a chance to talk to her about us.

I now waited the arrival of them both while I paced the floor trying to muster up the courage to confront her. Once again a knock at the side door, "It's open!" I yelled. We exchanged greetings and then she slowly carried our son to his bedroom where she gently placed him in his bed. "Now's my chance ," I thought to myself. I grabbed her arm as I had done so many times before I had pulled her in to kiss her. "Are we gonna try to work on our relationship or just deny we were ever married and in love?" I asked as I stared into her beautiful brown eyes. "Do you love me do we still have a chance?" I asked. "Tommy I will always love you no matter what, can we talk about it later though?" "Sure," I replied. Then she did something I would have never imagined she kissed me. It wasn't deep and passionate but gentle and compassionate. And though she had kissed me I still wanted more, an explanation, some enlightenment of what the truth for us would be.

What was the truth though? Several people had been telling me that they had been seeing our car at this alternative club when I was at work. It was undoubtedly our car, it displayed a motif cross in the center of the back window which was a distinctive symbol of the organization that I belonged to and I did not want to cause any reproach to my brothers and sisters who were associated with the organization. One night while at work, I asked my superior if I could take off for about an hour to take care of a few things. I drove down to her hang out spot with razor in hand and removed the cross from the car. This infuriated her because I could come and get the car if I wanted to and just leave her stranded, but I would have never done that. Seriously!

So the next day I received a call from her and she began to start in on me as if I did take the car. "Why in the hell are you following me?" she asked. "I'm not following you, maybe you should be more discreet with the company you keep, people are talking you know," I defended myself. "Well that's none of their fucking business where I spend my time and if you don't like it fuck you too!" "CLICK" she had slammed the phone down in a rage. So I called back "May I speak to Joy?" "This is she." "Hey look I didn't call to upset you and the only reason why I removed the decal was because I didn't want anybody to accuse me of being gay," I stated. "Well that's not the only type of people that hang out down there Tommy a lot of women go there because they just want to hang out without being hit on all night," she added. "Whatever, I just didn't need the accusations and all the drama," I replied. "If that's what you're into then that's your business I'm just protecting myself." "When are you coming at Treyon?" I asked. "I don't know when I get a chance." "CLICK" Damn it she did it again; now this infuriated me, but I decided to just let that somewhat sleeping dog lay.

As for the incident of the guy driving our car this was one of her male friends that she had come to know, and what bothered me the most about him was that I didn't know how long she had known him or what she had told him about me. What was even more bizarre was that he worked up the street from where we lived, about a mile. I never knew his name but he knew mine. Fate would have it that our paths would cross one afternoon. Now although Joy and I were separated nothing had been formally agreed upon by the court; I had only agreed to allow her to use the car due to the verbal agreement we had made. As I left my job that day I decided to take a more scenic route to the house and as I passed the local brewery warehouse there it was, our car. I thought to myself first, hmm that looks like our car. My second thought was what is she doing up here? My third thought was wait a minute its 3:00 she is suppose to be at work. I turned my truck around because something just didn't set right about the whole thing.

I walked inside the warehouse office and asked to see the manager; a man who looked to be about forty or so appeared and asked, "May I help you Sir?" "Yes Sir I need to speak with the person driving the burgundy car parked outside the door here." He strolled over to the intercom and called for the driver of the car. "Is there anything else I can help you with Sir?" "Yes as a matter of fact you can, I need you to assist me in getting the keys to my car." He was totally dumbfounded but stayed. The driver of my car came bee-bopping down the corridor totally unaware of what he had walked into. What the two of them did not know is that I had already retrieved the insurance and registration cards when I drove up, not to mention I had the other key as well. "What's up can I help you?" he asked. "Yeah you can are you on my insurance?" I asked sarcastically. "Excuse me?" "ARE YOU ON MY INSURANCE?" "I don't know what you mean," he explained. "Oh my bad it's just you were driving my car and I figured you were on my insurance or you must have obviously stolen my car," I continued with my plight. "Cuz I don't know what you're talking about," he explained. "Come with me." The two men followed me out to the parking lot where I asked the driver, "Who car is this?" "Mine, I mean my girl's, I dropped her off at work this morning it's been here all day." "Well first of all this is my car it belongs to me and my wife," I explained. The manager was totally baffled by now. "Look Sir I don't know what this is all about but, if we have to we can call the cops." "Oh there's no need for that I can clear this up in just a few minutes," I added. "Your girl, let me guess her name is Joy right?" "Yeah how did you know that?" "Because your girl is my wife and this is my registration and insurance card to my car, my keys which fit this lock and if I'm not mistaken you have the duplicate in your pocket which I would like you to hand over right now thank you!" "She said this was her car; she didn't tell me she was married," he explained. "It is her car but it's registered to both of us and since you don't have my damn permission to drive my damn car I would appreciate it very much if you would give me my damn keys." The manager at that time asked to see the documents and once he had confirmed that I was the owner he instructed his employee to give me my keys. And to add salt to a now gapping wound to his ego I left him with these words "Oh yeah when you start paying the damn car note and insurance you can come pick it up; until then stay out of my damn car and tell your girl to call me if she wants her car back!" I got into my car and drove it to the house and walked back up to the brewery to retrieve my truck which I had conveniently left parked on the side of the building.

During my brisk walk to reclaim my truck I was bombarded with a barrage of thoughts of her betrayal and infidelity. Not only was he driving my car but he was sleeping with my wife, but the latter part of my ludicrous thoughts had not been proven. As for now it was purely speculation. I never heard from her about the incident just mentioned and I was fuming over it. And the more I thought of how callous and cruel she would be about something we had worked so hard to achieve together, I became even more enraged to do something so desperate that it defied everything that I had been taught; inflict cold premeditated revengeful pain. All talk of the two of us getting back together looked bleak but looks can be deceiving. She called the house that evening to inform me that she had to bring our son home and when I questioned why she became irritated. "I've got plans," she stated. Therefore, I sat and awaited their arrival trying to remain optimistic about the possibility of a reunion with my wife.

Once again there was a knock at the side door. "It's open!" I yelled. We exchanged greetings and she slowly carried our son to his room and gently placed him in his bed. "Here we go again," I thought to myself. I grabbed her again by her arm like I'd done before. "Do you love me, are we gonna try to work things out or just keep denying we were ever married?" I asked as I stared into her gorgeous brown eyes. "Do we still have a chance?" I continued. "Tommy I will always love you no matter what, but can we talk about this later I'll call you later okay," she answered.

"What's wrong with right now?" I asked. Then she did it again, she kissed me, yet her kiss neither would her answer appease me. It was as if she was merely trying to accommodate the anguish I was feeling. Her kiss was not a deep passionate kiss it was more of a pitiful compassionate one and even I could feel the difference.

This particular evening she was with her friend Teresa. I, with an inconspicuous tone, asked what the two of them were up to for the night. Joy answered "Well I'm taking Teresa home to get changed then we are going over to some friend's house to hang out for a while," she explained. "Well you all have a good time and call me," I replied. "I will," she added. I knew well enough where Teresa lived and it was conveniently down the street from my Aunt Gloria's house. So I went back into the house and packed Treyon an over night bag and proceeded to meet or beat them to the other side of town. I arrived at my aunt's house just in time to see the two of them go inside. I gathered all of my son's things and went inside where I asked my aunt for two huge favors. "Hey would you watch Treyon for me for about three hours I'm trying to see what's going on with Joy; she's been acting like we have a chance but I'm getting mixed feelings." "Yeah that's no problem but don't you go out there and do anything to jeopardize your job and your boy." "I'm not," I replied. "Do you need any money?" she asked. "No but I need your car I'm just gonna follow her to see what's going on with her," I added. "You be careful and don't let this woman ruin you." She provided me with the keys to her car and I was out the door.

I left her house and I decided to just go back home and drink myself into a stupor, and as I sat there drinking and pondering all the things that the two of us had gone through recently engulfed my conscience. When I thought of how she could allow this man to share in something that we had struggled to achieve, mad thoughts of him being with her, had he been in my house had they shared our bed? I rose from my chair semi-inebriated grabbed my black leather trench coat, black ski cap and completed my disguise with my hand gun. I have to admit resentfulness and insanity makes a person do things that they normally would not do. I proceeded to go to the last place she was her friend's house. As I pulled up a block away from where they were parked I observed the two of them exiting the house. She had changed clothes once again, done her hair and was looking like she was on a first date. The two of them never knew that I was following them nor did they know of the sinister plot I had conjured in my head. They drove for several minutes and pulled into a nearby convenience store. I indiscreetly parked at a barber shop across the street. Teresa strolled into the store and got a pack of cigarettes and Joy proceeded to make a phone call; she chatted with the person for about two or three minutes and seemed elated once the conversation was done. The two of them started out again and headed toward the east side of town. As they drove I wondered what type of friends she had made that could make her smile the way I use to. They reached a part of town that I, as a grown man, would not have dared to enter at anytime of day. Full of section eight apartments, drugs, crime and a number of murderers along with gang infestation; certainly this is not the type of company my once beloved Joy was keeping. They continued on deep into the center of the complex and exited the car. The two of them walked some way across what was suppose to be a courtyard filled with thugs and hoodlums; polluted with forty ounce bottles and trash that seem to cover the entire compound. Once they came to the rat hole they were to enter I made my move to the terrace that overlooked the apartment they had entered. I stood there waiting, watching, and contemplating my next move for about thirty minutes. And when the rage had consumed me I advanced, then I was halted by the sound of the door opening. To my growing disbelief seven of the most thuggish brutes I had ever laid my eyes on emerged. They never knew the fate that could have awaited them as they exited the apartment. Nevertheless, my quarrel was not with them but the ones who remained inside. I positioned myself at the door, removed my pistol from concealment and tapped lightly on the metal door. "Who is it?" a male voice called from the other side. "T!" I replied. He undoubtedly had a homeboy with a similar nickname because without any hesitation he opened the door. The familiar, pungent odor of marijuana rushed into my nostrils. He was in a pair of boxers sporting a wife beater t-shirt. When I looked into his face my mind leaped forward and all I could hear was "BOOM" "BOOM". Rage and red clouded my vision I had placed two .357 slugs in the center of his chest. I stepped over him as he lay motionless on the floor; I could hear screams from one of the back rooms. There Teresa stood in the corner with her bra and panties on "BOOM" "BOOM she now lay unresponsive in a pool of her own blood in the bed. Joy sat on the bed adorned with only a large t-shirt I had bought for her on one of our trips to Florida. She sat at the head of the bed screaming, "Why! Why!" With no penitence I pulled the trigger "BOOM" "BOOM" it was finished the rage had been fed and for a brief moment the pain I had felt was quenched.

Many people would not dare admit anything this cold and callous that they have imagined in their mind, but for a long time this was the vision and the fate I saw of those I encountered that cold night. The truth is I've never shot a human being in my life. I did go to the place where my wife and her friend were but the account was not as such. I never removed my gun from my coat and when I knocked at the door a male called from the inside asking, "Who is it?" "Tommy," I replied. The thing that baffled me was when he opened the door he politely asked, "Can I help you?" "Yeah would you tell my wife to come to the door please?" I asked. "Hold on," he replied. He left the door partially open and I could hear the conversation he and my wife were having. "There's a guy at the door saying he's your husband." The door opened slowly and there she stood in the T-shirt that I had gotten while we were in Florida and a pair of panties on with a look of total frustration and perplexity on her face. "What are you doing here, why are you following me Tommy?" "I thought you said you were going to call me?" I asked. She let out this deep sigh, "You can't be doing this Tommy I can't handle all of this right now," she added. "So this is the type of life you want?" I asked with tears running down my face. "The dope, thugs and alcohol what have I done to you to deserve this, didn't I buy us a nice house, didn't I get you a nice car? What have I done to you to deserve this Joy tell me why are you doing this?" I asked. "I can't do this right now you need to leave." With that she slowly closed the door.

You see I never went into the house yet I knew her friend Teresa was there and I could only speculate what actually took place that night. I was dying inside. I had never felt such misery and despair like I had as I stood there motionless at the door that had just closed in my face. I couldn't move I was frozen. I experienced a sinking feeling as my heart and soul fell to the cold concrete under the crushing events that produced a sedative lackluster response. My intent before I arrived was to inflict as much pain as I could, but when I saw her I could not. Even though I had received the devastating news my soul sulked in its restraints. I finally moved from the spot I felt nailed to and dragged my wounded soul to the car and drove off.

I reached a set of railroad tracks and it was there I decided to end it all. At 1:30 in the morning I sat on the tracks with the ignition off, my head down sobbing and wishing a train would come by and relieve me of the torture. It can be said that I was definitely down but God had declared that I was not out. From out of nowhere it seems an old woman pulled up next to me and called to me, "Son you know you shouldn't sit here on this track like this baby," she said to me. And when I looked up I couldn't believe what my eyes were seeing this woman looked extremely old too old to be driving and especially at 1:30 in the morning.

"Yes mam," I replied. My brief encounter with someone who took the time to care about me gave me the strength I needed to drive to my mom's house.

I arrived at my mom's house and just sat on her porch. I could not bring myself to wake her so early in the morning. As I sat there crying her bedroom light shined through the mini- blinds and then I could see her peeping out. She was actually awake and came to the door to see why her son was sitting on the porch in the dark at so early an hour. The door opened and she called to me, "What's wrong?" she asked. "Nothing," I said trying to hold back the tears and the large lump in my throat. "Yes there is come in the house out of the cold," she insisted. But not even the comfort of my mother's home could eliminate the feelings that were bottled up inside my head and heart. "What's going on?" she asked again. "I just caught Joy at this guy's house," I whimpered. "Did you actually see her or do you think she's there?"

"No momma she came to the door in her t-shirt and panties and asked me what was I doing there. She told me that I had to leave and that she couldn't talk about it right then," I continued. I went on to explain to my mother and sister who was now awake, the bitter details of my heartbreaking rendezvous with my wife and her lover. My mom tried her best to console me, "My God Tommy I'm so sorry," my mom said. "I know you're hurting go ahead cry its okay cry." It felt like a floodgate in my mind had given way because everything that I felt every emotion that I could feel flowed from me all at one time love, hate, sorrow, joy, bitterness, anguish, despair they just kept pouring out of my soul. My mom went into the kitchen and brought me back a glass of brandy. "Here drink this don't sip it." It was just the sedative I needed to calm me down so that I could relax. I reached into my coat pocket and removed my hand gun and handed it to her. "Oh my Lord what is this," she asked with astonishment. "I was gonna kill'em momma I was gonna kill'em both, but I couldn't I kept thinking of my son," I confessed in tears.

Looking back now, our relationship it was doomed from the beginning. One thing I've learned at a very costly price is that the truth is paramount, self identity is vital and only what you do for Christ (in this life) will last. Our Lord and Savior Jesus Christ doesn't have a problem with these three attributes. When relating to Himself He said, "I am the way the truth and the life" (John 14:6). He knows who He Is and though He proved Himself through many infallible deeds people were still confused about His identity. We must know that if we profess the Lord as our Savior then we have become children of the Kingdom of God thus abolishing the most crucial identity crisis you may ever face. When you know who you are in Christ then no one or nothing you are confronted with is too large for God.

My spiritual immaturity would not allow me to grasp the principle that pertained to what God had ordained. When a union of matrimony is consummated there must be a spirit of oneness. The two who are together must be evenly yoked in order to become one flesh. This principle entails knowing your Lord and Savior, (Truth) and knowing what your purpose is for the Kingdom. (Identity) When these factors are rooted in faith then you become a person worthy of a help mate. Because you now have one purpose, one mind, one goal, and one flesh.

Now as a young person the very principles that were lived by Christ are the ones that I have tried to embrace daily in my life. 1 John 2:15 tells us, "Do not love the world or the things in the world. If anyone loves the world, the love of the Father is not in him." As a Christian this is also an essential principle to cling to. Note that the word says *things* of the world this could include people as well. Although the writer uses it to personify in-animated objects such as wealth, houses or cars there are some people who are yet in the world. These are considered to be the yokes we should not be given to. As an invitation to come to Him, Jesus instructs us farther by saying in Matthew 11:29-30, "Take My yoke upon you and learn from me for I am gentle and lowly in heart, and you will find rest for your soul. For My yoke is easy and My burden is light." In all of God's infinite knowledge He knows beforehand the things that would hinder us (stumbling blocks); on the other hand He knows those things that may be used to help others (miracles). Though we suffer He is glorified when we give Him the credit for seeing us through. Everything that we suffer through is not actually for us, although painful in its extent it is used to minister to others. When we are out of solutions for our problems He is the problem solver. This was not my mentality when I was traversing my present situation with my wife. I could not see due to the blinders that had decreased my spiritual vision. I wanted to restore that which I could not. I did not form her; therefore, I could not fix her. I knew nothing of spiritual growth nor of total submission to the Lord thus can it be said, "My people are destroyed for the lack of knowledge." And though I had been dealt a bad situation I refused to be destroyed for the lack of knowledge.

FIVE

Losing Joy

This was just the type of situation that should have propelled me into worshiping God but bitterness and rage caused me to stray from the very thing that I had been through since I was a child. The farther I wandered away the darker the path got and the more resentful I became. I started to view females as being good for only one thing expelling all of my sexual frustrations. I didn't want them to console me I didn't want to be loved by them I just wanted what I thought I needed sexual gratification. I spent the next four years in and out of meaningless relationships satisfying my desires.

Once again I moved out of the house that we were living in; this time for good because of all the stagnate memories that I could not escape. At my grandmother's house my son and I had our own room and she was very grateful for the company. This was not a very difficult transition because we had been there just months before. The two of us settled in and things were going great for the most part until Joy started to call. I started to resent the fact that my son was her son and we would have to share the task of raising him. That would mean that I would have to see her and I could not bear the thought of it at the present. She would call maybe once or twice a week to see how he was doing and my attitude toward her would be very hostile and more often than not I would deny her the rights of seeing her son. This was my juvenile way of returning wrong for wrong, and I have to admit now that it was terribly wrong to exploit our young child in that fashion. The very thing that I loved so much I started to use as a level to gain what I had lost and it was unfair to our son to make him a pawn in a struggle between two people which seem to be set out on destroying each other.

One evening while I was at the station she came by my grandmother's house and told my aunt that she was picking up our son. My aunt found it strange that when she came she was packing all of his things clothes, toys everything with the intent of him leaving for good. My aunt tried to reach me at the station but I was out of the house on a run. I didn't receive the news of it until later and when Joy called her tone and viewpoint of the legal kidnapping was very astringent. She later called me at work with the news of her ploy. "I don't know what you've been telling everybody but you're never gonna see your son again bitch!" "CLICK"

So I called my aunt to see what had happened and she told me how Joy had come and gotten Treyon. I paced the floor at work trying to think of a lie suitable enough to tell my captain in order to leave and again I received a second phone call which seemed to be the final knife thrust into my soul. "The next time you see your son it will be in court so bring your check- book bitch." "CLICK" I was furious by now and everyone at work knew my situation. I rushed downstairs to confront my captain about letting me leave but the wisdom he possessed hindered me from doing so. "Tommy I know things are bad right now but if I let you leave this station things are going to get worse so just go on back upstairs and simmer down," he said in his strong southern accent. "So you're saying I can't go," I replied. "Yeah that's exactly what I'm saying and if you leave here chief will have your job." I stormed over to the locker room to vent my frustrations on a metal locker that didn't know it had it coming. BAM! BAM! BAM! I launched into the locker with all the rage I had. My captain came in to see what all the commotion was.

"What are you doing?" he asked. "Nothing," I replied. "Let me see your hand," he commanded me. "You knot head you've gone off and broken your damn hand get on up to the chief's office show'em what you've done." I entered the chief's office where all the men would hang out and chew the fat. "Everybody get out!" the chief shouted. Once his office was clear of everyone with the exception of my captain, him and me, he asked, "What in the hell is going on Ashley?" "Nothing Sir," I replied. "Nothing Sir my ass let me see your hand you've broken it now tell me what's going on with you." So I began to explain the events that my wife and I had been going through and he listened attentively and showed a great deal of compassion for my present situation. He asked me if I needed any time off, a stress leave he called it to seek professional counseling. I declined the opportunity and he instructed my District chief to take me to the hospital for x-rays where I discovered that I had actually broken my hand in half and broke two of my fingers, a boxing fracture the doctor explained. Rather than allow me to go home for the remainder of the shift the chief ordered me back to the station where he could keep an eye on me and make sure that I could cause no more trouble.

I didn't see or hear from my son for a month I remained eaten up with animosity toward my undoubtedly now future ex-wife. Then surprisingly she called one night and we were on the phone for hours. In our conversation a lot of things were revealed to me. She shot straight from the hip and answered every question that I had. "What happened to us Joy?" I asked. "We grew apart," she replied. "But my love for you didn't depart, I still love you I've never cheated on you," I replied. "I know but I wanted to," she replied. "What do you mean who is the guy that made you feel that way; is he the one I caught you with?" I asked. "Who said he was a guy?" she answered. "What do you mean?" "Tommy I'm gay." "No you're not, since when?" I asked. "Every since I was thirteen you couldn't tell?" "No you're not you're just saying that because you don't wanna be with me," I said. "No that's not true I've had feelings for women every since I was a little girl and I didn't know how to deal with them." "So how do you explain Corey you had him when you were fourteen?" I asked. "Yeah I did but I never really wanted any children. When I got pregnant with him I didn't even know what I was doing I got pregnant the first time I had sex," she explained. "So what about us why did we have a child together," I asked. "Well honestly I thought if I got married and had another child that the feelings would go away. I never meant to hurt you," she continued. Right then and there I knew that she was telling me the truth. Only an insane person or someone with some type of psychological deficiency would cause another person to live a life of total misery and pain and receive fulfillment from someone else suffering. Joy was very bright very intelligent and when she made the confession of her lifestyle it was then that I drew the conclusion that she was very confused and any hopes of a normal relationship was null and void.

I started to feel regretful and humiliation for myself. I would now be labeled as the guy who turned a straight woman gay. Perceptions of inadequacy put me in a state of seclusion. I became a hermit; my social life consisted of sitting around the house with my grandma and going to church on a regular basis neither one being such a bad thing. I did a lot of reflecting during those times assessing the choices I made, the advice I took from others and scrutinizing every word that every woman had ever said to me in my life. There was a feeling of uncertainty as I sat and reminisced over my past and my future and I wrote down my thoughts and feelings once again.

"Uncertainty"

Uncertainty is something that we all must go through.
It's that feeling of doubt when you don't know what to do.
Afraid to take a chance, disappointed by an old romance;
Having to take that step again to find a real true friend,
Afraid to take a try, afraid to live or die, troubled by being
 deceived by
Another dressed up lie.
Uncertainty is a period that comes then it goes, driven by the
 feeling
Of reservation that seem so uncontrolled.
Be the problem large or small, the mountain low or tall
 you'll never
Know of triumph unless you're willing to fall.
And to fail is a certainty that has to be placed behind us, but
 fortunately
There is someone a Man we all can trust.
To sympathize and empathize to comfort and embrace, One
 who knows and understands the tribulations we all face.

I received plenty of words of encouragement throughout my endeavor some good some bad and others were down right absurd. Like the words some of the guys at the station offered in order to try and take the edge off of my mishap. "Well if it were my wife I would accept the fact that she liked other women and joined them," one of my peers commented. I didn't find that bit of advice helpful in the least not to mention I could never have shared her with anyone else. My brother in a harmless attempt to support me during a phone call one day gave me his bit of encouragement. "Look at it this way at least you know that another man didn't interest her," he said as we discussed women and their nature. "Hey man why don't you come down to Florida for a while and try to get your mind off of all that crap," he said. "I don't know maybe when Treyon gets to feeling better," I replied. "You need a vacation dude you need to come on down here and let me help you clear your mind for a while," he encouraged. "I'll call you next week and let you know for sure if I can or can't," I answered. Weeks passed and I had made the decision to call my brother with the news of my son and I coming for a little rest and relaxation. I informed my mother and grandmother of my intentions, packed our clothes and headed to Florida for the next two weeks. The ten hour drive was relaxing; just getting away and leaving my troubles behind started to feel exhilarating. I thought of the first time I had ever gone there and I smiled at the thought that it was our very first family trip and now I was making it again with my son who sat weary from the long drive yet ahead.

After driving for a good part of the morning my son and I stopped for a bite to eat. I decided to get something quick so that we could get back on the road. We stopped at this little diner in south Louisiana and got a few pieces of chicken, some sodas and something sweet for later. Once we were on the road again I reached into the box for a piece of chicken to give to my son and discovered that it was extremely hot. Having the temperament that most toddlers at his age has, he began to whine because I refused to give it to him under the circumstances. So being the ingenious father I was I took a leg and held it out of the window at seventy-five miles an hour and within a few seconds his piece of chicken was now suitable for any impatient kid ready to eat. I handed it to him along with a juice cup and settled myself for the remaining leg of the drive; snacking occasionally on my lunch. All of a sudden I heard whimpers coming from the rear of the car. I adjusted my rearview mirror to have a look at what had upset him and asked. "What are you cry about"? I asked him. And in a voice of total innocence he replied "My chicken flew out the window." I laughed at the thought that he was mimicking his old man but the truth of the matter is he saw me doing something as a solution to a problem but he had no knowledge of seventy-five mile an hour wind and what it could do to a piece of chicken in such small hands.

We arrived at my brother's home and were greeted once again by his loving family; his wife Jen conveyed her sympathy for my situation and agreed to watch my son who was now sleep after the drive down. Jen was from Michigan my brother had met her while they were both in the Navy. She was a sweet white woman who bore two handsome boys for him. Fats had shown me pictures of her when they had met, and she was and still is a beautiful woman and the reason for their divorce can be seen and understood in the up and coming paragraphs.

Out of all the people who offered their assistance during my crisis he was the only one who did not offer any advice. Whether it was because he couldn't believe what had happened or whether it was because he didn't know what to say. For whatever reason he sat and listened allowing me to spill my guts out over a few beers and a pack of Marlboro lights, and when I felt the urge to cry he presented me with some of Jamaica's finest marijuana. Mixed with the several beers it became the perfect sedative for the heartache I was experiencing. It's a peculiar thing about induced memory blockers they can't take away the problem they just allow you to forget them for a while and when the high subsides they are still present.

My brother and I were at one of his female friend's house one night we had been drinking and smoking all day. The evening was somewhat cool and breezy but nothing like the storm that I was about to encounter. We gathered with the two females and my brother introduced me to the young lady who would be entertaining me for the evening. Carmen was her name and she was a Latino beauty; long black flowing hair, a body that would make any Hollywood model envious and the willingness to please a man and make his jaw drop. The young lady who was engaged in satisfying my brother was a Cuban princess name Juanita, she was a little thicker than Carmen but just as pretty.

We started the evening off with some dancing and drinking, some talking and smoking and the entire time Carmen had only one other thing in mind getting me into the back bedroom which was pretty apparent. "What's wrong pa'pe don't you like me?" she asked in a seductive tone. "Yeah but I'm really messed up right now," I replied. "Ahhh why don't you come into the next room and let ma'me make it all better." My body was more than willing which was evident by the bulge in my pants but something on the inside of me would not let me get up. It was as if I was anchored to the couch and the weirdest thing happened that night there in the living room. Convictions of such unbelievable sorrow fell upon me that for once in my life I was compelled to listen to my inner man. The moment I vowed not to take her up on her explicit offer the weight was lifted and I could get up. I sprung from the couch with ease and headed outside for what I thought was for a breath of fresh air. I got to my brother's car and sat there with the sunroof open and within seconds the wind started to blow like I had never seen before. The most amazing thing was that I was no longer under the influence of the marijuana and beers that I had just consumed an hour ago. I was completely sober and the Lord was about to have His way with me. It wasn't like how people experience after drinking too much when they start pleading with Him or for the most part bargaining with Him by saying Lord if you get me out of this I'll never drink again.

No my friend He was doing all of the talking that night. All I could do was comply with what was being said. Which brings me to a very important point; we cannot stand or enter into the presence of the Lord any kind of way all of our iniquity must be dispersed. I am reminded of Jeremiah 23:19 and 20 which says:

Behold, a whirlwind of the Lord has gone forth in fury- A violent whirlwind! It will fall Violently on the head of the wicked. The anger of the Lord will not turn back until He Has executed and performed the thoughts of His heart. In the latter days you will understand it perfectly.

Although no harm came to me His fury was very prominent and it was an experience that I would never want to encounter again. The thing that frightens me the most was that I knew that He had cleansed me from my inebriated state. The power of the Holy Spirit was so strong that my body was totally restrained while my spirit quivered in fear. I was asked several questions during my conviction the first being, "Don't you know that you are destroying yourself?" My response was one of a child being chastened by their father all I could do was cry Yes! Again I was asked, "Do you know that you are not in control?" My reply once again was as a child being corrected with stern words because of the wrong I had done. Yes! I replied. "You are the oldest you are to be an example to your brother but you have surrendered to the ignorance of the younger don't you know that this is wrong?" Yes! Next a feeling of impending doom fell upon my soul as if the Lord Himself had flipped an emotional switch. "See you are not in control," He said. Afterward the floodgates opened I started to weep like I had never wept before. My soul grieved because of the destruction I had done to my temple. "Okay Lord, okay okay!" I remember saying as I sighed from being released from my restraints and without any warning it suddenly subsided just as swift as it had started. I sat there in the car trying to collect myself but there was nothing to straighten out He had done it entirely. All I needed to do was what He had commanded to do and I did.

If I were to guess I would say that the entire process took roughly four to five minutes; yet it seemed to be drawn out more extensively. I had fully comprehended what He was saying but in His unwavering promise to His word He had to reaffirm it for my sake. The trial which I had just gone through was repeated and this time the intensity was increased. Again I felt restrained as the Spirit of the Lord dealt with my iniquities; disciplining my soul as I replied to His questions once again, "Don't you know you are destroying yourself?" Yes! Yes! "Do you know you're not in control?" Yes! "Don't you know your behavior is wrong?" Yes! Yes! Then just as before my soul was flooded and I wept "Okay Okay Okay!"

Once this was over I moved with a sense of boldness and urgency as I proceeded into the house where my present company was. They were all still indulged in their immoral acts and I was now the thorn in their sides. "Fats get your things and let's go," I commanded my brother. "Man what's wrong?" he asked. "Nothing get your stuff and let's go now!" I could see his eye become enlarged and although intoxicated he could somehow feel or sense the importance of us departing. As we left, the young ladies were asking what was wrong and why were we leaving. I didn't feel that I was obligated to give them an explanation for our abrupt exit. I just knew that my brother and I were not to be there.

We got to the car and that's when the interrogation from my brother began. "Man what's the deal you don't wanna do o'girl, she was feeling you dog I know she was gonna let you tap that," he insisted. It seemed as though the one question that I had posed to him brought about a haunting revelation and an immediate sobering. "Man what the hell are we doing here?" I asked. "Trying to get laid," he replied. "Well it's not right," I replied. "Fats the Lord visited me and He was not pleased with what we were doing." His countenance had changed so dramatically it was as if he was witnessing a new birth. Then it began to happen again the exact same thing that I had experienced in seclusion the Spirit of the Lord began to manifest it in the presence of my awe stricken brother. In the process of trying to explain what had happened it was as if the Lord said, "Silence I can show him better than you can explain it to him." The previous questions that the Spirit subjected me to were now being revealed to my brother. I grabbed his hand and the power and glory of the Lord became so overwhelming that he too began to suffer the effects of His presence. The Spirit of God moved through me disturbing his soul and this time I was spared all the grief I had felt on the occurrences before. "Do you know that you are destroying yourselves?" the Spirit inquired. Yes! Yes! I replied. "Do you know that you are not in control?" Yes! "Don't you know your behavior is wrong?" Yes! Yes! "Be yea conformed." The Lord commanded. Then as before my soul was flooded and I wept without anguish "Okay Okay Okay Lord." The experience was horrifying to say the least to my brother who now sat in the passenger's seat shouting from the top of his voice. "Tommy what's wrong what's going on Tommy talk to me!" Desiring that he was conformed as well the Lord allowed me to speak calmly and convey the things he had just experienced. "Fats, Fats," I calmly called to him. "Yeah man what just happened?" "It felt like I couldn't move like someone was holding me down," he stated. "God is not happy with what we're doing," I confessed to him. "He said that we are destroying ourselves, that we are not in control that He is, our behavior is not pleasing and He wants us to be conformed to do the acceptable things."

The serenity of the evening was established once again and the two of us having an ample dose of admonishment by the Spirit of God we were inclined to spend the remainder of the night sober and reflecting on our transgressions. We sat in the parking lot of a well known shopping mart and watched the sun come up as we had done on many occasions. We did not speak of our spiritual encounter for some years later. It remained our mysterious conviction until we shared it at a family gathering. After our experience I desired to leave Florida and was all too eager to return home. All thoughts of returning to the Sunshine state were nullified in fear of reuniting with the demons that had possessed me during my visit. I would never allege that we were victims of any kind of premeditated injustice; we had well earned our chastisement and it was only when I had reached my spiritual maturity I was able to understand. Just as the latter part of Jeremiah 23:20 states *"In the latter days you will understand it perfectly."*

I returned home somewhat liberated yet revolted by my actions that I had exhibited during my retreat. I was relieved at the thought that I wasn't as troubled as I was before my trip. The problems were still present they had been put on hold, but I was determined to not allow my destructive mannerism to consume me once again. I tried to resolve any issues that may have hindered me from moving forward. I even called Joy to tell her that I had no hard feelings about our recent breakup. Though hard to do because of the love I had for her I had to put that chapter in my life behind me.

When I called her she informed me that she was no longer seeing the guy that I caught her with, but for some reason I felt that a bomb was about to be dropped and it did. She confessed that she was now seeing this young lady and the bomb was that I knew her she had attended my old alma mater. We even had a junior military cadet class together whereas she was one of my subordinates. Damn it I thought to myself. What was she trying to do? Was she trying to totally devastate me; was she that vindictive that she would do anything to persistently humiliate me? I wanted to reach through the phone and just choke the very life out of her. I really didn't want to hear about how happy she was or who she was involved with not that I wanted her to be miserable or anything. It was difficult for me to share that type of news with her. She was forcing me to cowboy up. (Get tough) A term I acquired while in the Army. There were many times in my life that I had to apply that principle to certain situations and although God's grace is sufficient for us, and His strength is made perfect in weakness it appeared that I would need the latter principle even more than ever.

The Bible tells us in Isaiah 54: 16 and 17, *"Behold I (God) have created the blacksmith who blows the coals in the fire, who brings forth an instrument (weapon) for his work; and I have created the spoiler (destroyer) to destroy. No weapon formed against you shall prosper, and every tongue that raises against you in judgement you shall condemn."*

However, once again spiritual immaturity would only allow me to understand this truth when I had submitted to the Lord, but to be under God's grace has enabled me to appreciate and respect Him sparing me during my time of ignorance. To God be the glory forever and ever.

I would face some bitter times after hearing about her new found relationship; not only bitter but detestable times. I began stereotyping every young woman I came across and if there were two of them together they were branded with a lesbian tag. Trusting a woman was difficult and I often had the propensity to convey to the couple in question just how I felt about their atypical increasing epidemic. I was not a bashing radical in the sense that I became physical but I would verbally express exactly how and what I felt.

There was a time when my untactful comments fell upon Joy's ears and in an attempt to correct and rebuke her I painted a picture of total hostility toward her and her girlfriend. I had to remind myself that I did not make her, I certainly did not break her and I absolutely unequivocally could not repair. Nevertheless, determination and persistence can often be our worst attribute when we are trying to reprove someone. In the hopes of helping we have the propensity of driving them away and that was precisely what I had done. She became so irritated by my tactics of conviction that she finally told me that if I could not deal with who she was and what she was interested in that I could go to hell. Her reply substantiated the adamancy of her decision to continue in the relationship although it was one that many had frowned upon.

I learned a very important lesson from her steadfast dedication to the things she had come to trust. That is I should have been more inclined to dedicate myself to what God wanted me to do versus what I thought I could achieve on my own merit. The possession of the right principles is often the factor that compels a person to become so adamant about a cause, but often the cause is not worth defending. I am reminded of Paul the apostle (formally called Saul) who possessed the motivation and steadfastness of persecuting followers of Christ. By kicking against the goads he had placed himself in the abominable path of unrighteousness. The Bible described him as being consenting to his plight even to his death. This implies that he concurred with what was being proposed by those (the Sanhedrins) who later stoned Stephen to death for preaching the truth about Christ. Not only does it imply that he consented to the callous deeds of the Sanhedrins but it also exhibits the pretentious nature of a person who has been mislead to believe that what they see and hear though wrong is tolerable and accepted. Therefore, we do what we believe is right and condemn the very truth of our spiritual guidance; dedicating ourselves to a cause that often has no social value and in the case of Joy no spiritual value.

It was not until the Lord intervened and revealed Himself to Saul causing his dramatic conversion from persecutor to preacher giving him the ability to move forward and find the first church of God. "Why are you persecuting Me?" "Why have you wronged Me?" "Why are you so adamant to commit such injustice toward Me?" All of the previous questions can be interpreted as being plausible to the situation he is now facing in the sight of the Lord. Saul's misleading notions kept him in a position where he was going against the will of the Lord. He had been conforming to what was not true and like Saul we have the same susceptibility. Jesus identified Himself to Saul and plainly tells him that it is useless, futile, and even pointless to kick against what God has ordained. In essence He was telling Saul, Saul you cannot win. Saul's heart and mind had to be transformed into a yielding vessel that the Lord could use to teach others and that is just what he became a loyal, committed, righteous servant of the Most High

God. With all of that being said the idea that I could change her became more and more absurd. I was still not able to agree with her lifestyle. I could only hope that a change would be made; that she would surrender to what the Lord wanted and not to what I had expected.

At present I'm able to write these things because of the change in my life, the awakening, the reviving. Before, I thought that I was about to go mad and that the things I was confronted with would be my demise. In the next chapter I write about filling the void and the point is this whatever you allow to be placed in the void that has been created in your life whether it is made by you or created by God. They ultimately bring you to the place He desires you to be. The void must be filled by Him. Who knows best the created or the Creator? It is my belief that the Creator knows what we need to fill that empty abyss.

The problem is sometimes we are not willing to be filled with that which He has to offer. God has a blessed offering that is so abundant and fulfilling that David the king of Israel simply refers to it as the Beauty of the Lord. As I have stated earlier bitterness and resentment was an unrelenting menace and they were factors which encouraged me to write

"Chaotic Asylum".

My poor unfortunate soul I watched lying in destitution;
In a cold and bitter place an abyss of immense pollution.
Seized by the vision that has been seared in my mind;
At times it's a befitting punishment for an unbefitting crime.
The crime, loathing hatred surmounting deep inside;
O' how I've yearned for that day that I had died.
To have ended it with a slash or an unrefined drink;
O' chaotic asylum of mine what other asinine thoughts do
    you think?
My thoughts at times were dark and my tentative notions
    would dwell;

In a place where I could hide things, secrets I couldn't tell.
A fortified solitude, a den of lonely seclusion;
Anguishly filled retreats and problems without solution.
Thoughts of despair are coupled with pain and agony;
A multitude of feelings but only one true enemy.
Unchained desires to lash out and destroy; to seek a type of
Vengeance not mines to employ.
I contend with reality and find pleasure in my dreams;
But of the first I find a horror and no one can hear me
   scream.
Curse or fate, mishap or misfortune I can't discern the
   problem;
And it seems that no one can save me in my chaotic asylum.

Sometimes we are overcome by the iniquitous depth of darkness that creeps into our hearts and mind; which causes so much chaos in our lives until we become complaisant. Before long darkness and sin seem to be the normal thing for those who have never experienced Christ. It is a dangerous place for any person to be. My appeal to you right now if you have not received the Lord as Savior in your life is to do so now. Join a church that will give you the teachings you need to further your relationship with the One who gave His life that we may live. Contrary to your precarious times God is able to work in you in ways you may have never imagined. Yet all He requires is that you confess with your mouth and believe in your heart that God raised Jesus from the dead and you will be saved.

SIX

Filling the Void (Fulfilling the desires of the flesh)

When the things which are new to us appear to be stagnant or fail to produce the results anticipated we as humans revert to that which we were once found comfort with and that is what this chapter deals with, the inability to wait patiently. After I came to the conclusion that divorce was an imminent reality my behavior became erratic. I exuded an air of self-gratification and I was determined to have what I wanted when I wanted it and as I mentioned in chapter five the principle of determination is good but the cause in which I applied it to was not. At this point in my life I didn't care who I had hurt with the exception of my family; others and their feeling, their emotions meant very little to me. If it didn't pertain to pleasing me you were disregarded like yesterday's trash. Cruel I know and not logical by any means but this is what I was reduced to after what I thought was a great injustice.

Feeling this void started out simple enough just let the young lady know what I wanted and with little or no encouraging from me it took off from there. If she was not interested then I moved on to another like some kind of untamed beast. It became a reckless and damaging way of life that left bridges burned and seemingly lifelong disfigurement for those who stood in my destructive path. The truth of the matter was that I did not have a clue to what I was doing.

The first of my victims was a young lady I had met while working part-time for an inventory company. I had inquired about her through a friend of mine name Michael. We were all taking a trip down to the "Big Easy" (New Orleans) to audit a huge department store and we were going to be there for at least a week. I first noticed Shelia when we all met at the office for one of our motivation meetings before we departed. My intentions were to just have someone I could have intercourse with while away on business trips. However, my scheme to make it a sexual affair backfired and I found myself falling for her hard.

I walked into the office surveying the potential candidates for my other than honest affair. She was sitting with her friend Paula and immediately there was an attraction to her. She was a high yellow, tall framed, well endowed woman both frontal and rear and somewhat timid at first glance. Michael and Paula were an item at the time and the two of them thought that we would make a nice couple. Shelia and I exchanged smiles as I walked by then I could see Paula whisper something into her ear. You ever have that eerie feeling as though someone was looking or talking about you? That was the feeling I had as I walked into the office. I would later find out that she thought I was nice looking. I didn't want to steer her into believing that I was attracted to her. So I played the game that many young men and women play with aspiration of not being overly enthusiastic about the potential of meeting someone.

During the drive south I couldn't help but notice how nice Shelia looked. I had positioned the review mirror in the van whereas I could keep my eye on her. Michael had mentioned to Paula that I was interested and like wise she had conveyed to Paula that she was interested in me. It was only a matter of time before I approached her. The introduction was not odd at all we had both shared our mutual interest for each other to others which made for an effortless union. "Hi, I'm Tommy," I said. "I know Paula told me who you were," she replied. "What else did she tell you about me"? "Why are you worried"? "No not at all," I said as I smiled. "So would you like to have dinner with me tonight so we could talk some more". "Well I was to meet Paula and Michael but I guess you and I could join them for a while". "What time"? I asked. "Six o'clock," she replied. "That's sound good so I'll see you then". "Okay," she answered as she and Paula turned to walk away.

We would spend a great deal of time together and our relationship grew into one that would lead us to start living together. She had a small one bed room apartment liberally furnished and things looked as if they would develop into a more permanent correlation. I introduced her to my family and friends; purchased a commit ring to signify how serious I was about being with her and after a year of committing myself to her exclusively she was swept off her feet by a fast talking car salesmen. I guess he had what she was looking for a great deal on a used car.

For a brief while she made me feel complete. Although my intentions were other than honorable when we first met my ambition to be with her for the person she was grew. We struggled together, shared a lot of pleasant times with each other. I'm reminded of the Christmas she and I were together and I purchased the commitment ring; I had taped it to the inside of an old video cassette box and placed it under the tree. We had agreed to invite our families over to open one gift during the eve of Christmas. Our families all showed up at the appointed time and had opened their gifts. I proceeded to the tree where she had several other gifts from me and I picked up the one that I had rigged for the occasion. Everyone looked on with anticipation as she ripped open its wrappings shaking it in the process as to guess what the content would be. When she saw the video cassette box her reply was, "I already have this movie." "I know," I replied. The looks on the faces of everyone who had gathered was totally blank. No one knew what to say and with a look of great disappointment she calmly set the box down and left the room. "That wasn't very nice," my sister stated. "Why did you do that Tommy?" my mother asked. "You need to apologize to her," my mother continued. "Shelia," I called to her. She came walking down the hall like a heart broken kid on Christmas morning. "Tommy I am so upset with you right now I don't want to talk to you." "I know baby and I'm sorry but you need to look in the box." When she gazed into the box and examined the contents closely she let out a scream that startled everyone. "O my God Tommy no you didn't!" she yelled. "What is it what is it"! Everyone asked. She ripped open the box revealing the content of the ring that I had taped to the inside and with a great groan of excitement everyone gathered for a closer look. She leaped from the couch throwing herself on top of me where I was sitting on the floor drenching me with hugs and kisses. Those moments though short lived were great and memorable. Once again I was happy and like the times I shared with Joy they were forever seared in my mind and every once in a while something would jog my memory whether it was the sight of something, or an unforgettable fragrance. The results have always been the same a journey into my pass that was both enjoyable and regretful. Nevertheless they are my memories which I have decided to share in hopes that you are helped and the humor of them are a soothing remedy in your times of need.

The breakup with Shelia was a terrible one. I guess it was because of how it happened. She began to come home late when she thought I would be asleep, or when she did come home she would have a ton of things to do that were imperative and required a better part of her evening. All conversation ceased and she was looking for any excuse to end it all. I, unintentionally, would give her that excuse she needed one day when I forgot to pay the phone bill. The phone had been off before and we would go downstairs to the pay phone which was right across the way and order pizza or take care of any business that we needed to. I got in from work that afternoon and she had left me a letter explaining her wishes.

~

Dear Tommy,

I find it difficult to write this letter to you because of all the things we have gone through with each other, but if I don't say it now I may never find the courage to do so.I think it is better to end this relationship before one of us gets hurt. I'm sorry for not being able to tell you this to your face. Please take all of your things, I need a change.

Shelia

When I read her letter my heart felt heavy. The pain of loss once again sent my mind spiraling to get a grasp of why or how this all happened. She had confided in her friend Paula who had divulged the information to Michael (her husband) who later told me why things had gone the way they did. During the process of looking for her a car she had met this guy who obviously swept her off her feet. Until then I was convinced that I could resolve what ever problem we were experiencing but the inevitable had happened her desire was for another and again I was alone. I left her this letter in the efforts to reconcile but to no avail.

Dear Shelia,

I don't understand why we can not work this out. All I know is that I'm very much in love with you. Let's talk about this call me.

Your forever
Tommy

I left a handful of quarters on the note on the floor I had written, grabbed my things and locked the door behind me. Hours passed not a word from her. The hours turned into days and days turned into weeks and after the first month of not hearing from her I closed that chapter of my life and moved on.

Before I turned the page of that chapter I sat and wrote these lines to express the way I felt when I was convinced that there was no more love.

"Love No More"

Love was given but never in vain; and
Love was received but no longer remains.
Like those who've died may never feel the pain,
Nor have the chance to taste a spring time rain.
A pity it must be to have love there no more,
Shut out and denied by a once open door.
To have had someone willing to give you his own life
Is without a doubt the greatest sacrifice.
Yet you would defy me and ultimately deny me,
From giving you a part of me that long to be with you.
Disavowed, and rejected alone feeling blue,
I have no one now to give my love to.
No peace of mind, no joy to bind, no one to adore,
A pity it must be to have love there no more.

Emptiness is excruciating and to have love inside of you with no one to share it with is devastating. I knew what I had to offer but it seems that the opposite sex was not interested in my proposition. I started to view myself as damaged goods and if they were not willing to accept what I had to offer, then I would be content with them exploiting my goods. For several years this was the mentality I possessed not knowing that I was jeopardizing my spiritual growth; increasing the distance between my Maker and myself. I was enjoying the satisfaction my flesh was receiving and became engulfed with the perversion of my pleasure. Pornographic paraphernalia began to pollute my heart and mind and the more I conceded to it the more perverse I became. The hatred and bitterness that was awakened in me caused me to do only the things which pleased me. If I was not able to have love then I would settle for lust. If affection was not attainable then sex would sustain me. As I began substituting one sin for another I also started to notice how my attention was averted from my spiritual growth. I became consumed with immoral acts. I lived to satisfy my flesh and I fed that which was slowly but surely dying.

A visitor came to see me at the station one evening which only added fuel to this fire that was consuming me. It was Angie my high school sweetheart. She had called weeks before and told me that she was coming state side and she wanted to see me. Angie and I were very fond of each other. Fate would have it that I would join the Army after school and some two years later she would enlist in the Navy. Until then we would only write each other occasionally to keep in touch, she once enticed me to visit her in Italy but finances would not permit. We exchanged photos and letters and suddenly without any explanation all communication ceased. A year later I ran into her sister and she informed me that Angie had gotten married. When she returned state side she called but the conversation was nothing I had anticipated; she talked of her husband's alcoholic binges, the physical and verbal abuse she suffered. I desired to take her away from it all but our careers made it impossible, not to mention she was still married. She would surprise me with a visit at the station one evening and she looked great, petite frame, dark smooth skin and a smile that could melt ice. She presented herself with an extremely affectionate hug one that lasted several minutes and she whispered softly in my ear, "I've missed you." "I've missed you too," I replied. "How's everything?" I asked. "I don't think that I can continue in my marriage," she replied. "Why what's wrong?" She went on to tell me how they were separated and that the probability of them getting back together was slim to none. I found this bit of information a little too encouraging. "Can I see you after you get off of work today?" she asked. "Yes yes yes," I thought to myself. "Yeah, what do you wanna do?" I asked with a coy demeanor. "Isn't it obvious?"

she replied as she ran her fingertips across the back of my neck, sending a shiver down my spine. She kissed me and I walked her to her car and made plans to see her that night.

That evening I picked her up at her mother's house. I had the pleasure of meeting her when Angie and I were in high school. I don't know what she really thought about me because she caught Angie and me making out in the back seat of a mutual friend's car while parked in the driveway of their house. Of course this was years ago when we were in high school. I pulled up at the house at 6:30 or so, it still looks the same I thought to myself. I went to the door and rang the door bell, and the feelings of a young boy with jitters came rushing back. Her sister answered the door, "Angie, Tommy is here!" she yelled. She emerged from the back of the house looking incredible. The scene took me back twenty years. "Why are you yelling," Angie asked. "Look we are adults now," Sonya went on to say. "Ain't nobody got time for you to be playing these high school games," she continued as to taunt her younger sibling. "Aren't you going to speak to my mother?" she asked. "Your mother is here?" I whispered. "Yeah she is in her room." "Hi Mrs. Twine, how are you doing?" "Hey, how you doing come in here and let me see what kind' a man you turned out to be," she replied. "Look at you gone now, Sonya tells me you're on the fire department." "Yes mam," I replied. "What are you two getting into tonight?" she asked. You don't wanna know I thought to myself. "Mama," Angie whined. "I was just checking," she grinned. "Well I was gonna take Angie to dinner and then to the movies," I answered. "Yeah right," she replied giving me every indication that she was aware of our intentions. For once in my life I could agree mama knew best. A wise man once said that "The anticipation of death is often worse than death." A horny young man also once said that The anticipation of sex is often more exciting than sex." Mmm, maybe not, but I can discreetly say that Angie was worth the wait.

At dinner she informed me that she wanted us to be together. We discussed the option of me giving up my career versus her giving up her career. We were both well established and found it difficult to give it all away. I think a fear of the unknown was the deciding factor. We were truly into each other and had a lot in common; both of us were single now, military, sons, and humor the list was vast, yet our careers remained an issue. At the end of the evening which was actually the early morning I drove her back to her mom's. We sat in the driveway and reminisced over that moment in time and laughed. "So what are we gonna do?" she asked. "I don't know baby I wish I could give you a clear cut answer," I replied. "Well I have choice of a couple of assignments, what if I got one that was closer to you and we tried that?" she asked. "That sounds great," I said. "I'll get working on it and let you know something soon." "I have to fly to Virginia tomorrow to take care of some last minute things but I'll call you," she continued. "So when will I see you," I asked. "Give me six months and I should be back." We kissed and I walked her to the door.

As the days fell from the calendar I anticipated the day of seeing her again. She would call me every day with the news of her progress. An assignment in Florida one in Biloxi, finally one she was eager to take in New Orleans. I was thinking about her but that didn't mean a thing. Her husband wanted her back and this added to her confusion not yet divorced he had every right to fight for her. I remember being in that exact same situation years ago, but this time I was egotistical and what he wanted didn't concern me. After the timeframe that she had given me had passed she came back to me still married but separated. In an attempt to get her back he had given her a gift that I would come to appreciate as well. Whether it was to try and change her or make her more appealing to him (which she didn't have to) or whether it was to buy her devotion I can speculate.

She called with the news, "I've got a surprise for you," she exclaimed. "What is it?" I asked. "You'll see I'll be there in two weeks," she explained. "I don't like surprises, not when they are surrounded with stipulation such as what we are faced with,"

I explained. "Trust me you're going to love them," hinting teasingly.

I waited anxiously to see her, wondering what the big surprise was all about. I tried to imagine what it could be but to no avail. One day while sitting around at the station I received a phone call from her. "Hello this is Tommy," I announced. "Hey baby come downstairs," the voice beckoned me. I exited down the pole hole and went to the back parking lot. I could not believe my eyes she had gotten breast implants. "Do you like them?" she asked. I was speechless. I was use to gazing at her warm smile, this was jaw dropping. "Ahh yes," I replied. "They are for you," she explained as she firmly embraced me. "What's wrong?" she asked. "Oh nothing," I answered. "I'm just shocked." All the fellows at the station were stunned to see such a bombshell calling on me. As I gave her a tour around the facility they were all too eager to make themselves acquainted with the fine specimen who came to see me.

This is where I think I hit my dismal depth; my infatuation for her was so strong that I pleaded with God to allow me to have her and I would concur to any punishment short of death and disfigurement. (What a foolish request, I know) Obviously some form of dementia seemed to be setting in as I discarded all rationale concerning the matter. At the price of whatever poignant punishment deemed I was going to have her. Looking back on the affair I can't recall ever wrestling with my conscience; I willfully submitted to the desires of my flesh. I was treading on ground that I had no knowledge of and my sense of logic seem distorted; just where Satan wants you to be. There was a way out of my situation and I declined to take it. It was as if I was trying to push the old proverbial envelope. I simply gave in to what my flesh had been wanting and waiting for.

Paul writes in 1 Corinthians 10:13 *"No temptation has overtaken you except such as is common to man; but God is faithful, who will not allow you to be tempted beyond what you are able, but with temptation He will also make the way of escape, that you may be able to bear it."* The thing is I didn't want an escape from my fleshy desires; I wanted to fulfill them and fulfill them I did.

After we had embellished ourselves in this abominable act my flesh was pleased, but something deep inside of me felt a sense of loathing. For days I carried on physically as though nothing was wrong but my spirit was afflicted. I waited impatiently for my just punishment and days later it happened. I and my oldest son were on our way home when all of a sudden a car came from a side street, he never stopped at the stop sign. He hit the driver's front side of my car and plowed us into a huge road sign. I placed my hand on my son's chest because seconds earlier I had told him to fasten his seatbelt. I slammed onto the brakes but by then we had gotten into some loose gravel; the car jumped the embankment and rolled onto its side into a drainage ditch inches from a natural gas main. "Got damn it," I yelled. "Are you okay?" I asked my son. "What happened?" "That ass hole ran us off the road," I responded.

With expired insurance and a mountain of bills I was left without transportation for eleven months. Neither one of us sustained any injuries but my car was trashed, twenty-seven hundreds dollars worth of damage. I looked up and thanked God that no one was hurt and to further demonstrate His wonderful grace and mercy He allowed the officer to not arrest me for an outstanding warrant. "You know Mr. Ashley I am supposed to take you in for this warrant, but under the circumstances we'll overlook it this time." "Thank you Sir, thank you I'll take care of it first thing in the morning. After the tow truck driver recovered my vehicle from the drainage ditch, I journeyed home for my extensive period without a car.

God does not categorize sin but there is an exception. The bible makes it infallibly clear that you cannot be forgiven for blaspheming the Holy Spirit (which I have never done) but how could I boast about something as atrocious as substituting hatred for lust. Notice that the bible tells us that the wages of sin is death it does not specify what sin because in the eyes of God sin is sin.

Proverbs 11:3 states it this way: *"The integrity of the upright will guide them, but the perversity of the unfaithful will destroy them." Verse six adds "That the righteousness of the up right will deliver them, but the unfaithful will be taken by their own lust."*

Paul did boast about his sins he stated that he was as the chief when it came to sinning. Yet after his conversion he taught that those things which he was once guilty of he no longer practiced, but he had to be filled with something other than himself in order to carry out the things God had called him to do.

The void had to be filled and this was the cross road that awaited me. Would I allow the Spirit to fill that void or would I choose a worldly substance instead? I wish I could tell you that I chose the Spirit of the Lord to lead and guide me but the truth was that I desired to nourish my flesh and it became fat with immoral deeds. Some would be ashamed to admit their transgressions and I would have to confess I wasn't at all that enthusiastic when I took on the task of writing the events of my life. Either I was going to be honest and present them all or I was not going to attempt this endeavor at all.

There was this other young lady I'll call her Ann for the sake of embarrassing her and her present family. I had met her when Joy and I separated; actually we met while we were still married but the affair began after I was denied the pleasures of lovemaking at home. Ann was very smart, goal oriented, independent and a true nymphomaniac. She was not ashamed of her excessive desire to have sex and at the time neither was I. She was just what I needed. The feelings we had for each other were genuine; outside of the unparalleled sex we shared she was a good person. Not only was she given to my sexual needs she would always have something for me. She wasn't selfish but she was a perfectionist one of her qualities I could not adapt to and the reason we would never marry each other.

The thing that kept our affair so persistent was that we both enjoyed the way we made each other feel. It was like an addiction for both of us, it didn't matter what time of day or night; my place or her place, my car or her car, motel or hotel it didn't matter she was always ready and I was only too eager to go along with it. Another thing that made the relationship so effortless was that we talked about everything in great detail we left nothing to chance. If she didn't particularly care for a certain act it was open for discussion. Come to think of it she felt secure with every proposition that I had confronted her with. We connected in a way that I've never connected with a woman before and it was not always about sex.

We would go to dinner usually after sex, or we would go to the movies sometimes after sex, hell we would even have sex after sex. I can't lie it was about sex but the two of us were alright with it because we talked extensively about it. At one point we thought that we needed to seek psychotherapy for our harmless affair. I remember that we vowed that if we were not getting it like we wanted in the future that we would call each for a tune up. The void was definitely being filled (no pun intended). It came with the greatest of ease, commotion free, without any apprehension or debates. The only problem was that we had pushed the envelope so early in the relationship until we were already searching for new and more exciting ways to fill the void. Ordinary sex was starting to bore us and we were looking for an extreme to keep us interested. I made the proposal one day to do something that was so extreme I just knew that she would question my sanity. "I have an idea," I blurted out. "What is it"? She replied. "Meet me at my security gig at midnight; don't wear anything too complicated," I added. "What do you have in mind"? She asked. "Well I can't wait until I get off in the morning so meet me at work". "Okay"! She replied. I was working as a security guard at one of the local hospitals and had access to every room in the building executive suites and all.

Ann arrived at midnight as she was instructed; she pulled into the parking lot and I observed her from the monitor in the office where I was sitting. She was wearing a mini-skirt and a tight blouse that complimented her well. She approached the loading dock and I could see that she was somewhat nervous. "Can I help you mam"? I asked. "Ahh yes Tommy told me to meet him here". "Okay hold on one second mam," I said. "Mam what's in the bag"? I asked. "A change of clothes for Mr. Ashley," she added. "Okay mam I'll buzz you in just a second". The look on her face was one of complete panic but she held her ground sticking to her story. "Mam what do you have on under that mini-skirt"? "Excuse me!" she asked. "Raise your skirt and I'll let you in," I added. "I don't think so tell Tommy that I'll leave his things here good night"! "Ann Ann it's me I was just playing with you, pull the door it's open"! I hurried to explain. I met her down the corridor and she was somewhat perturb with my gimmick I had pulled on her yet still willing to fulfill her purpose for her midnight visit. We ventured off into the executive suite and proceeded with our risky rendezvous. The scene was very erotic and explicit and for a couple of hours we were lost in satisfying one another like we had done many times before. This was our routine for several years a sexual escapade that took us into exploring each other like I have never experienced before in my life. We were not into drugs, S&M or anything like that we received an erotic high during sex that is why sex with her was so addictive. There were no limitations to our obsession only those we had set. I had convinced her once to participate in a three-some; she eagerly agreed once she found out that the third person was a young lady that we both knew and trusted. It never happened but to know that she was willing to was gratifying enough.

There was this one occasion when the two of us were so desperate that we decided to take a night drive into the country for a little sex session. We were driving around in an area that was predominantly known for not liking anyone outside of the Caucasian affiliation but that was not a dissuading factor for us. We found this tiny little dirt farm road that I managed to maneuver down in reverse when all of a sudden my car began to make this horrendous noise. "Damn it what the hell was that"? I asked. "I don't know but it sounds like you have four flat tires," Ann replied. "Don't say that you know how far we are back off in here neither one of our cell phones are getting reception and it is dark as hell out here," I replied in total fear. "Get out and see what you ran over," Ann instructed. "Are you out of your damn mind I'm not getting out of this car"? So I did the only thing I could think of, I put the car in drive and pulled forward. Again the bloody awful noise was heard and the entire car vibrated. "I don't know what that is," she replied. I finally mustered the nerves to get out and check my tires and to my delight they were all still in tack. "Are they flat"? She asked. "No their fine," I replied. "So what was it"? "I don't know but I'm about to find out". Any smart person would have known better to get out of there but when you are thinking with the head between your legs versus the one on your shoulders you make idiotic choices. I put the car back in reverse and drove back into the undetermined danger and again the noise along with the vibration was experienced. I pulled back far enough this time and turned my headlights on and to my surprise it was a damn cattle crossing. I blurted out to Ann, "A damn cattle crossing"! "What's that for, she asked. "It keeps cows from crossing through the gate," I explained. "So we're on someone's property"? She asked. "It's more than likely deserted because the gate was open," I tried to rationalize.

So there we were in the middle of who knows where we began kissing and getting undressed. By now we were both in the back seat of my car with the windows up and the radio going. Within seconds she had managed to straddle my lap and the passionate session began; the windows began to fog up from the heat that the two of us were creating inside, so I cracked the windows to get some air. The car was rocking in sync with every thrust of our bodies it was wild. Then suddenly I could hear something moving on the outside of the car. "Shhh listen," I said. "What is it"? Ann replied. "I think someone's outside the car". "Don't play Tommy," she whispered. "I'm serious I see something moving". So I eased into the driver's seat and went to take a peek out of the window when I heard the most terrifying sound in my life. "MOOOOO"! "What the hell was that"? I screamed. "I don't know"! Ann began to scream. "Drive drive drive"! She screamed. I cranked the car up and turned on the headlights we were surprised to find out that we were surrounded by cows. I had not seen one that close up before being a city boy and all. So I began to drive and I forgot about the cattle crossing which I hit at about forty miles an hour nearly jarring my teeth loose. Once we hit the main highway I realized that I was completely naked with the exception of my socks. What I didn't need right now was some red- neck cop pulling me over for speeding so I slowed down and Ann finished getting dressed in the back seat. Once she got dressed she joined me in the front seat with the most petrified look I had ever seen on a person's face. I thought she was about to start crying because she turned away and all I could hear was this whimpering sound. "What's wrong?" I asked. She turned to look at me and made the most side splitting remark. "Tommy look at us you're butt ass naked with a hard on and I got my pants and blouse on backwards." From that point on we laughed all the way to her mom's place. Occasionally she would look over at me and laugh as I tried to get dressed at sixty miles an hour. I dropped her off and told her to give me a call later.

As I stated earlier she had more than sexuality as a quality and I got to know the other attributes she had to offer as a person quite well. She would tell me of the things that interested her and where she wanted to be in ten years, but her perfectionist trait was more than I could handle. It's been my experience that most perfectionists expect you to perform at their level or above and unfortunately I was not willing to. We parted company some months later yet we continued to stay in touch and like the changing of the seasons so was our relationship. Sex became less and less until one day it ceased to exist. One day while at work I decided to give her a call after about a year of not seeing her. I was somewhat apprehensive about calling her but I thought to myself this is Ann the woman I shared a lot of intimate times with certainly she would be delighted to hear from me. She was which she expressed in our phone conversation; "Hello may I speak to Ann?" "This is she," the voice on the other end replied. "Hey this is Tommy how are you doing?" I asked. "I know who this is," she replied. "What are you doing girl?" "Me and my husband are out and about to go and get something to eat," she replied. "Your husband," I asked in surprise. "You're not married," I stated. "Yes I am he is sitting right her next to me hold on," she instructed me. "Hello, hey man how are you doing?" he asked. He greeted me as though we were old buddies. "I'm great thanks for asking, so you're Ann's husband?" I asked in an awkward tone. "Yeah we got married about four months ago, it was small just family Ann didn't want a big wedding." "Well I didn't mean to cause any trouble I didn't know that Ann had gotten married," I replied. "Oh it's no problem as a matter of fact I'd been waiting to hear from you because Ann had told me so much about you," he stated. "What do you mean," I asked. "Let's just say I have my work cut out for me if I want to please her," he laughed. "Well I'm glad that the two of you could go into your relationship with no secrets. Ann is a wonderful person and I know that if you treat her good you can expect the same. Well the best of luck to you both take care of each other," I responded. "Okay man here is Ann." "What did you tell him?" I asked. "I told him that I had been with a man that could satisfy me and I wasn't gonna settle for less," she stated. "So that's why he mentioned that he got his work cut out?" I asked. "Exactly!" she commented. "Well I won't keep you from your hubbie I wish you the best Ann I'll never forget you, stay sweet." "Okay it was good to hear from you I wish the same for you too stay sweet good bye now," she replied and that was truly the last time I had heard from her. Where ever you are Ann thank you.

There were others though, ladies I used obsessively too fill the dismal void. After Ann there was Toni she had a kid, a little boy. I met her one day while driving the strip; she was in a little sports car that caught my eye. I pulled her over, found out that she was an old school mate and things sort of just escalated from there. She fell in love quickly and I ended up crushing her heart. After Toni there was Krystal a very petite young lady I met one night while out getting donuts. I would end up having a son with her (Mike) but at one point I despised her terribly. She wasn't even my type; normally I go for the plus size women with a little meat on their bones. She came into the donut stand on a night when I had had a chip on my shoulder. I was upset about something probably a female. She started the conversation by getting in my business. "You know you shouldn't leave your child in the car unattended," she said with a hint of craftiness in her tone. "Oh he's not unattended; before you or anyone else gets to my car I would be all over them," I replied. "He's a handsome boy what's his name"? She asked. I'm thinking to myself "Bitch please all I want is to get my donuts and get out of here." "Tommy but we call him Trey," I explained. Until this point I could not tell you what she looked like because I had not looked into her face yet.

It wasn't until the cashier had given me my box of Southern Maid donuts and I was leaving the store when she said to me "Y'all be careful out there." and I looked at her to reply "Likewise." I realized then that she was actually cute. Not wanting to be too obvious I walked on past her and went to my car. I was leaving the parking lot and was in traffic when I realized she had pulled up next to me. I could see her looking at me and it was then that I asked her to pull over to get her name and number.

She was young, pretty and was running a lot of game. My assessment of her now would be she thought that the only way to get by was to get over and she did get over on a lot of folks and on me as well. I fell for it and I fell for her. Like the Joy I once had I thought that she was the one. I was willing to do whatever it took to maintain the connection we had. She talked a great game. I even trusted her with my child and the keys to my car while I was at the station. Strangely my son started to withdraw from her and word had gotten back to me that she was hanging out in promiscuous places. I had left the fire station on two occasions and found her alone with her ex-boyfriend, but the thing that did it for me was the time I had come from work and my son was in bed sleep. I went to check on him and he had been playing opossum with her and when he saw me he began to cry. He raised his shirt and pointed at this gash on his chest. She said he fell. He said she pinched him. I wasn't a forensic pathologist but I could tell the difference between the two injuries. My son began to distrust her and I had had enough of evidence to feel likewise. She was not who she had claimed to be and in the past neither had I. It's funny that way what goes around comes around.

Then there was Chirley she had made several inquiries about me when I had joined the church my sister and brother-in-law attended. She was a beautiful woman, with two marriages, three grown children and one grandchild to her credit. I liked Chirley a lot but she made me feel like the character Winston from the movie "How Stella got her groove back," and all though this woman was fifteen years my elder I had no problem with it. When the two of us would go out to the movies you could never tell that this fine specimen of a woman was fifteen years older than me. The trouble was that she had more experience in relationships than I did and she knew all the games that young men played. Getting over on this beauty was going to be damn near mission impossible. We eventually agreed to end the relationship and remain friends.

Lynn was and still is a good friend of mine. She was introduced to me by one of my cousins who was visiting my mother one day. I came in and there she was sitting on the couch. I knew from the moment I saw her that something was going to transpire. What struck me about Lynn was that she was a voluptuous full-figured woman. She was a lot bigger than the previous contenders. She was very outspoken once the old proverbial ice was broken, and those eyes they were pretty; not like a hazel or an odd color pretty but they were deep as though you were looking into reflective pools. If that was not enough she sported very nice breasts. She made the cardinal mistake; she showed me too much interest. Remember I'm filling a void. There was this one time when we were talking, we mutually agreed to have sex. Well it turned out that Lil' Tommy didn't want to play that night. The mind is a strange thing; it didn't matter how much I wanted this woman the message was not being delivered. I was definitely attracted to her, but it was as if a block had been installed which diverted the signal for pleasure. Yeah sure the night was devastating and somewhat of an embarrassment but little did we know that something more was brewing. That very thing that started to develop resulted in a friendship. There is not one subject that Lynn and I feared to discuss. Our conversations were very explicit, thought provoking and long. On average I have spent more time on the phone with her than I have with any woman. She became my sound board. Yet just because you have someone to listen and offer sound advice, it doesn't necessarily mean that you are going to take that advice.

I can't pinpoint why Lynn and I never settled with each other. She had very few faults in comparison, she was independent, pretty, smart, so why not? Huh! Good question. We did eventually end up going for it again. It was okay, not my best performance; so again why not?

I can only offer this one explanation, "The mind is a strange thing." My wounded ego from times past would not allow me to live down the none inspiring, lackluster, semi-performance of our first rendezvous. And the desire of the flesh had not been totally fulfilled.

Lynn would be replaced by Laurie who lasted for several months until her boyfriend found us in bed together. Laurie and I worked together at a restaurant. She was a very flirtatious white woman with a nice shape who was into horseback riding, sports and things like that. She had been to my place a couple of times and we had gone out a few times before sex had even happened. The stage was being set though for it to happen, she would hint at having sex with me on occasion, but I never took her serious and then one day while at work she asked me "Why hadn't you approached me about us having sex," and I replied "What are you doing this evening,"? She sarcastically turned to me and replied. "Having sex with you this evening at my place at about six are you coming"? With a discreet nod of my head I eagerly accepted her invitation for an evening of fornication that was almost to die for literally.

Prior to going to her house I had gone to the trouble of showering and going to the store for alcoholic drinks. Once at Laurie's place she made us several drinks then she told me to make myself at home while she freshened up. She returned from the bathroom some fifteen minutes later or so, hair down and wet, looking good, smelling good and definitely feeling good. She grabbed me by the hand and led me to the bedroom where we remained for a couple of hours. Suddenly while lying there talking and laughing about what had just transpired the bedroom door slowly opened. There standing at the foot of the bed was a man I had never seen before and the look on his face and the tone in his voice was enough for me to have blacked out like a startled white woman. "What da hell"! I shouted. "So this is why you are not answering your cell phone huh bitch." he commanded. "Oh my God," Laurie cried as she scrambled to find her clothes. I desperately looked for my underwear that was now dangling on the door knob like some type of sex flag. She had taken her tip earnings for the day and set them on her dresser. "What's this are you paying this bitch for sex"? He asked me. "HELL NO." I replied. "Hey look let me get my clothes on and we can straighten this out," I pleaded. "How in the hell do you think I got in here? I got a key motherfucker," he injected. "Well I got an invitation," I replied not trying to be sarcastic. "Nigger what da hell did you say," He yelled. "Tommy don't," Laurie stated. "Bitch we need to talk," he commanded her. She grabbed a sheet from the bed and wrapped herself in it and the two of them stood in the doorway as I frantically got dressed. "Where are my draws, where are my draws, got damn it where are my draws"? I think I got dressed in thirteen-seconds; I can't really be sure, but the one thing I do know for sure was that he had just acquired a pair of recently used underwear.

By now the two of them had made it to the living room where he proceeded to call her everything but her name. I being dressed now could tackle the situation at hand. "Laurie what do you want me to do"? I asked. "You can get the fuck out," he implied. "I'm not talking to you I'm talking to her," I replied. She could not answer me she was in a state of shock. "Bitch you need to choose who you wanna be with, him or me," he demanded. "Hold on there cuz what do you mean choose she told me that you were married and it looks like you are about to jeopardize your marriage over a piece of pussy," I stated. "You been telling this nigger my business"? "SMACK" he gave her a fresh one across the jaw. Her face was red from the previous strikes she had received and she just stood there whimpering in fear. By then I had made myself around the room so if I had to make a dash for the door it would be in my favor. I had been told at an early age that opportunity stands at the door knocking and I was not gonna let this dick head stand between me and my opportunity of getting out of there alive.

"I know how to settle this shit," he added. "I'm going to my truck and getting my pistol and when I come back I'm killing both of you motherfuckers. Everything seemed to slow down. I had my hands in my pocket on a rather sharp knife that I had managed to open while still buried, and when he headed for the door that's when I had to deny him the privilege of leaving this little dance. "Hold on there podnuh you ain't going no damn where talking bout pistols and killing and shit." I had removed the knife from my pocket and inadvertently cut my leg in the process. The adrenaline was coursing through my veins and the maneuver happened so quickly I never noticed that I was bleeding. I had grabbed him in the collar and placed the knife firmly against the side of his neck swearing to cut him if he had even said the word door knob. "Nigga you even say door knob I'll cut your damn jugular and plead self- defense, I've tried to settle this with your dumb ass but you wanna act all brand new and shit," I warned him. "Laurie Laurie what do you want me to do"? "Put the knife down Tommy," she pleaded. "Oh hell no that's not an option!" I added. I could feel his heart pounding. "Do you want me to leave you here with him or what," I asked. "Yeah nigga you can leave," he replied. "Shut the hell up I'm not talking to you I'm leaving whether she asks me or whether I have to cut your damn throat," I warned him again with all sincerity. Laurie finally gave me the okay to leave the three party tango; her safety was in her own hands I presume.

I guess there was a certain amount of guilt on her part for getting me involved in this mess. I left the house and drove down the street where I called the police. That was the last time I'd seen her. She called the following day crying for forgiveness. Forgiving her was not hard to do because I, for one, had made up in my mind that I was never going to see her again and sex with her was not to die for and it was obviously not yet my time.

I didn't know it then nor could I acknowledge it but God had spared me. How many times have you heard of love triangles gone bad with multiple homicides and then the person kill themselves? Why did he spare me I didn't know? The answer to that phenomenal act of mercy was forthcoming when I was willing to submit to the will of God and commit myself to a life of obedience. That didn't mean that He was going to force His will upon me; it simply meant that He was going to allow my eyes to open to the sinful nature of man and be able to make a collective choice between a righteous or unrighteous lifestyle (conversion). When we have chosen to live a righteous life we become perfect in the eyes of God. Yet our perfection is not based on what we have done; our perfection is based on our belief in Him. To try and live a life that is pleasing to Him and not to us. Although a Christian life is not easy it is possible. The thing that is impossible is trying to live your life according to the standards of this world. Learning that vital lesson almost came at the cost of my life, and what good is a lesson learned if one is dead.

Some time after that I pursued a neighborhood sweetheart Le La. As young kids I was sweet on her and she was sweet on me, but we were young. She would have my third and final son Ty. Prior to our marriage she would marry and moved to California where her husband enjoyed extra-marital affairs so the story goes. Both Le La and I entered the relationship still carrying baggage from our previous relationships which made for a difficult journey toward matrimony. She knew about my sons; as a matter of fact during my break up with Krystal she told me that she was pregnant, but due to the fact that I caught her alone in my house with another guy I didn't believe she was pregnant by me. I shared that with Le La because I felt she had a right to know. I had been in too many relationships where I was only given half of the story. Consequently Le La was not able to trust me after I shared with her my many indiscretion and nature would have it I would continue to add to the distrust. Yet the choice was hers to make she knew the truth which was more than I could say.

Our titter-tottering relationship continued on its course. I would become upset about something and leave, weeks later we would make up and the cycle would start over again. I would always tell myself if I leave this time I would never go back and like an addict returning to a tavern for more of his intoxicating brew I would always return to her.

There was this one time when we got into this big fight and she started to demand that I give her some answers. My reply "I don't have to put up with this shit I'm leaving." I shouted. "No you're not you ain't going nowhere," she exclaimed. She began to rip off my clothes and the only logic I could come up with was that she thought that if she got my clothes off I couldn't leave the house. The scene reminded me of the Looney Toon character The Tasmanian Devil it was like she was swirling around me with this sharp knife cutting my clothes away. When she finished I was literally standing at the door butt ass naked. If I hadn't experienced it myself I wouldn't have believed it could have happened. I would go on to marry her some years later and the anxiety of getting married would grow more and more. The only thing I knew that would satisfy the anxiety I was feeling was to surround myself with the one thing that made me feel good, sex.

SEVEN

Resentment at its worst

Resentment is a strange emotion in that something or someone could prompt you to feel or act in a hostile way and the problem may or may not be about them. It could be a comment they may have made, an unexpected appearance or anything that would produce the sensation or even something that they've experienced in their childhood. Failure to accomplish a goal may also lead to resentment which may be accompanied with bouts of depression. Thoughts of abandoning the things and people you loved the most, why because you feel cheated, hoodwinked. I was a grown man with boyish thoughts of just running away and damn did I want to run. I would spend quite a bit of time yearning, wishing, longing for the chance to do it all again. I shared with you some pages back how my writing reflected the moments in my life. Hope was one of those poems that was crucial in the sense that it was a warning of my possible destruction and a reminder of how much I needed Christ in my life.

"Hope"

My troubled mind longing to find;
A way to make things right.
Courageous heart searching the dark;
Where it stumbles upon a light.

My wounded soul sat losing control
Reluctant to carry on.
Devoid of all understanding;
Of those things that seem so demanding.
Who did I forsake, what law did I break;
What road did I take and why is there no escape?
Is there more for me to bear or does it all end in despair;
Or do I continue on my own without a single care?
On some days I just wonder, trying to simply cope;
Waiting on tomorrow in which lies my hope.

Something that added further resentment was not being able to obtain something or someone you have grown to love. There was this young lady (Janetta) who I consider to be a very good friend once we got to know each other. I never noticed her on the job until she came to the station where I worked and began her probationary period. I didn't talk to her at first and a month or two went by before we actually began to hold lengthy conversations. We would stay up for hours talking about past relationships and we started to bond in a way that left me feeling a need to be around her. Call it infatuation or obsession either way I wanted her something terrible.

We made plans to go out some days later; all the guys were meeting at a local bar to have a few drinks and unwind from a long tiresome shift. The guys were surprised to see the two of us show up together they had no idea that I had asked her out. Janetta and I had a splendid time when we ventured out. One of the things I enjoyed most about her was that she wasn't concerned with who would pay she wasn't frugal. There was this one time when we had gotten paid and child support had taken its toll on my check and my outlook on life. I was confronted with a $180.00 pay check for two weeks and a $210.00 electric bill. I had come to the bitter gut wrenching conclusion that I was going to have to ask Joy to take care of our son. I resented the idea that I was lacking even the basic ability of caring for him and now I would have to go to the woman I tried to ostracize from our lives and ask for her help.

It was during times like these that Janetta seemed to step-up to the plate like a savior. "What's the matter Hon? Talk to me," she would say. "Well I know that I asked you out tonight but when I got my check it was no way that it was going to happen," I explained. "I've had to send my son to stay with his mother because I can't give him what he needs," I added "Hey don't worry about it I got you Boo whatever we need," she said. From that moment on she had me and I believed her. It was a feeling that I hadn't felt in a long time and the overwhelming emotions that engulfed me gave me the hope of possibly loving again.

She lifted my spirits with every kind act she performed toward me, she made me smile with every appearance that she made, she inspired me to write with every word that she spoke, she was a bridge I needed to cross to get me over the counterfeit relationships I had experienced. She was sexy I thought and yet I looked past her voluptuous figure into a person who was genuinely generous and I wanted to be a part of whatever she had to offer.

We had some great times together like the time we sneaked onto a military base and crashed an N.C.O. (None Commissioned Officer) New Years Eve party. The two of us were looking for something to do on that snowy night and it was obvious that we wanted each other for companionship for the evening. She allowed me to make the plans and before the night was over we had scored four bottles of champagne, all we could eat and drink and danced until we were exhausted. She confessed that she hadn't done anything that bold in a long time and we still talk today about the time we crashed the party of a lifetime. So unforgettable was the night that I sat up for the rest of the night penning

"The Sweetest Dream"

Unable to sleep for the fear that I may not dream;
I close my eyes and wonder what all this could mean.
I dare not slumber unless you await me in my dream;
Then and only then will I understand what it all mean.
The taste of your kiss shall stay upon my lips and every
Once in a while the chardonnay that you sipped.
I remain intoxicated by the scent of your perfume;
And smiled at the thought that I would see you soon.
Sade sing to us "The King of Sorrow" and once again
I smile at the thought of seeing you on tomorrow.
Departing from you was indeed bitter sweet; but it allowed
Me the memories that I will forever keep.
Breathtaking kisses, feelings of the little school boy;
A moment that would last a lifetime,
Remnant no words could destroy.
Thank you for "The Sweetest Gift" and "Every Word"
That was said and I thank you for the memories of you
Forever in my head.

Sex with Janetta was something I didn't press; it didn't matter then any way. We were having so much fun it never came up. There was this one occasion when I received an early morning invitation to her place to go work out with her and was given the brief privilege of viewing her incredible body. After that I couldn't stop thinking about her. In the pursuit of getting her to fall for me I would come to learn that labeling, titles or anything that remotely defined a committed relationship was not what she desired at the time. This made me even more determined to win that place in her heart as her steady. So what did I do I pushed her, I gave her an ultimatum. "Look what's the problem I like you, you like me why can't we be exclusive," I asked. "Why do you want to ruin what we got?" She asked. "What is it that we have?" I asked. "What we're doing hanging out and stuff," she replied. "Why do we have to label what we are?" She asked. "Because it clarifies what our intentions are for each other," I explained. "We don't need titles to communicate what we are to each other," she insisted. "Okay whatever," I commented.

Some nights later she asked me out; I all too eagerly agreed. I drove to her place and we found ourselves at one of the city's hottest clubs. Feeling somewhat attractive that night I thought that I'd turn the table on the conversation we had some days prior. We proceeded to have a few drinks and by now I had mustered the confidence of a full grown charging rhino. "Let's dance," I asked her. "I don't want too," she replied. "Okay I'll be on the floor," I replied. Seconds after I hit the dance floor I was approached by this woman she wasn't drop- dead gorgeous but she was a nice looking white woman. She had seen me dancing and motioning Janetta to come and dance with me; that's when she asked me "Is that your wife?" No, I replied. "Is she your girlfriend?" She asked. I paused for a moment "No we're just co-workers," I replied. I presumed I had given her the impression that I was lying or something. So she strolled over to the table where Janetta was sitting and asked "Do you mind if I dance with your husband?" "Oh we're not married," Janette replied. "Is he your boyfriend?"

The woman asked. The look on Janetta's face was keepsake as I stepped in and asked the woman "You wanna dance?" "Sure," she replied. Once we were on the dance floor this woman came alive. I had recently shaved my head and she could not keep her hands off of it. It was like a scene from the movie "Dirty Dancing" where Patrick Swayze and Jennifer Grey captivated the crowd with their gyrating pelvis thrust.

Janetta seemed to be bothered by the show on the floor and to add to the insult once we finished dancing my new tango partner joined us at our table. "So what's up with you two?" She asked. "We're just co-workers," Janetta implied. "So you wouldn't have a problem with me screwing his brains out tonight?" She asked. "No I guess not," Janetta replied. Her candid and bold comments must have gotten to my now spiteful co-worker; she motioned for me to ditch her but I was having way too much fun watching Janetta sweat this one out. Once again she was beguiled to the dance floor when the latest butt shaking song blared through the club. She immediately grabbed my hand and with no permission from Janetta she pulled me to the floor. I was eating it up watching the dissuaded look on the face of my co-worker as I was being groped and fondled by my indiscriminate dance partner.

Things could not have gotten any better oh but they did. Cheri the nurse I was dancing with invited a friend of hers to join us on the floor. This young lady was stunning. She was wearing a spaghetti strap sun dress, which was about thigh high, which was a thin nylon type of material. I could feel her soft skin as she draped her arms around my neck. Feeling confident in the present situation I threw caution to the wind and pushed the envelope even farther. As the two of them constructed this human, dark meat sandwich on white bread, which consisted of me in the middle. I proceeded to run my hand up the leg of my partner who had joined us. I started at her knee and slowly allowed my hand to glide up her thigh. I reached her waist stopping there to investigate the goods and I realized that she was not wearing any panties. She was grinding and gyrating on my leg which she had straddled and I was in La- La- land. She was tossing her blonde, shoulder length hair around and around and I could just make out the words that were falling from her lips. "Yes yes," she moaned. "Oh my goodness," I thought to myself. The scene was so hot she was having an orgasm and I was right in the middle of it. Talk about a blissful predicament. Once the song ended I joined Janetta at the table where she was nodding her head in utter repulsion. "You don't have any shame do you?" She asked. "Not tonight besides this was your idea, you should've danced with me," I teased. "Well I'm glad you're enjoying yourself," she said sarcastically.

I sat there like some big shot mob boss gloating and grinning from ear to ear. And suddenly Cheri emerged from the crowd carrying two bottles of beer one for her and the other for me. Janetta looked at me with the most vicious look I had ever seen in a while and shouted the words "I'm ready to go." My first intuition was to toss her my car keys and bid her goodnight. My second instinct was to call her a cab. "I'll take you home Tommy," Cheri insisted. "No that's okay I picked her up I need to get her home," I replied. "Are you coming back?" She asked. "Hell yeah!" I replied. "Okay I'll see you back her in a bit then," she stated. She got up from the table and passed flauntingly by Janetta, came over to where I was sat in my lap and kissed me on the cheek. Janetta looked on as to say bitch gone. I could barely maintain my composure as I looked over at my now astonished co-worker and calmly reply "You know I could die and go to heaven right now." "Shut up, you make me sick," she replied. "I know come on let's go third wheel, I added jokingly. Contrary to popular belief I did not go back to the club. I would like to tell you that Janetta and I went back to her place and made love until the sun came up. The truth is I returned to my house after riding around for a few hours. I was just as perplexed as I was before. It didn't make sense.

At work the next day a few of the guys drilled me for the details about our outing. "Ask Janetta you wouldn't believe me if I told you," I replied with a smirk. "Oooh somebody got some booty, was it good?" Steve sang. "Come on dog tell us what happened." "There's Janetta ask her yourself." As she began to tell what happened all the guys jaws dropped in admiration. I sat back like the big man on campus as the climax of that evening was being told. She left no particulars out of the story with the exception of the conclusion. The guys were on the edge of the seats and the first question was "So did you go home with Cheri?" I thought of leaving them all wondering; I could see Janetta looking at me for the conclusion she seemed anxious to hear. "No man I drove around for a while then went home." I finally confessed. "Ahh man that story sucks," Jeff yelled in disappointment. Everyone laughed. "You mean to tell me that Janetta didn't put out and you had some thrown in your lap and you didn't hit it?" Jeff continued. "That's when you should have told Janetta to put out or get out." "I'm disappointed too," Steve added. "You could've lied to us or something." I never felt a need to exaggerate the outcome of an evening with a young lady it either happened or it didn't. Lying about it was not going to make me feel any better about myself or the lie that I told.

Why was this woman so intriguing and why can't I stop thinking about her. Reflecting on the situation now it seemed all too contriving. A well orchestrated conspiracy to get me to remove my shoe and walk comfortably on this Persian rug and then without any warning snatch it from under me. I couldn't have her so I decided to put an end to it before I became too entangled and started stalking her (Not that I have in any other relationship). The wound she created would soon be exposed to the salt of her callousness. The finale that played out was humbling to say the least; a sense of numbness accompanied with spitefulness would present themselves when Janetta and I talked. While at the station one afternoon sitting at the table reading the paper she strolled in as usual as though nothing had happened; smelling good and looking as good. "Hey Tommy," she called in a teasing voice. My attitude was anything but polite as I mumbled a funky "Hey" to her greeting. "When you get a chance I need to talk to you," I replied. "What's wrong with right now?" She asked. "What's on your mind Hon?" "I think I'm going to just leave you alone don't call me and I won't call you," I stated. I anticipated her responding in a way that would convince me that she was at least hesitant about losing what we experienced. Without batting an eye she quickly and sharply replied "Okay" and walked away seemingly unaffected at what had just transpired.

The tension that lingered around the station between us two was like stumbling upon artillery fire. Several weeks went by and we would argue, fuss and carry on like an obstinate old married couple. I don't think our supervisors knew what to do with us. The fellows at the station would try mending the situation but to no avail. She would come into a room and I would get up and leave; I even stopped eating dinner with them. It came to the point that I resented going to work. I would do all that I could in the shift to avoid her. The smell of her perfume around the station was once a delight but now it had become repugnant a vile venom. The fragrance was sweet but it only provoked bitter thoughts of her.

"Duality" was a poem that reflected the turbulent changes that we sometime experience but on the other hand are too afraid of sharing or acknowledging.

> What have you done to make me feel the way I do?
> Concealing mixed emotions with no guarantees you.
> Thoughts of you I would love; some I'd come to hate.
> In all I have become jaded but in the beginning I couldn't
>   wait.
> To see your angelic face a vision I would adore;
> In all I have become jaded detesting it all the more.
> A strange duality raging deep down inside;
> An unbecoming persona that of Jekyll and Hyde.
> Separation of the two seems so inconceivable;
> The reality of your denial completely unbelievable.
> A difficult bridge to cross;
> Leading to God knows where;
> A bridge I must not burn;
> Because it connects an intricate pair.
> My goals, my accomplishments, my victories and defeats;
> The joy of you, the pain of you, the bitter and the sweet.

People are not perfect and what lies within them that makes up the commonality of men are the imperfect thoughts, values and the sense of incompleteness. Strangely enough to be incomplete is to be lacking, unfinished, missing a part or wanting. I'm reminded of the story in the book of Daniel where he is called upon to read and interpret the handwriting on the wall in the palace of the king of Babylon (Belshazzar). Due to his imprudent heart in dealing with the things of God and the outright disrespect for God, God revealed to him through Daniel his own fate. "God has numbered your kingdom and finished it, you have been weighed in the balance, and art found wanting." What has God numbered and finished in your life; an unyoked spouse, a dead end job, disease or debt? And when God weighed your heart in the balance were you lacking any of the spiritual attributes that are found in Him? So the story goes that after Daniel revealed to him what was written and its interpretation the king died that very night. You may ask what does the story of Daniel have to do with Janetta or me for that matter and the answer is everything.

Whom should we look to, to finish us God? The word of God tells us that "We should look unto the hills from whence cometh our help. My help cometh from the Lord which made heaven and earth." Glory to God. Jesus is the author and finisher of our faith, Creator of everything in heaven and earth. Too often we look to others or even ourselves to be made whole; never realizing that we do not have the power nor the resources. How can something that was made from the dust better or save himself; they can't the Creator must restore that which is imperfect. It has been my understanding that when God is changing the essence of a man the spirit of man yields. It yields because it knows that God is at work and allows the Creator to transform us by the renewing of our mind. The spirit needs not to be transformed it is from God and therefore perfect; it is the carnal mind which needs to be perfected. This is where resentment comes in because of the two forces working against each other. The flesh desires to do evil but the spirit desires to do good. Thus the mind has to be renewed; deprogrammed because what the flesh feels the mind must first sense and if the flesh's perception is that it feels good, it tells the mind that it likes what it is feeling and therefore the mind stores the data of pleasure that only the flesh knows how to acquire. Likewise God simply speaks to the spirit of man and the spirit is quickened why because the spirit is from God. He says in the book of Isaiah 55: 8, 9 *"For My thoughts are not your thoughts, nor are your ways My ways," says the Lord. "For as the heavens are higher than the earth, so are My ways higher than your ways, and My thoughts than your thoughts."* Just imagine if your thoughts and ways were that of God, but because of the flesh of man that lusts after the things of the world enmity is between God and man. So much enmity in fact that God announced in the book of Genesis 6:6 the Lord God was sorry that He had made man on the earth, and He was grieved in His heart.

As the Spirit of God was bearing witness to my spirit Janetta came to me one evening and asked if we could talk. I had no idea what to expect. She came to me in a manner that was submissive but strong, loving but brotherly. "Don't talk just listen," she started. "We've had some good times together and I really care for you. I don't want to lose you as a friend. I told you in the beginning that I was not ready for serious commitment," she reminded me. "I really miss talking to you so can we be friends; I know that you are a bigger person than how you've been acting toward me because I've experienced the real you before and the person you've become is not attractive," she continued.

"Just think about what I said you don't have to answer me right now, but I miss you." The revelation hit me like a bolt of lightning. My eyes were opened and for the first time in my life I had made a female friend that I didn't have sex with. After all the relationships that I had been in this one was rare we could actually converse with each other; talking mostly about our own personal growth.

There was a time when I saw two females in a car and I was convinced that they were lesbians. Satan deceives that way in that he tried to convince me that something was wrong with Janetta in the sense that she was gay. And when there was not enough evidence there to persuade me he tried to trick me into believing that something was wrong with me. I have never questioned my heterosexuality as a matter of fact my sexuality was a big part of my problem. So how did I get over that O'whoa is me complex? I didn't God did it. When we understand that the physical flesh is not who we really are but the person that is within, then racism, chauvinism, prejudice and bigotry can be eradicated. What do we do to obtain harmony? Understand that we wrestle not against flesh and blood, but against principalities, against powers, against the rulers of the darkness of this world, against spiritual wickedness in high places.

Let's look at Ephesians 6:12 a little closer. There is no rationale for one human to fight or kill another human being we're all human. It is the second clause that Paul makes that gives us a definitive reason why doctrine, opinions, practices or beliefs are offended. Principles are comprehensive and fundamental laws, doctrine, or codes of conduct that govern people. Knowing this it can be applied to situations where conflict is prevalent. Take slavery for example it started as an assumption or a belief that Africans/Negros would be a lucrative investment for inexpensive labor. True by all means according to thousands of slave traders who invested in ships to search out such a nation of people, but we did not share in their ideology. When the white man saw that the black man was different and did not possess a strong defense for himself or his home, he violated the black man's principles; his comprehensive fundamental law, his doctrine, and his code in which he conducted himself.

In Paul's third clause he gives us another description of the thing we wrestle against those forces or powers that are at work that we cannot and often do not see until it is too late. Everything someone says or does is manifested in power or force. When you say to someone I love you the power to do for them is released. Yet the powers and forces of evil become just as evident when someone claims to hate as well. These are the powers in which Paul speaks of frustration, anger, malice, wickedness, bitter resentment and the power of sin that we act upon are all associated with evil spirits that bring about contention.

I have often shared with people that Satan is a persistent adversary. He is the ruler of the darkness of this world. He is also a cunning rival who identified his intentions twice in the book of Job when God asked him "From where do you come?" "From going to and fro on the earth, and from walking back and forth on it." God knowing all things was not asking out of curiosity; Job was about to be tested and Satan would be all too willing for the challenge. Notice how Satan answers God as to not divulge too much of his plot. This is often his tactic half of the anecdote, then an all out assault on everything you own. As soon as God gave him permission his whole intent was to get Job to forsake God. We should be as Job when any calamity falls upon us unyielding, steadfast and holding fast to our integrity.

People react to adversity differently but those who have confessed Christ as their Lord and Savior should govern themselves according to Proverbs 3:11,12 and not despise the chastening of the Lord. Nor should they detest His correction; because whom the Lord loves He corrects, just as a father does to a son in whom he delights. Sometime a person can become so overwhelmed with hardships until they faint under the constant pressure but Paul tells us that if we faint not while doing good we shall reap our reward. The manner in which a child of God should respond to such a crisis is to be exercised by it; That is to say receive instruction from it, even the bible tells us that discipline is unpleasant and painful. However, it produces a harvest of rewards and peace for those who have been trained by it. The big question seems to be why me God or Why did God allow that to happen? Well I can't say specifically why due to Isaiah 55:8, 9 but I can offer several reasons why we should suffer. First, our suffering yields development that furthermore enhances our ministry to others.

Attributes such as endurance, joy, wisdom and growth are traits that give us the strength and assurance we need for God to use us effectively. Third it confirms the word of God in us as it pertains to Satan; there is no truth in him, he is the ruler of the darkness of this world and he walks to and fro seeking to devour what God has sanctified. When we suffer God receives glory after we have gone through, but just as such we should glorify Him while we are in the midst of our calamity. When we concentrate on God the period or timeframe does not seem to be as extensive. Another reason why we suffer is to make us more Christ like; when we experience the type of persecution as He or for His namesake we shall also be glorified with Him. How can we understand lest we suffer? To inherit the kingdom of God for our suffering is a reward that far outweighs any payment that we could receive. Change is inevitable when we suffer it is a humbling experience and a process that validates just how weak we are in the flesh. We are forever changing, forever learning as He reveals to us the roads we travel and the startling contrast of the avenue which leads us to God.

No parent should allow their children to continue doing wrong and spare them from rebuke. Although Job had done no wrong he was still delivered into Satan's hands. Suffering is a way to deter us from sinning; it is Jesus' power to restrain and a child of God needs only to suffer once to realize that sin is not worth suffering. In all, our suffering should lead us to total dependence as Christ instructed Paul in a vision in 2 Corinthians 12: 9 *"My grace is sufficient for you, for My strength is made perfect in weakness."* Although we may be weak when trials and tribulations evolve His grace is enough to sustain us. Vitality is attained if we faint not; our faith is strengthened as a matter of knowing that the entire time we were going through God will protect and provide for you.

"Oh, that I were as in the months past, as in the days when God watched over me." This expression made by Job in chapter 29 verse 2, was a plea in his defense. It is a reflection of how we all feel when Satan is on the attack. A sense of self-righteousness had set in, and as the Word of God states there is none righteous no not one. All I had experienced in the past was preparing me for work that only God could call me to do. The corruption and perversity that had overtaken me needed to be done away with. Only God could change me. Only my God could heal me.

The healing process is a difficult one and just like our physical wounds, scars can develop within us that only God can heal. Someone once said that time heals all wounds, but it is my sincere belief that only God can repair you entirely. When I was seven my parents decided to go to a local park one Sunday afternoon for a family outing. We all loaded up into the back of my dad's old 57 pick-up truck and headed to the park. The day was filled with typical family fun, food, reminiscing, loud music etc. As children this would soon prove to boring; my younger brother and I sought to entertain ourselves by throwing rocks at a large fifty-five gallon drum which was lying on its side at the top of a hill. The drum was partially filled with water and was held in place with a stake that was driven in the ground. The two of us had been hitting it and the echoes could be heard throughout the park. "Hey let's see who can hit the stick in front of the barrel," one of us suggested. And so it was we spent the next twenty minutes or so before one of us actually hit it. I can vividly remember turning around to fetch another stone and as I turned back around I was confronted with the barrel which once sat on the hill. I was leveled in my tracks; not even given the opportunity to elude it. The feeling was like having a three hundred pound defensive end hit me during a full blitz without any opposition. I lay there for a second trying to figure out what had happened; then my brother came over to help me up. "Are you all right?" He asked. "Yeah," I replied as I staggered to my feet. We walked over to the park bench where my folks were sitting. "Why are you so filthy?" My mother asked. "That barrel ran over him," he explained. "Come here are you okay?" She asked. "Yeah," I replied still stunned from my encounter. She began to help me tidy up when she noticed blood running down my white shoes as she raised my pants leg, the most horrendous cut you could imagine was revealed; needless to say that was the end of our outing. I was rushed to the hospital where I received twenty-six stitches in my lower leg. During our intense drive to the hospital I couldn't feel any pain. I could, however, see my bone which was protruding above the surface. In due time the wound would heal and I would be back on my feet. As for my leg it bares a hideous scar that remains to this day. It is a constant reminder to me of how disobedience does not go unpunished. I don't feel that it was a cruel lesson to learn. My life and leg were spared and it became a testimony to God.

EIGHT

A TIME TO HEAL

I found it difficult to begin this chapter; it wasn't because I didn't feel healed. I think it was more at the length and the process in which healing takes place that makes it so extreme. There are situations or instances that come up and I relive them in my mind, so the cliché goes forgive and forget. I truly believe in the principle of forgiveness but forgetting is sometimes taken out of perspective. How do you not remember centuries of coercion, the brutality of battle, and the malicious murders of a group of people based on the color of their skin or the devastation of a storm that not just happens to a certain group of people but occurs world wide? Unfortunately, as I write these lines, the city of New Orleans is in the process of evacuating tens of thousands of its residents due to the catastrophe of hurricane Katrina. Thousands are left without homes, jobs and sadly enough without love ones. Healing for the individuals who may survive the event will be painful, to some it will be unbearable, yet in the wake of recovery some will come to the conclusion that it is very possible. The misperception of forgetting is often hinged on forgiving which are two totally different principles. Forgetting is the inability of not recalling or not remembering; but forgetting in the spiritual sense means that we are gracious enough to overlook what someone has done to us. To see beyond the fence you must overlook it and if the fence consists of barbed wire you must look through it. Yet you are reminded that the obstacle still remains and the wrong doing of another will not hinder you from the goals you have awaiting you on the other side nor what God has in store for you. King Solomon tells us that, "*To everything there is a season, a time for every purpose under the heavens: A time to be born, and a time to die; a time to plant, and a time to reap; a time to kill, and a time to heal.*" Attesting strongly to the statement made by the wise king we find many have searched the world over for the meaning and satisfaction of life; only to find that nothing is attainable without God. Life becomes wasted searching for foolish things, tangibles and hopeless riches that can neither buy nor sustain our health.

Frequently those foolish matters are the things which cause us the most harm; subsequently, leaving behind wounds that later become scars. Scars are the body's testimony to an event in our lives in which we will never forget. They are visual reminders of lessons learned and experiences that have changed us forever. To this very day I refuse to go or do anything on a Sunday that is not associated with worshiping God or relaxing. "Remember the Sabbath day, to keep it holy," as His commandment says; a principle I adopted from my mother which she as a result began to administer to her life after our terrifying ordeal. What if our emotional scars were worn as those that adorned our body and gave a testament to our sensitive situation? We would be an uncomplicated group of people if our dysfunctions were worn as a label. We would know up front what we were dealing with; as a result we would not be hoodwinked. "How did you get that scar on your chest?" A person would ask. "Oh my husband/wife broke my heart," the other would reply. An even better scenario would be; "Why do you make me cry?" Another might ask. "Because I was abused as a child and being that I was hurt the only thing I know to do is hurt," They may respond.

Healing is essential in order to live life. If we do not allow the body to regenerate or repair itself infection sets in and rapid deterioration occurs, and if further unimpeded death is most certain. So what are the prerequisites for healing? Several biblical accounts are referred to when healing is an issue, it derives by four means: repentance, prayer, faith and the Word of God. Used alone each one is an extraordinary method of receiving healing, but when used in conjunction with another they become even more powerful.

Even in fulfilling my fleshy desires I was able to notice the opportunity to repent. At some point I would have to come to the conclusion that I was not able to be healed unless I invited Christ in and denied myself. Repentance consisted of me turning from those things which I thought I needed and trusting in Him for all I needed. It not only denotes changing it also embodies profound sorrow and an honest confession. "I am sorry Lord; I am sin sick, Lord I need You to change me, I need You to heal me, deliver me from the bondage of sin that I may be used to serve You." Let your request be made known to God; if we confess our sins, He is faithful and just to forgive us our sin and to cleanse us from all unrighteousness.

Something kept me from truly believing that God could forgive me for some of the things that I had done. Satan had painted such a picture that I was convinced that my sins were unforgivable; therefore I continued to wallow in them. We at times are our own worst critic we become so defeated with what we have done that we can't see or understand how God can forgive us let along heal us. He wants nothing more than to heal us; confused in our understanding of who He truly is we remain lost in our sins. God gave me these thoughts as I struggled to begin this chapter. Within hours it all came together; it is advice given to a hurting child that sought to find his/ her way. Poetically put I think the discourse would go something like this,

"If and When."

If you could see the scars that are seared within My soul;
You would know the wonders of the stories they have told.
If you could feel My heartache or share with Me the pain;
Then you could come to appreciate the sunshine after the
    rain.
If you could look beyond the darkest cloud, far beyond the
    veil;
You would see that heaven awaits; an image that never fails.
If you would just submit yourself, giving Me total control;
Then you could receive the promise of eternal life foretold.
If you would trust Me to heal you, excepting My Word and
    Son;
You would see that heaven awaits; and life has just begun.
If you could hear my plea before the storms of life arise;
Then you would know the mysteries and there would be no
    surprise.
If you could taste the triumph of all I have achieved;
You could come to appreciate the calmness after the breeze.
And when you walk through the valley of death, far beyond
    the bend;
Look toward heaven for it awaits you, a journey that has no
    end.

Prayer is the way we communicate with God. The Hebrew word *siyach (see-akh)* implies to ponder, i.e. converse with oneself, aloud. It also denotes commune, complain, declare, meditate, prayer, muse, speak or talk with. As the poem suggests God also speaks to us whether it is by His Word, dreams, visions, His angels or His voice. In the beginning both Adam and his wife Eve heard the voice of the Lord God during their plight to hide themselves from God's face due to their sin.

God has always been audible and He changes not, so why is it that we do not hear Him when He speaks? Christ gives us the answer in the gospel according to Matthew. His word is not to be used as a platform for debate, but rather for changing the hearts and lives of men. Christ says, "I speak therefore to them in parables because seeing they do not see, and hearing they do not hear, nor do they understand." He continues by quoting the prophet Isaiah, "For the heart of the people has grown dull. Their ears are hard of hearing, and their eyes they have closed, lest they should understand with their heart and turn so that I should heal them." Life for us is filled with distractions of the things we must get done, there is no wonder why we can't hear from God. We must disconnect ourselves so that we can retreat to a quiet place to meditate. Another variable that adds to the difficulty of healing is the constant reminder of your shortcomings by friends and love ones. Once again I would have to regress to Job who was persistently compelled from all sides that he had done something to anger His God. What seems even more daunting was the advice given to him by his wife after Satan's second assault. "Do you still hold to your integrity? Curse God and die!" Theoretically his integrity was the only moral fiber he had when his friends and family had forsaken him. He was continually in prayer with God and relied fervently on his faith that God would restore him.

During the process of compiling this manuscript I would be placed in a situation where my prayers and faith would be indispensable. In light of my ignorance to the devastation hurricane Katrina had just dealt to the Gulf coast I had made the statement that I would not go down south for the relief efforts. Like many others who may not admit I was not directly affected and I felt that it was not my problem. I stereotypically thought that they should have heeded the warnings and evacuated, but as fate would have it there were thousands who had no way out. I found this out firsthand. I had taken my younger sister to Houston (240 miles) to do some recording for a documentary; the trip was a turn around for me in and out, no sight seeing, no fellowshipping just drop her off and return home. She instructed me to give her a call as soon as I had gotten home and I complied. As the evening went on I received several more calls from her informing me that all was well and that the session was about to wind down. As I watched the news that night and I was surprised to hear that a category four hurricane was headed straight toward her.

Galveston, Texas had received a mandatory evacuation twenty-four hours earlier and Houston was next. This was all in light of hurricane Katrina which had just devastated the coast lines of Louisiana, Mississippi and Alabama. I was not able to sleep knowing that I had driven my sister down there and left her in harm's way. So finally at about eleven o'clock I called her; "Hey what's up," I asked. "Oh nothing much just got to my room, watching some T.V," she replied. "How long do you plan on being down there?" I asked. "I'm leaving Sunday; Keona is coming to get me, why?" "Well I was watching the news and from the looks of it you need to be out of Houston like right now," I exclaimed. "Why what's the deal," she asked. "They are reporting a hurricane for the area," I replied. "Oh my God I'm looking out of the window and these people are scrambling to get out of this hotel," she replied. I woke my wife and informed her of what was going on. "Are you going to get her?" She asked. "I don't have a choice I couldn't live with myself if something happened to her after dropping her off down there," I replied. "Are you going by yourself?" She asked. "No I'll find Fats and the two of us will go get her, but if I can't get in touch with him I'll come get you," I explained.

I found my brother and called home to inform my wife that the two of us were headed to pick up Tina. My brother and I got on the road at 12:45 and made the trek south into the unknown. As we drove into the early morning we could see a great sea of white light exiting the southeast portion of Texas. The thought I had was to stop and fuel up, and by the time we retrieve our sister the majority of the traffic would have dispersed making our journey home one of ease. To our dismay it would prove to be the most excruciating trip you could ever imagine.

Our sister was staying at the Marriott in an area of Houston that was not at all familiar. After driving around in downtown Houston for an hour we found her hotel and proceeded to go to her room where she had fallen asleep. The lobby of this high-end establishment was deserted, with only a handful of occupants remaining behind to ride out the storm. We grabbed her luggage and loaded up the car only to be met with the early morning traffic fleeing the area. We did not plan for such a delay. As we headed out we found that every road leading from Houston was in gridlock. Traffic was backed up for miles as the residents from Galveston and surrounding cities made their efforts to vacate the area.

Every highway, county road, side road, and back road was congested with bumper to bumper traffic that would move several feet then shut down for hours. In the beginning the three of us found it to be simply a nuisance but by the tenth hour with no northern progress everything about Houston seems to become painfully detestable.

We sat in traffic just on the outskirts of Houston and watched the sun rise. With less than a hundred dollars between the three of us we sat in the middle of I-10 westbound and began our painstaking trip home. While sitting in the mayhem, I observed one of my favorite eateries I had visited countless times at home. "Hey do y'all want something to eat?" "I'm not hungry but I could really use something cold to drink," Tina replied. "What do you see?" My brother asked. "Look over to the left off of the interstate isn't that a Jason's Deli?" "It damn sure is," he exclaimed. "What are we gonna get?" He asked. "I was thinking about a couple of sandwiches, some chips and sodas," I added. "Oh hell yeah!" He replied. "I just want something cold to drink," Tina kept insisting. With traffic moving periodically I remember having the fear of it suddenly moving forward and becoming disoriented; separated from my siblings, and wandering around trying to find them. "If traffic starts to move do not leave me," I remember telling my brother. "Man we ain't gonna leave you," He replied. "I'll stand outside the car and keep an eye out for you," He assured me. I dashed across four lanes of I-10 traffic, picked up the items we would need and made my way back where I found my brother standing outside the car twirling a large red and white umbrella. By now we were just thankful to have something cold to drink and filling to eat. We moved up in the gridlock traffic about twenty or thirty yards and there we would sit for the next four and a half hours.

We scanned the local radio stations to get traffic updates and frankly the news was anything but encouraging. "It's fifteen before eleven here on your favorite radio station and if you're stuck in traffic give us a call and let us know your situation," the radio personality announced. Hour after hour we tuned in to hear how traffic was backing up on 45 north, 59 and 79 north, and to make matters worse we had burned three quarters of a tank of gas idling in traffic. Our next necessity was to find fuel and every convenient store we visited gave us the same reply. "We won't have fuel until Monday." Which wouldn't have been so bad but the day was Thursday and bad news seems to have only added to our frustration. It began to look as if we would be spending our time in Houston looking for shelter from the storm.

As the hot afternoon slowly dragged to a close we were starting to run out of options; we became desperate to leave the somewhat inhospitable city of Houston. Aggravated at our present situation I asked my brother to take the wheel for a while. Since that this was not his first hurricane evacuation he proceeded to drive in a manner that bought us precious time. Any shred of forward progress we could make he took it; driving on the shoulder, rudely cutting off motorists and occasionally shouting obscenities from the window as we drove by those sitting idle. We were making some advancements north, but without fuel we would surely be stranded. You may be asking yourself what this excursion has to do with prayer and faith. Well I'm about to make my point. The sun was starting to set as we found ourselves scrambling westward out of town on a misleading impression that there was fuel in the adjacent town. While on this back county road nearly twenty plus hours into this horrible nightmare I exited the car and began walking trying to get a grip on what was happening. That's when I heard something inside of me ask, "What is it that you need; pray and believe and your Father in heaven will answer your request." At that point all I could think of was being at home drinking a bottle of nearly frozen water. I knelt down outside of the car, placed my elbows on the hood of the car which was extremely hot by now and began to pray. I asked God to give us a safe passage home and to intercede for us in whatever we needed during our trip home. When I returned to the car my sister was crying and I assured her that it would be okay. Earlier we were joking and laughing but now the mood was one of impending doom.

We finally made it to the gas station we were searching for and once again we were met with the news that fuel had run out four hours ago while we sat in traffic. By now I was beyond frustration; I wanted to hit something hit someone it didn't matter. I needed to vent my anger but no one person was responsible for our circumstances. If anything could be said about our present situation it would have to be that inexperience and ignorance of the severity of what could develop under the conditions faced would make for a good lesson.

With only an eighth of a tank of gas remaining we decided to spend the night in the parking lot and get an early start in the morning. We made signs which read "Need gas" and "Will work for gas." Our only rations were three gallons of hot water and no way to cool them. I don't know if you have ever had to rely on hot water to quench your thirst it doesn't it only added to the misery. All thoughts of us leaving that evening were dismal. This is when I took the time to pray once again, "Lord God You fed the children of Israel while in the wilderness with manna from heaven. I pray right now that you would hear my request to provide for Your children those things which we need to get us safely home, I ask it all in Your Son Jesus name Amen. The response received was overwhelming.

The Lord sent an angel in the way of one of the store owners; he pulled up in a huge maroon Hummer. "Good evening, how are you all doing?" He asked. "Tired and thirsty," Tina replied. "What do you all need?" "Gas," I replied. "We are out of gas, it's probably gonna be Thursday before a fuel truck comes," He added. "What about ice?" My brother asked. "We have three gallons of water but it's hot," "You all sit tight I'll be right back," He said. The mystery man drove off and returned about five minutes later with the most promising words. "Go over to the store and ask for Frankie, tell him that you are friends of Tony and he'll get you what you need." It was what I had prayed for; the three of us locked the car and strolled over to the store where we proceeded to ask for Frankie. We explained our situation and he was all to willing to meet the need of three traveling weary souls. "Sorry about the fuel guys but we are slap out all we have is diesel," He explained. He went to the back and retrieved two huge bags of ice and went on to say "I charge two dollars a bag, how many do you want?" "We'll take them both," I responded. "Hey it looks as though we are gonna be stranded here for a while can we purchase a few things to get us through the night?" I asked. "Yeah man what do you need?" "Just a few snacks some chips and cookies, we don't have anything," I replied. He went back into the store and returned with a couple of bags of chips and two huge bags of trail mix along with these encouraging words; "Take them no charge, I'll be back in the morning and if you need anything else come and see me." "Thank you Sir God bless you," we bidded him.

That night we sat beneath the stars and dined on trail mix as though it was filet mignon and was filled not only physically but spiritually with the hope that we would make it safely home. Neither of us could sleep that evening because of the overall feelings we were experiencing due to our recent blessing. A better part of the night was spent reflecting on how God had shown us so much favor. There were many other people in the parking lot but we seem to find favor in the eyes of strangers named Tony and Frankie.

We began to watch the traffic as it started to dissipate on Highway 2920. We then formulated another plan, we decided to let the traffic move forward and then move in behind it. At 1:40 a.m. the road was totally empty; we packed our signs, water and the little food we had and headed out. We drove for about fifteen minutes and found the rear of the pack once again. So we employed our strategy, we pulled over onto the shoulder, two slept while the other stayed awake and watched for our chance to advance. We would repeat this process over and over throughout the early morning hours until we got to a place to buy more fuel or until we had run out totally. At times we would reach speeds of 100 miles per hour in order to put as much distance between us and the storm as possible. We'd race into small towns slowing down long enough to observe plastic bags displayed on the pump handles a wretched sign indicating that they were out of fuel. As I raced down the back roads of little towns I never knew existed, I glanced down at the gas gauge. "Damn it," I thought to myself. "We have got to find a gas station," I mentioned to Tina. "Hey didn't that sign say Navasota thirty miles?" She asked. "Yeah why," I asked. "I've been there before. The last time I went to Houston we came through there; they have two stations where we can fill up there," She explained. "Cool let's do it," I replied. We managed to make it to the little town called Navasota where we found ourselves in dire straits once again. The local sheriff was parked at the exit ramp and confirmed what I had suspected. "Sorry folks the town is dry we're out of fuel and every hotel is filled to capacity." Tired from driving all morning we felt it would be best if we shut it down and wait for the sun to come up.

While our brother lay asleep in the back seat, Tina and I thought of ways to get home; none seem to be any more promising than the next. "Hey what type of insurance does mom have?" I asked. "She has full coverage," Tina replied. "What about roadside assistance?" I asked. "Look in her glove compartment," I instructed my sister. She removed the contents from the compartment and began her search. "Oh my God," She screamed. "What, what," I asked. "A roadside assistance membership card and one- eight hundred number," She shrieked.

It was like a voucher of victory. She promptly called the number and spoke with one of the operators. Tina went on to explain our situation; the gentlemen on the other end put her on hold and remained gone for about four minutes. He returned to the line with the most devastating news yet. There was a service there in Navasota but they were accepting cash only. "You mean to tell me that they run a reputable business and can't accept a major credit card. We're trying to get home," Tina insisted. Whatever the man said on the other end Tina simply remained calm and politely responded. "Well thank you Sir, you to" and hung up the phone. She explained to me the situation and it was all but optimistic. I felt defeated once again but took some gratitude that we had made it this far. Several minutes passed and Tina's cellular phone rang. "Hello, Yes Sir, Navasota N-A-V-A-S-O-T-A," she continued to give the operator mailing address, credit card number etc... "Okay and thank you to." She ended her call. He said someone will be here in about thirty-five minutes.

I was a little relieved and yet apprehensive at about the news. We woke our brother to inform him of our progress; to tired too express himself he simply responded, "Wake me when they get here." It seem to take forever the sun would be up in another three hours; then out of the darkness like a tow truck cavalry, yellow lights could be seen in the distance. The driver pulled past us then slowly started to back up. After some small talk the young man oddly named Luscious began to fuel the car. "Sir would you turn your ignition on to see where your fuel hand is?" He asked. With great anticipation I watched as the fuel hand rose from "E" to an eighth, from an eighth to a quarter. Policy was that they could only provide us with enough fuel to make it to the next city for fueling; not at all encouraging but at least it was a start. The finale to our nightmare seem to sum it self up like a twilight zone, master card commercial, two bags of ice four dollars, all the trail mix you can eat zero dollars, five gallons of gasoline sixty-one dollars, leaving Houston before all hell broke loose priceless.

We had done the math on how many miles we could go with the amount of fuel that we had. From hatch mark to hatch mark we could go forty miles or so. Desiring to put as much distance as we could between us we headed out once again. I don't advise anyone to try what I'm about to share with you but desperate times sometimes require desperate measures. We finally got the break we had been looking for in traffic; with our flashers on we began to hit speeds which exceeded ninety-five miles per hour. We finally made it to this little town called Hearne where we filled up. It was a grueling journey and to be able to find fuel was like winning the lottery. With a full tank of fuel we continued slowly and entered Buffalo, Texas. We were still a long way from home, but with a full tank of gas I was comforted in the thought that we would be there within three or four hours.

My siblings slept as the sun rose above the trees and we pressed on northward. At 10:45 a.m. we arrived at our mother's house. I exited the car, got on my knees and literally kissed the ground. I had never been so thankful to see familiar sights; I embraced my mother with a hug that affirmed how much I had missed her and thanked her for supporting us. "Thank you God." "Thank you momma."

I have learned to never say what you are not going to do in life. Just as I was placed in a position as those trying to escape the coastlands I try daily to choose my words a lot more vigilantly. I had no idea that I or we would be among the multitude of people scurrying for their life. Yet God is faithful in all that He does. Upon our return like so many times I sought the comfort in sharing all I had experienced with a legal pad and pen.

"Unwinding Roads" reflects the events that took place.

In a state of desperation the mind becomes creative;
Searching every possible means for conclusive mitigation.
All possibilities explored, every stone overturned;
Seeking the ultimate solution while the heart continues to
    yearn.
Yearning to escape the passion of one's sin;
Travailing only to find that the answer is from within.
A source of infinite knowledge, a sea of endless bounty;
Unworthy host I am yet His spirit abides in me.
Forever rebuking, forever challenging, continually willing to
    guide;
But the soul of man bares secrets, things he wishes to hide.
Lustful things of the flesh, sinful things of the mind;
All types of atrocities and every unthinkable crime.
No unity is found in the trinity of the mind, body and soul;
Each one imperative and all want to control.
The essence of man is a battle of what he is and what he
    aspires to be;

Contention from all three, no man is entirely free.
Like a poorly planned journey he has to adapt and overcome;
Not knowing that his voyage will be a difficult one.
But in the hands of the Creator his journey is made straight;
Because the Master knows the way and He also knows my
    fate.

I can now confess that I know that He is a healing God. He
has equipped me with the tools needed to receive healing; His
Word is one of them which I try to apply to my life daily. My
repentance has brought about a certain part of my healing which
is a blessing as well, but my faith keeps me anchored in knowing
that whatever arises He and I can handle it. For I can do all things
through Christ who strengthens me. When it comes to spiritual
healing we are all recovering patients and sometimes we need to
go to the hospital for re-evaluation (the church). My pastor once
told me that the church is a place filled with sick people but God
will meet them there every Sunday to heal them. The coolest
thing I think God ever established was a way to contact Him. We
don't have to make an appointment, we don't have to talk to His
receptionist and leave Him a message; all we have to do is call on
His name and make our petitions or requests be made known to
Him (pray) and He will hear and answer our prayers.

I stated earlier that we suffer some things in our life and
although they seem unfair or unjustified we must suffer them.
I relate this to the suffering of Christ. He had committed no
crime nor was he guilty of any illegal conspiracy. He was falsely
accused, mocked, beaten and put to death by crucifixion. Was
that a fair sentence? Not at all, was it unjust absolutely. Yet He was
led as a lamb to the slaughter, and as a sheep before its shearers is
silent, He opened not His mouth. God knew that there would be
suffering, oppression and all sorts of injustice in this life, but He
loved us so much that He became the perfect example of suffering.
Not only that but He became the infallible example and source
of our healing.

The fact is that Christ conquered all that He was sent to do. His accomplishment even under the most adverse conditions should be an inspiration for all believers. Just when you think things are going bad for you take some time to reflect about the things that our Lord and Savior Jesus Christ had to endure. We are all guilty of fanatically scrutinizing what we don't have, complaining of how unfair life is and wishing we had just a little more than the Johnson's. Excess seems to be the craze for most, but Christ achieved every task He was sent to do using less, the inferior, and the discarded. As 1 Corinthians 1:27-29 tells us *God has chosen the foolish things of the world to put to shame the wise, and God has chosen the weak things of the world to put to shame the things that are mighty; and the lowly things of the world and the things which are despised God has chosen, and the things which are not, to bring to nothing the things that are, that no flesh should glory in His presence.*

Our healing is no exception even though we receive it by faith, repentance, prayer and the reading of His Holy Word; time and again too much credit is given to medicine, technology and even the doctors which are only a tool that God uses to bring about healings. I'm not knocking modern science by any means. However, some sing their praises as though God does not exist and yet He has had His hand on the conception of all medicinal treatments and cures every since the beginning when He stepped out into the spans of time and spoke the words, "Let there be" and it was. The book of Revelation speaks of a time for God's people when He will wipe away every tear from our eyes, where death will be no more, sorrow will not exist, neither crying, nor will pain, the things we suffered before here on this earth will pass away, all things He declares to make new. Sounds like the perfect place; it is and you can enjoy the same beginning if you believe in your heart and confess with your mouth that Christ is the Son of God, who came and died, was buried and raised from the dead, who now sits on the right hand side of our Father in heaven interceding on behalf of all of those who trust and believe in Him. Amen.

NINE

Joy Cometh in the Morning

I want to try something with you, but this little exercise will not work unless you read it out aloud and preferably in the company of a friend or love one. After that if it does not register to the senses have them read it aloud to you. "Eye we Todd did, eye we Todd did, eye we Todd did, I so we Todd did". Did it register? I thought it would. This was shared with me by a young lady name Jamie, a paramedic I worked along side during the relief efforts while in New Orleans. Like many others I have played this joke on I found myself trying to make sense out of its sentence structure and punctuation, reading it slower and slower with astute pronunciations, not knowing the hold time that my partner was sitting in the passenger seat laughing hysterically to the point of tears. It was only when she caught her breath that she was able to decipher it. "What's so funny?" I asked. "You can't hear yourself?" she asked. No! Then as all good friends do at the expense of your humiliation she enlightened me. "I retarded." she explained. As you would expect when I heard it I joined her several minutes of laughter. I've shared this with all of my family and friends and now with you.

The joy that I write about is not of the former Joy but the present and everlasting joy. It is not of a woman or material possessions but of a Man. A Man that has been there through it all and His name is unequivocally called Jesus. We often search for God and when we find Him we can't see Him clearly; we don't know Him as Adam knew Him. God formed man from out of the dust of the ground, and blew into his nostrils the breath of life; and man became a living soul (Genesis 2:7). This establishes that God knows us well; so much in fact that He gave us some of what He has in Him. God created the man in His own image; in the image of God He created him. He created them male and female (Genesis 1:27). As I dissected the latter verse, He created us in His own image; in the image of God.

I found joy in knowing that a God so awesome thought so much of me that He gave me a part of Him and that breath/spirit is His it will return to Him one day; just as man has to return to the earth, so does the spirit return to its rightful place. Which brings me to this point, I was having a very profound theological discussion with a co-worker one day and I posed this question to him.

"If God can become angered, jealous, delighted or pleased; which are all human traits, can He become bored, lonely, sadden, or frustrated?" He thought for a moment and with a look of total perplexity he finally confessed, "Man I don't know that is a good question."

I'd learned early in my life that God is a Spirit and He made us in His own image. We are spirits dwelling in a slowly deteriorating shell, and although we possess a body, we also share some very similar spiritual characteristics of our Creator. Tugah (*too-gaw'*) which is a Hebrew word that denotes a deep depression- heaviness of one's heart or sorrowful in their spirit. It can be seen in Genesis 6:6, 7 when God declared that He had sorrow because He had made man on the earth, and grief was in His heart. The reason for His grief is given in the previous verse the Lord saw that the wickedness of man's thinking was only evil continually. So, as He would have it the rains came, the flood waters rose and the wicked died. Now the very opposite of the word tugah is euthumos (*yoo'-thoo-mos*) it is defined as having a fine spirit-of good cheer, but the word I want to concentrate on is *tobe* (tob) when used as an adverb to describe the acts or works of God it encompasses or signifies something (well), to be beautiful, the best, better, bountiful or cheerful. Therefore, it can be said that in the beginning when God called all of the firmaments together it was beautifully done, it was the best that any human could hope for on this side of heaven, it was better than either one of us could have ever imagined or planned, its span and its stature was sufficient enough to incorporate both man and beast and above all it pleased Him to provide for us such a place and give us dominion over something that He has created.

"A Priceless Portrait" was a poem I was inspired to write as I laid on my back one day and watched the sun set. God does some awesome things with color but you would have to slow down long enough and gaze into heaven to really appreciate it. I've come to enjoy the sounds of the day as well; there is a certain tranquility to hear birds singing by day and crickets chirping at night. The Michel Angelo's and Leonardo DaVinci's were masters of their trade but they could not compare to the works of God.

> You are a Creator of the finest art;
> And the firmament is Your canvas.
> You place hue in its background;
> And add colors that are not amiss.
> Shades of white cascading into pink;
> It all seems soothing to the sun,
> A constant, perfect reminder of the work You have done.
> The journey of the sun is an early one at best;
> It makes no haste as it travels slowly to the west.
> Sliding behind dancing clouds that never seem to rest.
> Stars set to appear as darkness begins to approach;
> And yet the moon cannot be seen because the clouds are a
>   cloak.

But with a blast from His nostrils the clouds hurry and give
    way;
To a vision of millions of lights that are as beautiful as the
    day.
With the setting of the sun You have created a wonderful
    masterpiece;
I yearn for tomorrow when there's another You will release.

One of the most breathtaking sights I have ever witnessed was
the view of the sky while on an airplane. The weather was ideal
for traveling, clear with no chance of rain. I was flying north to
Emmitsburg, Maryland for a hazardous material class for the
department. As the plane took flight I became elated to see the
view from above but what was more overwhelming was the view
above the clouds. It was a very liberating and spiritual experience.
I found comfort in knowing that the clouds we had just soared
through were called the chariots of God by the Psalmist David in
Psalms 104: 2-3 *"He wraps Himself in light as with a garment; He
stretches out the heavens like a tent and lays the beams of His upper
chambers on their water. He makes the clouds His chariot and rides
on the wings of the wind."*

With millions of commuters flying daily one would think that
a person would find joy in knowing that God is closer than they
think. Nevertheless, the stark reality is that material possessions
have become joy to most; which deters our attention from the
one true joy in our lives, God. As children of God and to those
who have not yet confessed Christ He wants nothing more than
to give you a life of joy. The type of joy that surpasses everything,
that kind of joy which enables believers to praise Him even when
they are penniless, or allow you to declare those things which are

not as though they are and revealing His glory as He brings all things to pass.

Jesus was teaching His disciples the correct way to give and pray in Matthew chapter 6. His instructions to the men were concise but pertinent so that they could reap the rewards that their heavenly Father would bless them with. The premise of the lesson was to teach His disciples how to give and pray. He instructs them to do it in secret and our Father who is in heaven shall reward them openly. All of the principles that Christ was introducing to His followers would result in rewards of joy and the peace of mind God wants for His children. All that you need give no thought of it, all that you eat, drink, or wear, but "Seek first the kingdom of God and His righteousness; and all these things shall be added unto you." No one, I mean no one, knows joy the way in which Christ knows joy. He is the very essence of it and it is His desire that we experience it Godly and to the fullest.

Other lessons in the bible are also equated to finding joy. David tells us once again to "Delight ourselves also in the Lord, and He will give you the desires and secret petitions of your heart." The word of God makes it all so clear those things we need to do to receive the comforts of this life. I believe that so many people are depressed and lonely because they have not received the ultimate source where they can find all that they need. King David understood that everything he needed God not only had access to He owned it and if you are a child of the Most High God you have access to it as well. He continues to exalt the Lord by saying that there was one thing that he desired of the Lord and that one thing is what he would seek; and it was to dwell in the house of the Lord all the days of his life, to behold the beauty of the Lord and to inquire in his temple.

Dwelling in the house of the Lord is beneficial for God's children; it is a delight as well. Attributes such as blessings, knowledge, protection and joy can be found in the presence of the Lord. If you want blessings then first seek the kingdom of God. Knowledge, protection, joy or peace of mind they are all from the Lord and if you seek Him you shall find them. I particularly like the way God said that wisdom and knowledge are with Him and those who seek after them find Him. He makes no separation of Himself or from wisdom and knowledge because of His omniscience (knowledge of all things).

David declares that he was once a young man, and now being an old man he is able to confess without a doubt that he has never seen the righteous forsaken. Only a faithful servant of God could speak such a bold statement. He was able to say it because of the trials in which he had suffered; without grief he would not know joy and without joy he would not be able to bare his grief. It is the things that we have fear of happening to us that bring us so much sorrow. David's heart was heavy because his enemies had enlisted to destroy him namely his son Absalom and other conspirators. God was allowing him to taste the possibility of defeat so that David would rely on Him for total deliverance from the hands of his enemies. Being the wise king that he was David employed spies into the midst of Absalom's counsel to bring back every word that was conspired against him and it worked. David defeated his son's army and maintained his kingdom. That is why he is able to write such heartfelt poems that gave God all the glory.

If you would take a moment to analyze the trials and tribulations of events that caused you so much grief in your life you would observe that they caused you to run to God. We seldom run to Him when all of our needs are being met and I think it is because we are self-reliant creatures when the chips are stacked in our favor, but when the chips are down we embrace the pity of our neighbors and strangers alike. Yet all the time God was bidding for our attention, but we could not see over our chips; therefore, adversity arises and it seems as if they are reducing us to nothing. Remember we serve a God that owns it all. Let Him increase you and your enemies can never defeat you.

God has continually given me the increase; not just financially but with the knowledge of knowing that He is my source for all that I need. He is a capable God, He is omnipotent (invincible). He is a willing God, He is omnipresent (everywhere), and He is more than able because He is omniscience that is He (knows all).

Before, I would rely on myself to make imperative decisions at the cost of who knows what and would later become inundated with a rash of problems with no viable solution. I'd find myself stressed to the point that I became engulfed with it, and all of those who were around me would in some way suffer. What I failed to realize was that God was and is a problem solver. It is a daily walk in trusting God, what you want may not be good for you, it may cause you to oppose Him and He will not test us with things that would ultimately destroy us, but the more you surrender to His will the more automatic it becomes to walk with Him. You see Him working in your life, you watch as He makes a way for you and stretches an income of $114.00 every two weeks to pay your bills, He transform you into a sincere believer while He takes the taste of alcohol and promiscuous women out of your life. He elevates your awareness of how far He has brought you and you can't help but to praise Him. That's the type of joy that I'm referring to.

What anchored me more in the Lord was I knew that He would bring things to pass whether good or bad. As a young boy I was involved in J.R.O.T.C (Junior Reserved Officers Training Corp) where I excelled. By my sophomore year I had tested for the position of Command Sergeant Major and was promoted, and while in high school I enlisted in the military. That summer was spent carousing about enjoying my freedom. Due to the fact that it would not exist once I put on the uniform. My father didn't want me to enlist, my mother was more supportive, and I thought it would be a great way for me to pay for school. NOT! At least it wasn't for me. The one thing I remember vividly was the advice my parents gave me before my departure. My father advised me to watch my ass and find me some true friends who would do the same, but what has inspired me the most is what my mother simply said, "No matter what you're going through trouble don't last always," she said.

I would call home from time to time to assure them that I was well and complain to them how the drill instructors were making our lives a living hell. My mother would encourage me not to falter; "Stay strong and pray," is what she would tell me; she would also convey to me that she missed and love me. Being the spiritual example in my life she set in motion an amazing inheritance when she introduced me to Christ. Whether it was insisting that I go to church on Sunday or dragging me there as a kid I'm very grateful that she introduced me to the Man. Without them I would have certainly faltered and died in my sins.

There are many things that I have found joy in but there is only one that has stood the test of time, and it is true that they cannot be compared and they all hold a unique place in my mind and heart. The joy of Christ is like none I have ever experienced. He gave up so much when He came from heaven, and so often while on this earth he was constantly rejected by family, friends, kings and others who thought of Him as merely a carpenter or a devil trying to convince a nation that He was the Son of God. My joy of Him is better defined when I think about the persecution He knew He would incur, the mocking, beatings, whipping, thorns and nails He would subject Himself to because He knew that I could not. I can see Him in the Gospel of Luke 22:41-44 as He prayed. The humanistic side of Him felt tremendous agony before His death and like any human He inquired of His Father if there might be another way. "Father if thou be willing, remove this cup from Me. Nevertheless not My will, but thine be done." His body would be torn and cut beyond recognition; the beating would be so severe that no flesh could bare it. That is why God dispatched an angel to minister and strengthen His Spirit. Even then the flesh was in agony, that is a struggle to man up; but how could one prepare the body to receive such a horrific punishment. In all of this I can recall the Lord telling His disciples once before, "Indeed the spirit is willing but the flesh is weak." Now with a strong spirit He can endure it, painful still but He had you and I in mind. He was wounded for our transgressions, bruised for our iniquities, the chastisement of our peace was upon Him; and with His stripes we are healed.

The disciples remained doubtful I know because the bible states it. They thought that the death of Christ was permanent. They could not fathom a dead man living again, but if they were to simply believe that His death would be just a short sleep, they could have rejoiced when Christ said that in three days I will rise. The God that watches over us as we slumber in our beds at night is the same God that watches over us in the grave and He will not let us over- sleep. What follows the day after the death of Christ is not unlike what would happen in today's society. Bereavement takes place and we reflect on the memories of our love ones. This reflection on Christ's life inspired me to write this poetic epistle to His mother.

Epistle to Mary

I write to convey my deepest heart felt sympathy.
It wasn't until now that I understood what He's done for me.
O' how you must regret that Your loving Son should die.

There is no way to repay you or any gift that I could buy.
I read the news of how He was mocked just before His
    death;
And the way He called out for us before His final breath.
Three days later without a doubt He appeared once again.
He said to all that gathered that day that He would send a
    Friend;

To comfort us when we moaned,
To console every sorrow and pity every groan.
So much was given by Him,
Salvation, redemption and peace;
Gifts He even promised to a hell bound thief.

He assured us that He would be with us forever and always.
O' how He is worthy, so worthy to be praised.
I thank you for receiving such a precious gift.
I often sit and wonder, pondering what if;
What if you were not chosen to bring us this sacred Child?
What if they hadn't condemned Him the day He was on
    trial?
What if He had rebelled, denied His ordained calling?
What if He didn't catch me whenever I had fallen?

As we reflect upon His life and relish His immaculate birth;
We are reminded of the miracles He performed while here
    on earth.
He made the mute man talk and gave sight to the blind.
Do you remember the feast when He changed the water into
    wine?
I'm delighted I got the chance to meet your beloved Son.
I'm thankful His Father sent Him to be the only One;
To model myself as Him, to become as He is, and
To try and make a difference in this world that we must live.

Some find it difficult to be thankful that Christ died for us
but without the shedding of His blood no atonement for our sin
could be made. Atonement in the bible means that man's sin is

covered by the shedding of blood; that satisfactory reparation for an offense has been made. In the Old Testament it was done by sacrificing animals but as sacrifices became tainted and the rituals taken for granted God provided for us a greater sacrifice in the New Testament by allowing His Son to die for our sin. Christ was the only medium that could reconcile us to God in a word Christ is our Redeemer. Every time I think about Jesus and what He's done for me my soul rejoices and I receive strength.

I have had the misfortune of losing a very close friend; he was so close in fact that he was my next door neighbor. I had moved into a small two bedroom house with my oldest son when his mother and I divorced. For several months no one occupied the house next to us; that all changed when Paul and his family bought it. Paul was an ex-drug dealer that had been reformed by the gracious and merciful hands of the Lord and what I loved about him was that he would be the first to testify that he was a scoundrel. His testimony also contained the persistent praises to the Almighty God that saved him.

Our encounter didn't seem to have a beginning, and I'm comforted in knowing that I will see him again one day; it felt as though I'd known him all my life. He was like the best friend you grew up with and never lost contact. Paul was several years older than me but he never treated me like a little brother he treated me as an equal and he treated me that way because he saw in me something he had struggled with in his life. Our friendship began to grow by the day; we would somehow manage to be pulling up in front of our homes at the same time almost daily. "Hey neighbor," he would call out. "What's going on neighbor," I'd reply. Before either one of us retired to our home for the evening we would sit on the brick wall which divided our property and talk about everything; work, women, politics, religion, the worst thing we had ever done versus the best thing we had ever done and so on. I noticed that our greetings had changed over the years since meeting each other. One day he called out to me, "Hey friend," and I instinctively replied "What's going on friend"? And later it would come to be "Hey brother," and my reply would be "What's going on brother"? Sometimes his wife would have to come out and remind him that he had other things to do and he would regretfully tuck his lunch box under his arm and go in for the night. I found out some days later during our meeting on the wall that he was a minister and I confronted him about it to try and get a better understanding of how God had called him to preach; more particularly how did he know that God was calling him. "Brother Paul how did," "Hold up," he interrupted. "I know exactly what you're about to ask me," he continued. "You wanted to know how I knew that God called me to be a preacher," he asked. "Yeah," I replied. "You know brother when I first saw you I knew that it was something peculiar about you," he continued. "Let me tell you something and it's not the first time you've heard it either, man you're a preacher," he stated. My mouth struck the ground and it seem as though my soul was crying out "Say yes, say yes." I couldn't I just stood there astonished. Before I could process what he had said I heard him say in a chuckling voice "You've been running ain'tcha Doc"? All I could do was join him in laughter; the two of us would share a lot of comical moments and as I reflect on the person he was; I find myself missing my neighbor, my friend and my brother.

Brother Paul was very astute and proficient when it came to biblical topics. His bible bore the markings of a well worn sword that had been used frequently in war. His generosity with his time and money was of a good steward. He taught me a great lesson on sowing and reaping in the Kingdom and what it means to bless a man of God. A lot of his time was spent ministering at the local correctional center were he would teach and preach to the inmates of the facility. He would ask me to join him in this ministry, but the thought of walking into prison and being subjected to an atmosphere of convicted criminals was something I couldn't grasp at the time. He began to assist me in any way he could when it came to my spiritual growth he purchased for me my first Matthew Henry concordance. I remember this one time when I was strapped for cash, his wife had made spaghetti and with an almost heightened instinct he brought to my door a hot meal and a warm word from the Lord. Every Friday when he cooked fish he would bring me a mess of them for my enjoyment, and it was then that I turned him on to my famous blackened catfish.

During one of our meetings on the wall one day Paul disclosed something to me that shocked me. He shared with me that he had hepatitis. My thoughts were modern technology was available and he could get the necessary treatment he needed to get well. However, it was in its latter stages and the irreversible damage to his liver and immune system was already done. He asked me to pray for him and I did that every moment. I prayed that God would comfort him and allow him to defeat his illness. Several weeks passed and Paul was hospitalized due to injuries he sustained in a car wreck; nothing serious but they kept him overnight for evaluation. He would be in and out of the hospital in the coming weeks for complications stemming from his illness. I would go to sit and pray with him during that time and like a shot in the dark my wife would call me one morning with the news of his passing, it devastated me. I couldn't believe that he was gone, a relatively young man cut down by a debilitating illness.

His funeral was some days later, I stood before a crowded assembly and spoke words that confirmed to others what kind of person God had inspired him to be. He was a man put in the position to do what God had called him to do. He helped save a few souls for the Kingdom more than any of us may ever attribute. He was my neighbor, he was my friend and he was my brother in Christ Jesus.

I can't help thinking what type of impact Paul's life had on mine; seemingly brief, it taught me several things. First, no matter how brief this life is only what you do for Christ will last; the people he introduced to Christ their lives were changed forever. Second, "If you meet someone you don't owe them anything initially, but if you are to become their friend the very least that you owe them is the truth." Last, but certainly not the least, it doesn't matter where you come from, what wrong you have done in your life, how immoral or unworthy you think you are of having a relationship with God. He's not concerned about who or what you are His ultimate interest is who or what you can become for Him through Christ Jesus. I was able to smile the next day as I thought how blessed I was to have known him and to have had him as a brother so I sat and wrote this poem.

"Brother"

An unselfish neighbor you were even from the beginning;
Not at all absorbed with vices or too zealous about winning.
You presented yourself in a very humble fashion;
And I not knowing we'd share the same heartfelt passion.

An unselfish friend you gave until it hurt;
Leaving your job, rushing off to eagerly do God's work.
Ministering to souls to get one saved;
Not concerned with retirement or what would be your wage.

An unselfish brother you taught me in your living;

Sharing with me the importance of heavenly Kingdom
  giving.
Helping to nourish my body in time when I couldn't do it;
Feeding me the Word of God enlarging my starving spirit.

An unselfish servant of God who hardly ever complained;
I look to the day when I would see you once again.
Rest now brother, take comfort in your labor;
The Lord has removed your yoke and has shown you His
  great favor.

Sometime people's paths cross for whatever the reason. Maybe and in the process of getting to know that individual we learn things about ourselves. We try to analyze the specifics of how you met which are significant to a point, but most important is the reason for such destiny. Some people live a lifetime never knowing the reason for their union; some claim it to be their fate while others might think it was by coincident. Understand that your reason for meeting Christ is neither coincident nor chance. We are all predestined to have an encounter with Him before we leave this earth whether or not you answer when He calls is a different story. Romans 8:28-30 tells us *"And we know that all things work together for good to them that loves God, to them who are the called according to His purpose. For those whom He foreknew, He also destined from the beginning to be molded into the image of His Son (that inward likeness), that He might become the first born among many brethren. And those whom he thus foreordained He also called, and those whom He called, He also justified* (exonerated, made righteous, and reconciled us).

The latter verses I think are a stronger testament of a lesson taught to me by my friend Paul and are a source for drawing strength and joy. He knew without a doubt that he was a child of God and the sickness was a means to a greater end, that end is eternal life with his Father in heaven. *If God be for us then who or what can be against us? Who* is used as an indefinite pronoun that denotes any person, place or thing so the meaning of the remaining verses should answer any question about our love for Christ. *Who shall separate us from the love of Christ?*

Shall tribulation, distress, persecution, famine, nakedness, peril or sword. As it is written For thy sake we are killed all the day long; we are accounted as sheep for the slaughter .Nay, in all these things we are more than conquerors through him that love us. For I am persuaded, that neither death, nor life, nor angels, nor principalities, nor powers, nor things present, nor things to come, nor height, nor depth, nor any other creature, shall be able to separate us from the love of God, which is in Christ Jesus our Lord? Knowing these things brought great joy to my life. Thank you brother.

TEN

A New Joy

There's no feeling like the feeling you get when you receive something new. It doesn't matter what the occasion is receiving produces the same sensation every time. New shoes, a new toy, a new look or whatever it may be it elates the soul. The recipient is taken away in blissful glee. So why aren't more people just as invigorated when it comes to receiving spiritual matters? The answer to that I think is for a lack of knowledge. In the Word of God joy is an attribute of Deity and a significant part of the fruit of the Spirit. Joy is occasionally compared to happiness; nevertheless, they are two totally different principles. Happiness stems from happenings, it is dependent on the outcome of events; happy friends, bills paid, health and wealth, etc. A Happy person and an unhappy person at a party are hard pressed to get along, but a joyful person and a sorrowful person at a funeral are in harmonious fellowship. I've experienced this antonymic situation plenty of times to know that you can't party forever and trouble don't last always.

The incident I wrote of some pages back concerning hurricane Katrina was as such; to be with my siblings was joyful yet the situation we were faced with caused us tremendous sorrow. Both Paul and Silas were met with a similar trial while in prison which is recorded in the book of Acts; the uniqueness of their situation and how they would respond to their adversity was the motivating force for the other prisoners as well. *Having received such a charge, (the jailer) thrust them into the inner prison, and made their feet fast in the stocks. And at midnight Paul and Silas prayed, and sang praises unto God.* Their situation was one that many would agonize over, but their trust and joy was in the Lord their Savior.

The ultimate demonstration of joy and sorrow lies with the character of Christ. Isaiah calls Him a Man of sorrow one who is acquainted with grief, a man rejected and despised. Yet He responded to this negative display in a proof positive manner. The author of the book of Hebrews projects another side of our Lord and Savior; He is justly portrayed as the One who took joy in the divine task set before Him. He endured the cross despising the shame and is set down at the right hand of the throne of God.

The notion of having something new is exciting and that was what I had anticipated when I decided to rededicate my life to Christ. Promiscuity was such a lifestyle for me that change seems unattainable. I honestly didn't want to be addicted to sex or use it is as an instrument of false liberation. I would try to resist all depravity without any aid from an outside source only to descend farther into my vices. It seems hopeless depression sat in once again. I was ready to change. I knew I couldn't continue like this.

I was sitting in front of the television one night aroused beyond containment. I fumbled through my address book searching desperately for a victim to exploit but to no avail loneliness would be my companion tonight. As I thumbed through the channels my attention was drawn to an evangelist screaming at the top of his voice on the subject of change. Coincident, I think not. He went on to say how change was impossible unless we first recognized the Spirit of God. "The Spirit of God is sent to us as a Comforter, a teacher and a guide; how then can you change or expect change unless the Spirit of the Almighty God is received," he continued. He spoke from a passage of the bible that was not familiar to me Isaiah 43: 18, 19. *"Do not remember the former things; neither consider the things of old. Behold, I am doing a new thing! Now it springs forth; do you not perceive and know it and will you not give heed to it? I will even make a way in the wilderness and rivers in the desert.* This message from God, to the children of Israel, spoken by the Prophet was a message of inspiration and somehow I could relate it to my present situation. I could not press forward because of the things that held my mind captive, but God tells us in His Word not to dwell on those former things; to do so would cause us to waver and lose focus. He continues to say nor shall you consider the things in the past; the way God delivered them from the hands of Pharaoh was unparalleled and although He could do it again to reflect on it or becoming fixated on it would hinder their growth and trust in Him to do even greater things. Therefore, He says to them "Observe, I will do something different a new thing! And when it happens will you not know that it is I and pay attention to it? I've done it once before and I can do it again." *I even I, am He that blotted out thy transgressions for Mine own sake, and will not remember thy sins.*

He said in his Word that He will not remember our sins so why should I? Why then should I dwell on my past transgressions? Why should I stunt my spiritual growth by concentrating on the past when He is more concerned about my future. He blots out our sins for His sake because He is holy, incorruptible and He does not want to see us in that state; just as He hid His face when Christ took upon Himself our sins He also cannot bare to look upon us in our sin.

The first human sin committed was done by deception. Yet there was adequate understanding and of their own free will which made it a deliberate rebellion toward God. I was only perpetuating what my forefather had fallen to. The chain of self indulgence had to be broken, but the links in the chain were sturdy and I had become weaker; due to the length of time I had been bound by them. As I listened attentively to the minister on the air waves the answer on how to break the chains became apparent. "You can do all things through Christ that strengthens you," he boldly announced. "Your Father in heaven wants to deliver you, He wants you to live a life of liberty, but you have got to open your mouth and be careful for nothing; but in everything by prayer and supplication with thanksgiving let your request be known unto God and your Father who hears you in secret will bless you." He also ascribed the following passage of scripture to further make his point on how to break the chains of sin. "*Whatsoever things are true, whatsoever things are honest, whatsoever things are just, whatsoever things are pure, whatsoever things are lovely, whatsoever things are of good report; if there be any virtue, and if there be any praise, mediate on these things.*" There was the answer setting before me in its entire splendor all I needed to do was apply it to my life and hope for the best.

In the process of application or the trial and error you may never get it right the first time. I needed to know and feel that the process I was employing in my life was not futile.

I began to pray and ask God to remove the iniquitous thoughts from my mind and to cleanse me of all unrighteousness. It would take some time and He would answer my prayer; I stumbled upon a verse that changed my prospective of how I viewed myself in times past I wasn't looking to be vindicated only assured that my walk with Christ would be a beneficial one. Proverbs 24:16 tells us *For a just man falls seven times, and rises up again; but the wicked shall fall into mischief.*

It was very reassuring to know that even a just man may fall but he has the strength from God to rise again. There were no more excuses to lean on, nor any reasons not to submit to God; my way was not even close to being a solution but as I pressed on daily with my hand in His hand He began to expose me to life situations that would ultimately challenge me to look to Him for the answers. He undoubtedly took the taste of strong drink and loose women from my mouth along with the desire to frequent the local clubs, and like other recovering addicts I had an occasional relapse but it remained my hearts desire to be cleansed.

When something we are use to is taken out of our lives it is only human nature to try and replace it; in this case something productive was needed. Hobbies are fine but you want something that will inspire grow and self improvement. My substitution was reading, studying and writing poetry not on just any subject. I began to pick up the Word of God and apply a somewhat unorthodox method of finding answers. I would start with a particular person or subject matter in the bible and read the conclusion of events first; then I would pose questions as to why the person and events unfolded the way in which they did. Often I would find that the outcome of events were directly linked to the choices that the individuals made or did not make. God began to allow me to get an understanding of how and why things happened; which led to teaching Sunday school and evening bible study. To see the look on the faces of people as we dissected the Word of God delighted me and to be able to answer some of their lifelong questions about a certain event of the bible filled that void that had been created. Yet I could take no credit neither did I want any it was all made possible by Christ. Once I submitted myself to Him, He used me as He willed and gave me such thoughts as "In life and death."

Rejuvenated, regenerated, reunited and reborn;
No longer living rebelliously but in life now I am conformed.
A purpose and a plan You have revealed unto me;
No longer bound by chains but living life with liberty.
No longer regretful or ashamed of my past;
A life and a love You have giving me to last.
No longer dying anxiously because through death I am
    transformed;
Rejuvenated, regenerated, reunited and reborn.

One of the bible's most joyous accounts can be found in the four Gospels. They all tell the story of Christ from his birth to His death and give different narratives of the accounts but all concur that it took place. In the Gospels we find that both Mary Magdalene and the other Mary visited the grave of Christ. The visit was one of grief and sorrow as they undoubtedly recalled the manner in which He had died. They came for the purpose of anointing His body with the sweet oils they had prepared; with the expectation that His body would still be there. When they saw that He was not there they thought that someone had stolen the body of Christ. It was not until the angel of the Lord spoke to them and told them that He has risen just as He said. With this great proclamation they ran with great joy to inform the others of the great news.

There is an old saying that bad news travels fast, and it's never too late for good news. Yet what the women are about to share with the others is received with doubt and even when He appeared before them doubt is still in their heart. *The other disciples therefore said unto him, (Thomas) We have seen the Lord. But he said unto them, Except I shall see in His hands the print of the nails, and put my finger into the print of the nails, and thrust my hands into His side, I will not believe.* Christ makes a statement to Thomas that is a promise to this day. *"Thomas, because you have seen Me, you have believed that I have risen, but blessed are they that have not seen, and yet have believed."* If we are faithless, we are Christ less, graceless, hopeless and joyless. Thomas was ashamed of his unbelief, and cried out, "My Lord and my God." Great is the joy of men who believe in the death, burial and resurrection of our Lord and Savior Jesus Christ who have not witnessed it with their eyes but believe.

The Gospel of John tells us that while Christ was with His disciples He performed many other signs and miracles in their presence but they are not written in the book, but the aforementioned accounts are written in order that you may believe that Jesus is the Christ (the Anointed One), the Son of God, and that through believing, cleaving to, trusting and relying upon Him you may have life through His name.

Something I've taken for granted in the past was peace; you know when everything is in its place whether it is your family, your job, the cars or even something as insignificant as your golf game unless you are a professional. No bad hooks in the family life, no fading slices at the job today and you're not in the bunker when it comes to the car and any mechanical problems that could arise, everything is up to par or better. When I was first invited to play a few rounds of this challenging sport by my co-workers, I approached it with too much confidence, an arrogant, conceited mentality that this was easy. Beside I had been watching the sport for months now and I could mimic the swing of some of the best players on the circuit. We all agreed on a 7:00 a.m. tee time at one of the local courses that was known for breaking the spirits of novice golfers. I wasn't intimidated I was ready to swing'em hard, drive'em far and eager to two putt to show these fellows how it was done.

The first hole a par three; I loved par threes short and to the point, basically just get it close and tap'em in. One of the guys a more seasoned player addressed his ball, slowly drew his club back, and suddenly uncoiled let go of a beautiful drive straight down the middle landing a few feet from the hole. Everyone erupted praising him for an outstanding shot, "Good shot Steve," one of them called out. "Way to let it fly," another shouted. The game we were playing was called "Best ball;" you and your partner played the best ball lying closest to the hole while you competed with other teams for that hole. The team with the most holes wins. I was paired with a guy name Leland he was an average player at best; he knew the game and had his weak points as we all did. He addressed his ball, pulled back, released letting one fly high and a little wide, missing the green landing about twenty-five feet or so on a grassy knoll, rolling back about six feet to give him a little work to make par. "Damn it," he yelled. "Not bad," D.J. called to him. "Yeah you've got a little work left don't get frustrated buddy it's too early we've got 17 more," he continued. D.J. was up next he boasted of how he was about to get a hole in one, he pulled back, released the ball looked good as it left the tee. "Get in the hole," he yelled. The ball hit the green a foot from the cup, "STOP STOP STOP STOP STOP," he continued. It rolled an additional ten feet or so and came to rest. "I'll take that one any day boys," he boasted. "You're up T.A. take your time buddy hit a good one, no pressure," they all screamed.

I approached the ball feeling confident that I could produce the same results or better than these guys had just displayed. "Feet apart, keep your head down, pull back, explode and follow through," I repeated to myself. I envisioned my shot leaving the tee coming to rest inches from the hole. I pulled back slowly and released ripping one high and 90 degrees into the parking lot. "Medic!" D.J. yelled in laughter. As horrific as it was the ball hit the concrete between two parked cars, bounced, landing between a Mercedes Benz and a Cadillac, bounced again and landed in the grassy median under a rose bush. "Damn T.A. you're trying to kill the ball, "Leland laughed. "Where are you going Steve?" D.J. asked. "I'm going to move Brenda's car I don't think my insurance covers acts of golf balls," he laughed. "Hey T.A. where did you buy that 90 degree slicing wedge," D.J. sarcastically asked.

I felt terrible. Steve came over and gave me a few pointers as to why it all happened. "Hey T you're trying or you're swinging to hard let the weight of the club do the work, this is more about fineness than power; that will come later, here try again," he urged. "Hey what iron are you using T.A.?" D.J. asked. "A seven iron," I replied. "Too much try a nine instead," he encouraged. "Hey that's way too much club grab your nine iron and try it again," Steve added. That would be called a mulligan and as I later learned, a penalty stroke applies toward your whole score.

I approached the ball once again this time somewhat apprehensive. "Take your time T.A.," Steve encouraged. "Remember don't try to kill it swing easy," he continued. I pulled back steady and gently, released and the sound I heard as the club struck the ball was one I'd never forget "TINK". The ball left the tee approached high but was headed directly for the pin, it landed twenty feet or so from the hole and rolled 19 feet to the left of the cup. "Damn right T.A. good recovery shot you still have a chance of making an honest par," D.J. said. We all gathered our bags and walked down to the first hole. "I guess we are playing your ball T.A.," Leland laughed. Since I was the closest to the hole I had the option of hitting first or last. I opted to hit first. I lined my shot up pulled back on my putter, swung forward and plop in the hole. "Yeah baby that's how you play best hole, in your face," my partner yelled. "Good shot there T.A. way to save par fella," D.J. encouraged. It felt great but I knew the victory was short lived; we were only on the first hole and just like life there was going to be plenty of obstacles ahead.

Golf and life are somewhat similar in that they both contain novice, intermediates and masters; they also share a commonly used terminology that equates to dilemma (hazards). Hazards are golf's little seen or unseen stumbling blocks that add to the frustrations and penalties of the game. Often called bunkers or roughs they are parallel to life's trials and tribulations. With every bunker there is a viable solution just as in life there is a viable absolute for every obstacle. When standing on the tee box you are confronted with options; you weigh them to find the best means of mitigating the situation at hand; not at all different from life circumstances. You face them head on, you face them with the tools that you are provided with to negotiate over, through or around the obstacle. Sometimes we still find ourselves in those hazards we've tried to avoid, but like any master golfer who becomes embedded in the sand now is not the time to panic. Remember you have a viable solution. In golf it maybe a sand wedge, a pitching wedge or even a mulligan, but in life it is the Word of God.

Four words come to mind when I've stood on the tee box or consider my life: examine, recognize, establish and implement. First, always examine the problem or situation from every possible angle; often I have found that if you look at it from a third person's point of view you gain a better perspective. Try removing your emotions and yourself from the equation. Recognize the hazards just examining it does little or no good if you do not identify it as a hazard and associate the risk that may accompany it. Third, establish the best plan to mitigate over, through, or around the obstacle. Never be afraid of asking another how they overcame a problem. I have this friend name Ray, he's one of the smartest and well experienced people I have access to. Yet many people are intimidated by him or have the wrong perspective of him. He has that quiet knowledge and ingenuity he's not the boasting type; you probably would think he didn't know anything if you met him, but as you get to know him you come to find that he is a tremendous asset as a friend. And fourth, implementation, there's this saying that I once heard that simply states "Don't just talk about it be about it." Take the necessary steps to get the plan rolling. Many people say what they want to do, or what they ought to do; only to fall victim to procrastination the dream killer.

God's word is relevant to every situation you may ever face. The answer may not be clear or the source may be even cloudy but 1 Corinthians 1: 27- 29 tells us that *God chose the foolish things of the world that the wise might be put to shame, and God chose the*

weak things of the world so that He might put to shame the strong things. And God chose the low-born of the world, and the despised, and the things that are not, so that He might bring to nothing the things that are, so that no flesh might glory in His presence.

Every golfer has a good caddie; a helper or assistant, his job does not just consist of carrying the golfer's bag; he is a valuable commodity, he also advises the golfer on the slope and speed of the course, he provides vital information on club selection, change of wind direction and possible ways of negotiating obstacles. In a like manner the Spirit of God is a caddie someone who is always there and willing to advise and instruct us but we must be willing to receive Him and His counsel.

As it pertains to the game of golf or life there are times when you wish you could have just stayed in bed; nothing seems to be going as planned, either your short game is too long or your long game is too short or maybe the car seems to have a mind of it's own. The key to days like this in the terms of golf is to "Keep swing'em." Occasionally we are put into situations that are challenging to the development of our ability to cope with problems. How we react when faced with such obstacles is crucial. Walking blindly into a situation with no expectation of a challenge is dangerous in itself. The one thing I am sure of is that you will inevitably end up in a bunker. Practice and Preparation however will help you in negotiating those obstacles both in life and on the course. With that in mind I sat and wrote "Par".

> The day is great for a challenge; the course is set for battle;
> Morning dew cascades the field as nerves began to rattle.
> I wait patiently as the master starts to prepare;
> He looks to be unnerved as though he doesn't care.
> Flying straight and true my master seems so proud;
> He knew I had missed my mark by the groans from the
>   crowd.
> Anxiously he searches for me and I'm soaring once again;
> Yearning to find my mark that some would call a pin.
> The grass beneath me rough, there's no sight of the cup;

In times like these I worry but I know he won't give up.
Suddenly I hear him there's commotion all about;
"Over here!" I heard his trusty comrade shout.
As I looked up at my master his countenance strong with
    detest;
"Pull yourself together," he said. "You can get out of this
    mess."
With great resolve my master approached and again I'm
    flying high;
"Get down get down," he cried and it obliged me to comply.
Plummeting near the target the crowd erupts with cheer;
"This is the place," I thought "I've finally made it here."
He approached me once again, kneeling as to pray;
He finished his task with a tap and then went on to say.
"Thank you Lord for deliverance and bringing me thus far;
Thank you Lord for the birdie, I'd been content with making
    par."

Golf has taught me a lot; it was just the antidote I needed
to help reduce certain stressful situations along with helping
me develop more patience. I've learned that you cannot become
patient with anyone or anything unless you first become patient
with yourself. I became frustrated initially when I started playing
the game. Taking those things that you're taught and applying
them to your current circumstances will assist you in evolving into
a better player and person.

Impatience is such a childish quality; nonetheless, it seems
to spill over into our adult lives. To see a grown man throwing a
temper tantrum is appalling. It is a good indicator that he is not
spiritually astute. I have got to admit that use to be me; sulking
in my anger when things didn't go my way (childish I know), but
it is a tool that we as humans use to subvert another's will or way
when ours is not being fulfilled. When I looked up the definition
of the word sulk I was surprised to see its true meaning: - (to be
silently angry) to refuse to talk to or associate with others as a
show of resentment for a real or imagined grievance. You may

be asking yourself now, "What does that have to do with a new joy?" In part everything; it has to do with self awareness, knowing when you are wrong, knowing what caused you to behave in such a manner and most importantly knowing when to admit it and seeking deliverance from it through Christ.

One of the most transforming things God has allowed me to experience is self awareness. No, not like an outer body experience it was more like a mirror encounter. He allowed me to see the real me and guess what. I found myself to be repulsive; not so much physically but spiritually, but those things that seem to be lying dormant within has the propensity of manifesting outwardly. The reality of what I saw caused me to seek for what He wanted me to be. It would ultimately shed light on this truth God has done some rending in my life; He has also done some building. Through it all I could not have been in any better hands.

In the dispensations of both Isaiah and Jeremiah they share a metaphor of the Potter and the clay that is parallel. Isaiah writes: *But now, O Lord, You are our Father; we are the clay, and You are our potter; and we all are the work of Your hand.* Jeremiah writes: *And the vessel that he made of clay was marred in the hand of the potter so he made it again another vessel, as seemed good to the potter to make it.* In their analogies they both acclaim God as being the Potter. In like reference we are the clay that is set a top of a wheel and is fashioned in the manner in which God sees fit. Jeremiah alludes that one particular vessel was defective upon examination so the potter made it again. The thing that caught me was the clay was not thrown away or destroyed, but the shape of the vessel was altered; he continued to work with the same piece of clay until it was without any blemishes. I've had the opportunity to work with clay and when you make something if there is a void or flaw in the object when placed in the kiln many times the finished product is ruined. God loves us too much to just throw any old thing into the kiln we are precious to Him. Notice that the potter caught this defect before it was placed in the fire. He knows clay in fact during the period when Jesus walked the earth, the men of this particular trade gathered the ingredients needed to make the finest clay. He knew well in advance that the elements in the clay had a certain property and would be tried in the process of becoming a useable vessel. The conditioning of the fire was to harden the vessel, seal it so that the works of the potter could bring him honor. When God makes us and put us in the fire of trials we become a vessel worthy to hold within us His Word and expel it upon the hearts and minds of men in this world that would gladly receive it.

A vessel that has not gone through the sealing fire of God is an ineffectual piece. Whatever He put into it would not or could not hold it. Imagine going to someone and you were dying of thirst and they presented you with a beautiful crystal goblet, but it was riddled with holes. To try and drink from it would only frustrate you more. The purpose it was created for was to hold something precious, something desirable and useful, but when it is unfinished or marred it serves no useful purpose. Being a vessel of God is and should be a joy to all who are called. Christ tells us that we are the salt of the earth, but if the salt loses it savor, how can you make it salt again? It is then good for nothing but to be put out and crushed under feet by men. Everything God has made has a purpose, we may not see the significance in it but it is of value to Him. We are important to Him, we would only have to come to know Him in order to walk in the joy of the Lord and once you have walked in His presence it is a place you yearn to be.

Christ teaches us that we are special to Him; when we read Matthew 6:25 & 26 this is affirmed in us: *Therefore I say unto you, Take no thought for your life, what you shall eat, or what you shall drink; nor yet for your body, what you shall put on. Is not the life more than meat, and the body than clothes? Behold the birds of the air: for they sow nothing, neither do they reap, nor gather into barns; yet your heavenly Father feeds them. Are you not much better than they?*

We are much better than they are which is evident by what He desires every man to have inside of him and that is the Spirit of Him. *What is man that you are mindful of him? and the son of man, that you visited him? For you have made him a little lower than the angels, and have crowned him with glory and honor.* It is my belief that this reference is made of Adam the first man even though it could be implied of Jesus. Let me elaborate, in Genesis 1:26 God gave dominion to man over all the earth. Why not give it to His Son? One word redeemer, it is not a coincident that Christ would have to come in the same sinful like flesh, yet he never sinned. God knows the beginning and the end and He knew that the world would need a redeemer and not a ruler. What is man that God would remember or recognize us along with the descendants of the chosen people and that He would care for us? Although we were the last of His creation it was fitting that He placed us as rulers over His works; in His provisions we would lack nothing once created.

After some forty-two generations Christ would also become flesh. (As mentioned in the Gospel according to John)He was born of a virgin named Mary, the only begotten Son of God. The only plausible reason why Jesus Christ may be called the Word, seems to be, that as our words expound on our thoughts to others, so was the Son of God sent in order to make know the divine thoughts of His Father's to the world. His message is clear receive My Son today for tomorrow will be too late.

In reflecting on what God has made so readily available for us it seem to come to me as many other thoughts have as a "Poetic plea".

If it had not been for sorrow;
I would not have appreciated the joy.
Yesterday is of no value to me;
Tomorrow has yet to deploy.
It is true I've not known death;
Yet life will hastily pass,
Yesterday is of no value to me;
Tomorrow is approaching fast.
Eternity is indefinite,
Grief seems just as long,
Yesterday is of no value to me,
Tomorrow is a distant song.
Yesterday will be no more,
Tomorrow maybe too late;
To deny ones self eternal life,
A day that surely awaits.
Salvation is of today,
Yesterday has come and gone;
Tomorrow may never come,
Like the melody of an unheard song.

ELEVEN

Joy in living, learning and sharing

The Apostle Paul wrote to the early church at Corinth when several problems disrupted the forward movement of the assembly. Dissension within the group, incestuous marriages, spiritual gifts and proper observance of the Lord's Supper were only a few of the problems he had before him. In an effort to dispel any erroneous thoughts or behavior he penned the first of two letters to them in the hopes of correcting and clarifying anything that may have caused them to falter or misinterpret the Word of God which they had received through him from Christ. Paul starts the body of his letter not with reproof but with thanks to God for the grace that was given to them by Christ Jesus. An important note because when people receive mail they are more prone to discard it if the first words out of your mouth are of scorn. No one likes to receive bad news nor be the one to deliver it, but it was the purpose for his calling and his letter. In this letter Paul exercises his authority as he firmly deals with division within the church. He admonishes the church with words he selected carefully in the hopes of helping them help themselves. *Now I implore you, brethren, by the name of our Lord Jesus Christ, that you all speak the same thing, and that there be no divisions among you; but that you be perfectly joined together in the same mind and in the same judgment.* In part he shows his concern for the church, condemns their immoral acts, and counsels them through their difficulties.

To farther reprove their actions he challenges their maturity as a concerned father would by adding that the things they were preoccupied with were childish and needed to be put away. *When I was a child, I spoke as a child, I understood as a child, I thought as a child but when I became a man, I put away childish things.* Knowing that their engrossment would cause further division Paul uses himself as an example to convey his discontentment for their behavior.

Earlier followers found it difficult to receive him due to him being a former persecutor of the church and a participant in the death of Stephen, but this was no longer an issue, the church's problems stemmed from the superstitions of one group and the sinful conduct of the other. The only way that Paul could eliminate this division would be to educate the church on the will of God. When we take into account all the obstacles that he was facing it appears that he would certainly fail. Failure, I once heard is a certainty if one never tries. What Paul had begun he was very eager to finish. *I do not write these things shaming you, but warning you as my beloved children.* Though the apostle spoke with authority as a parent, he would rather implore them in love, and as a minister he was to set an example.

As a parent I have found that it is a commendable responsibility to be able to pass the knowledge you have to your children. I find it equally important to pass along any experiences whether good or bad and to share any mistakes you have made in the efforts of having them grow into a more productive person. Thinking back to my childhood years it was my mother who gave me the most affection, the most attention, and the most affirmation which has made me partly the person that I am. My father's role was more of a disciplinarian, one to be feared and not crossed.

I wanted to incorporate both of my parents' method in order to develop a healthier relationship with my children. I've noticed that our relationships with our heavenly Father seem common to the features of the relationship we hold with our earthly father. And as a father I anticipate the same things of my sons that my heavenly Father expects of me. Ten facets of our relationship with our heavenly Father seem to be closely related to the qualities we have with our earthly father which are:

- Obedience
- Love
- Devotion
- Diligence
- Fear

- Trust
- Invoking
- Integrity
- Sanctification
- Righteous

Not all of the aforementioned characteristics are easily found in our earthly father yet they are the basis for developing and sustaining a relationship with our heavenly Father. These are a few verses that I have employed in my life to strengthen and better my relationship with Him.

☐ The supreme test of faith in God is our obedience; *You are My friends if you do whatever I command you.* The scripture tells us that Christ was/is our example of obedience so much in fact that He was even until His death.

☐ Our love is displayed when we keep His commandments but the ultimate show of love is displayed in Romans 5: 8 & in John 3:16, *God demonstrates His love for us while we were still sinners by giving us His only Son to die for our sins.*

☐ In devoting something to God it is not like a sacrifice or offering that can be recalled before a ceremony; it shall not be sold nor redeemed. *Every devoted thing to God is most holy, set apart unto the Lord.*

☐ *But without faith it is impossible for us to please God. For it is right that the one drawing near to God should believe that He is, and that He becomes a rewarder to the ones Seeking Him out.*

☐ *For God did not give us a spirit of fear, but of power and of love and of self-control. Be not wise in your own eyes; reverently fear and worship the Lord and turn away from evil.*

☐ *Trust in the Lord with all your heart; and lean not unto your own understanding. In all your ways acknowledge Him, and He shall direct your paths.*

☐ *In my distress when seemingly closed in I called upon the Lord and cried to my God; He heard my voice out of His temple (heavenly dwelling place), and my cry came before Him, into His ears. As for me, I will call upon God, and the Lord will save me.*

☐ *The integrity of the upright shall guide them but the perverseness of transgressors shall destroy them. Let integrity and uprightness preserve me; for I wait on You Lord.*

☐ *Sanctify the Lord God in your hearts and be ready always to give an answer to every man that ask you a reason of the hope that is in you with meekness and fear.*

☐ *For the Lord knows the way of the righteous but the way of the ungodly shall perish. Be glad in the Lord, and rejoice, you that are righteous and shout for joy, all you that are upright in heart. I have been young, and now am old; yet I have not seen the righteous forsaken, nor His seed (children) begging for bread.*

I can't say what worked for me would work for you but I do know that He and His Word works for me and can work for you as well. As unique as you are your relationship with Him should be just as genuine. I relate it to the relationships that I have formed with my own sons; they are all different and the relationship that I have with each of them is as distinct. The only similarities are that what I do for one I do for the other. The method may be different but the motive is the same I love them. God is as such, He is willing to bless His children equally yet His means of doing so may be different. The place that we are in in our lives also depends on how and to what degree we are blessed; for example my sons are ages twelve, eight, and seven. I can't give to my seven year old what I would give my twelve year old; it is all relative and based on their maturity level. Just the same God will not give His children anything they are not mature enough to handle. Observe how Paul enlightens the church members of Corinth in 1 Corinthians 3:1 & 2. *Brothers, I was not able to speak to you as to spiritual ones, but as to fleshly ones, as to babes in Christ. I fed you with milk, not solid food, for you were not yet strong enough [to be ready for it]; but even yet you are not strong enough.* Although the Apostle is referring to spiritual immaturity and not physical immaturity it can be plainly perceived that the two are synonymous as it pertains to maturity.

In growing we often face things that are confrontational, but with the understanding from the Holy Spirit we are able to discern between that which is spiritual and that which is of the flesh. In the continuation of Paul's teachings to the children of Corinth he further explains the cause or reason why we are disconnected from the things of God. The following scriptures make it apparent that the flesh and spirit of man is contrary to one another. *The natural (flesh) man is not able to understand the things of the Spirit of God; for they seem foolish to him, and he is not able to have knowledge of them, because such knowledge comes only through the Spirit. For those who are according to the flesh and are controlled by its unholy desires set their minds on and pursue those things which gratify the flesh, but those who are according to the Spirit and are controlled by the desires of the Spirit set their minds on and seek those things which gratify the [Holy] Spirit.* What are men most confident in is it their flesh or the spirit, the old man or the new nature, depravity or the grace of God, which of these do we make more provisions for and which ones have we allowed to control us in our daily walk?

☐ Another eye opening lesson that the Spirit of God instilled in me was the importance of obedience. I was sitting observing my boys at the park one day when the Spirit placed this on my heart. God is our Father and He has blessed me to be a father, the park represented the world which was jam-packed with plenty of seen and unseen dangers, along with enticing situations both good and bad for a child to get into. The scenario reminded me of one of the great parables of the bible. I had specified clearly to them the boundaries and the do's and don'ts when we arrived. I also explained to them that any failure to obey the rules would be met with punishment. "Treyon keep an eye on your brothers, and the two of you mind your big brother," I instructed. Like any excited kid the message would be received but would be placed in their short term memory bank.

They seem to adhere for about twenty minutes or so when I noticed them being led away by a very pretty and persuasive little girl. She was just adorable and the three of them all seem to be smitten by her beauty and charm. Before I knew what had happened she had coaxed them to the other side of the park out of view. I went looking for the three stooges and searched for ten minutes to no avail. For whatever reasons the youngest of the trio Ty wandered off. Both Treyon and Mike strolled up to me as though everything was okay. "Where is your brother"? I asked. "I don't know," Mike answered. "I thought he was over here with you," Treyon explained. "That's it as soon as we find your brother we are leaving"! I shouted. "Come on here so we can find Ty," I ordered. We searched the park calling for Ty and several minutes passed before we found him. He was sitting with this father and son watching them catch fish. I was relieved to find him but I was upset as well. "Boy where have you been"? I asked. "Treyon and Mike wouldn't let me play with them." he explained. "I saw him walk over here I kept my eyes on him he was just curious about what we were doing," this strange man said. "They were being ugly to him so he came over here," he continued. "Is that your little girl"? "No Sir just these three right here." "I appreciate you looking after him thank you Sir," "No problem." he responded.

Now I told you that little story to say this, our heavenly Father wants obedient children; I know this because He made it as plain as day when He showed it to me "Just like you want your sons to obey you, I want My children to obey Me." Then I began to recount the number of time throughout the bible when God's children disobeyed Him, the things which they suffered simply by not doing what they were told. The children of Israel could not see the consequences of their action, just as children are today they may see the clear and present dangers, but those that lie and wait in dark places are the ones that normally go undetected. So you can imagine how I felt when my boys didn't mind me. It frustrated me, it angered me. All which are traits possessed by the Father and all though He is slow to anger we should not provoke Him to it.

☐ Love is the apparent theme throughout the entire book of 1Corinthians, it is Paul's wish that the church comes to understand the advantage and necessity of love. In chapter eleven he bids the church to imitate him, just as he also imitated Christ. The Apostle Paul goes on to pen the most profound definitions of what love is and what it is not.

Though I speak with the tongues of men and of angels, and have not love, I have become as sounding brass, or a tinkling cymbal. And though I have the gift of prophecy, and understand all mysteries, and all knowledge; and though I have all faith, so that I could remove mountains, and have not love, I am nothing. And though I give all my goods to feed the poor, and though I give my body to be burned, and have not love, it profits me nothing. Love suffers long, and is kind; love is not envious; love does not boast of itself, is not puffed up, does not behave rude, seeks not her own, is not easily provoked, thinks no evil; Rejoices not in iniquity, but rejoices in the truth; Love bears all things, believes all things, hopes all things, endures all things.

Love never fails but whether there be prophecies, they shall fail;
whether there be tongues, they shall cease; whether there be knowledge,
it shall vanish away. (But love will never fail)

In his conclusion he tells the church that it doesn't matter
what deeds he had done but if they were done without love they
would all amount to nothing. Everything he had done, did or was
about to do he suffered it in faith, hope and love yet the greatest
of them all was love.

☐ As it pertains to our devotion to the Lord we are to honor
Him with our possessions, and with the first fruits of all our
increase. I'm reminded of a song we use to sing that goes "You
can't beat God's giving no matter how hard you try." Once again I
would have to revert to a previous statement, He gave the ultimate
to us He gave us His son. Our reasonable service to Him is
to present our bodies as a living sacrifice, die daily from some
immoral act or thought and live holy which is acceptable to Him.
Paul later tells us in 1 Corinthians 6: 20 that we are bought with
a price; therefore glorify God in your body and in your spirit,
which belong to Him.

In reference to our earthly father the bible tells us regard (treat
with honor, due obedience, and courtesy) your father and mother,
that your days may be long upon the earth the Lord your God
gives you. It is a statistical fact that a great deal of households
today are without father figures and mothers are left with the
burden of being provider, comforter, disciplinarian and teacher.
It's true that it is difficult for single parents but I've read and have
witnessed to many success stories to even think it to be impossible.
In the up and coming pages I'll introduce you to a woman, a
Queen who provided for her family. She wasn't single but she
worked, planned and invested as though a kingdom depended on
her and in essence it did.

☐ Diligences denote a persistent effort, persistent and hard-
working effort in doing something as when we are seeking God.
People are always hard at work doing something but only what
you do for Christ will last. Many people will miss their salvation

calling due to being busy doing other things. It is my prayer that you want to be saved, if you haven't received Him do it now. He wants you to have eternal life. Christ said it Himself *"Just so it is not the will of My Father Who is in heaven that one of these little ones should be lost and perish."*

☐ There was a slogan coined some years ago that simply read "No Fear." It was my motto, I foolishly lived by it, the implications of it were all wrong. It is true that God wants a certain boldness of His servants but the connotation in which I lived it was strictly worldly, a foolish bravery the kind that often gets young (black) men killed. It was not of God because I didn't know Him the way that I know Him now. I was hoodwinked, without a clue and Satan does not concern himself all that much if you're living recklessly it's where he wants you. It's only when you decide that you're going to follow Christ that bothers him, and that's when he becomes busy.

☐ "In God we trust." So our currency says, "Yeah right." Trust is relying on somebody or something or to place confidence in somebody or in somebody's good qualities, especially fairness, truth, honor, or ability. What happens to a nation of people when they stop trusting in God? They fall into perilous times; they are handed over to their enemies so the bible says.

And the nations shall know, understand, and realize positively that the house of Israel went into captivity for their iniquity, because they trespassed against Me; and I hid My face from them. So I gave them into the hand of their enemies and they all fell into captivity or were slain by the power of the sword. So how do we prevent something this catastrophic from falling upon us? That's simple first we repent, and then stop allowing the immoral liberalist society to back us into a corner by trying to convince us that homosexuality and same sex marriages are natural. Psalms 118: 8 & 9 tells us *It is better to trust and take refuge in the Lord than to put confidence in man or nobles.* Therefore, we should Lean on, trust in, and be confident in the Lord with all your heart and mind and do not rely on our own insight or understanding.

☐ Calling upon the Lord is a privilege that some have not known and others seldom use. In life difficulties sometimes mom or dad may not have the answer or the doctor may not have the remedy for what ails you, but God is waiting for you to call on Him. The Lord is near to all who call upon Him, to all who call upon Him sincerely and in truth. We have both a necessity and a right to call upon Him but we must do it now, because there will come a time when He will not hear our voice nor pity our cry.

☐ Responding to life tribulations with integrity can be quite challenging yet it can be done. Integrity is the quality of possessing and steadfastly adhering to high moral principles or professional standards even when things are going bad around you. " Be it in private, public or peril let us always do the right thing," was a motto which we would recite daily as a member and graduate of the Firemen Academy. It seems corny then probably because I was young and thought it was just cool to be a fireman. As I matured and realized that more people were watching me to see how I would respond to different issues, it became a better practice to maintain a greater degree of integrity.

☐ I wish that I could tell you that it is easy to live a Christian life but the truth is, it isn't but it is very possible. Sanctification of one's self is even more demanding, but again very possible. I've learned that I have strength for all things in Christ Who strengthens me. I am ready for anything and equal to anything through Him Who gives inner strength to me; I am self-sufficient in Christ's sufficiency. Although we can sanctify ourselves we can't make ourselves righteous.

☐ There is none righteous, just, truthful, upright or conscientious, no, not one. *Even the righteousness of God through faith of Jesus Christ is toward all and upon all those believing; for there is no difference.* There is no difference between Jew and Greek, black or white; it is the prayers of Jesus for all that are His that they may be made holy. Even the Disciples of Christ must pray for sanctifying grace. This grace is from God it lies in His truth, His word which is truth, His Son which is truth and we are to be set apart for Him and His service. Jesus devoted Himself entirely to the task before Him not half- heartedly but with eagerness once again exhibiting the ideal character of one faced with the distressing commission.

Not all of life situations have to do with who's right or who's wrong; sometimes it is a matter of who is more mature. My wife Le and I were dealing with a certain issue in our marriage that kept surfacing. Every time it started we would have an argument; it seems more to me like a nagging convention or a let's irritate Tommy day. I was so frustrated with the thought of talking with her that I was willing to give her everything and leave. That's when I noticed an intriguing pattern developing; Satan was trying to disrupt yet again another family, to kill the family charter and shatter any hopes of us having a constructive Christian family. His tactic once again was deception and confusion. What I perceived to be nagging from my wife he amplified with a biblical scripture. *It is better to dwell in a corner of the housetop [exposed to all kinds of weather] than in a house shared with a nagging, quarrelsome, and faultfinding woman.* (Proverbs 21: 9) The uniqueness of this verse seem to answer a multitude of questions but Satan only wanted me to see the negative side of the verse if there could be one. I focused on the part of the verse that emphasized how it is better to dwell in a corner of the housetop. The message I received from that was "leave" but that wasn't the answer God had proposed.

At no point in the scripture does He say leave but rather "separate". They both needed to clear their head and it wasn't going to happen with the two of them under the same roof arguing passionately about who they thought was right or wrong. I had developed a "Me complex" from dealing with the women of my past and God was about to shatter everything that I had learned about a woman.

Further dissection of the verse was needed to get the full ramification of its meaning. What was the woman nagging or nitpicking about the bible doesn't say but in the case with my wife her speech reveres her fears and with my wife it was about finances, not seemingly having enough. Was it a valid complaint, it didn't seem so at the time but time and the Word of God has a way of making things plain. I started to feel like a host for a colony of leeches having my money and my blood sucked out of me. It was threatening to my ego to become henpecked; I didn't want to become a "Yes Dear" type of man. To a certain degree it was a form of selfishness and as Paul taught us in the definition of what love is love is not selfish. In essence if I was not providing for her she had every right to nag me, it was only when the two of us had gone to counseling and I learned that as a husband the best possibility of obtaining happiness is to make her happy. In providing her with all that she needed, she is happy and in turn she is a blessing to her husband.

Proverbs 31: 10-31 gives an account of a woman who is truly virtuous. In reading and studying the scripture they are words of wisdom spoken by a loving mother to a growing king; although it is presented by the king, it is apparent in the opening verses that this advice is clearly accredited to his mother who wants him to live a righteous and prosperous life. His mother in an attempt to provide for her son the best advice possible may have taken her knowledge from the former king by observing the way in which he managed his affairs. She appears to be the type of woman that submitted herself too totally to her husband and king for the benefit of the earthly and heavenly kingdom. One thing is for sure she is smart. She has her husband and family as well as her servant's interest at heart; she even makes way for strangers who are of need. She is a hard working woman who spares no day light and who often works into the wee hours of the night in preparation for the coming day. The multitalented woman has a business savvy that profits her husband and family. The mother refers to the woman as a merchant ship that brings goods and food to her family by the goods from her garden and the works of her hands.

The way she speaks reveres her fear and respect of God. A woman worthy of honor and praise she receives it from her children, husband and acquaintances. In summation of this advice the mother notes, *Fair looks are a deceit, and a beautiful form is of no value; but a woman who has the fear of the Lord is to be praised. Give her credit for what her hands have made: let her be praised by her works in the public place,* (Proverbs 31:30 & 31).

Some women may read Proverbs 31: 10-31 and say, "Please, I'm not trying to be that busy." Others might read it and reply, "Wow! This woman has it going on." Yet a great majority of them will never be able to relate to this Queen whether it is because of bitterness, resentment or a lack of understanding her. Bitterness causes a slew of problems ranging from the inability to trust, commit or love. Its depth can become so immense that people seclude themselves from society and even love ones. Consequently time is spent leaping from one down spiraling relationship to another, self worthlessness strongly impinges on our esteem and we began to just settle for the next viable victim. I no longer wanted to be associated with that type of lifestyle nor share its potentially violent outcome with anyone. So what did I do? Well, to quote a line from one of my favorite movies Forest Gump, "I just kept running."

Was running a viable solution? Certainly not, it only prolongs the situation at hand, but it was the only conclusion that I could come up with at the time. What people fail to realize is that running puts you on a path that veers directly into the path in which you started; I call it the "Y" affect. The path you start on is either good or bad, then you come to a point or a fork in the road that either takes you left or right. It is in this time of your life that you must choose wisely. Going left leads to hardship and adversity, while going to the right leads to growth and privileges. Take note that both choices come with a certain degree of difficulty but the right road is less harsh and you don't have to make a u-turn because there is no dead end. Unlike the road to the left it is a dead end and what has made the journey so lengthy for some is that once they realize that the road is ending they return to the intersection and travel the same road again.

Contrary to belief life is a journey not a party as some would think. Along this journey we are tried and tested in a number of ways that produce in some a testimony, in others it builds ministries that go on to help people who are not linked by chance or consequences.

I believe we are all linked in some way the bible tells us that at one time we all had a common language. Genesis 11:1-7 says And *all the earth had one language and one tongue. And it came about that in their wandering from the east, they came to a stretch of flat country in the land of Shinar, and there they made their living-place. And they said one to another, Come; let us make bricks, burning them well. And they had bricks for stone, putting them together with sticky earth. And they said, Come, let us make a town, and a tower whose top will go up as high as heaven; and let us make a great name for ourselves, so that we may not be wanderers over the face of the earth. And the Lord came down to see the town and the tower which the children of men were building. And the Lord said, "See, they are all one people and have all one language; and this is only the start of what they may do and now it will not be possible to keep them from any purpose of theirs. Come, let Us go down and take away the sense of their language, so that they will not be able to make themselves clear to one another."*

Their pride and arrogance of heart cause the division of their language a division that can be seen in today's society with an inability to understand each other and live in harmony. Where there is foolish pride there is no desire to do the will of God. In their dire attempt to obtain excellence they forgot the One who had blessed them. Their thought was, "Let us make a great name for ourselves," not "Let us bless the Lord our God with a temple to worship Him." In turn their language had been reduced to mere babbling. It would prove to be impossible for them to continue in the efforts of building a city because communication would be the key and without understanding all efforts would be futile at best.

I read some time ago about a theory that anyone on earth can be connected to another on this planet through a chain of acquaintances that has no more than five intermediaries.

The theory "Six Degrees of Separation" was first proposed in 1929 by the Hungarian writer Frigyes Karinthy in a short story called *"Chains."* The concept is based on the idea that the number of acquaintances grows exponentially (rapidly growing in size) with the number of links in the chain, and so only a small number of links are required for the set of acquaintances to become the whole human population.

I don't consider this theory to be far fetched its application has great potential. In 1967, American social psychologist Stanley Milgram devised a new way to test the theory, which he called "the small-world problem". He randomly selected people from various places in the United States to send postcards to one of two targets, one in Massachusetts and one in the American Midwest. The senders knew the recipient's name, occupation, and general location. They were instructed to send the card to a person they knew on a first-name basis who they thought was most likely, out of all their friends, to know the target personally. That person would do the same, and so on, until it was delivered to the target himself/herself. Although the participants expected the chain to include at least a hundred intermediaries, 80% of the successfully delivered packages were delivered after four or fewer steps. Almost all the chains were less than six steps. Milgram's findings were published in Psychology Today, and his findings inspired the phrase *six degrees of separation.*

Impressive nonetheless, but my confidence is strongly anchored in the genealogy of the bible. Genesis gives us the descendants of Noah after the great flood Shem, Ham, and Japheth. Shem was the distant father of Abram who later would be called Abraham from these came all the nations of the earth after the great flow of waters. Without going into much detail and for the sake of time and repetition the account of all their sons and daughters can be found in Genesis chapters 10 and 11.

After reading the history of how nations were established and how kings came to be I was moved by its complexity and wrote "A Nation;" it reflects some of the situations of our past and some of the current events in the world today.

A nation is born and another one dies;
One will rejoice while the other one cries.
One will hale a president, while the other buries a queen;
One nation soars while the other one dream.

A nation will build while the other lies in rubble;
One will know war while the other averts trouble.
Her people will remember her, her noble men will panic;
Her name will not die for the meek loves to chant it.

She will rise and she will fall;
O' Beautiful is her name but to others she will appall.
She is not a perfect nation, but men yearn to abide;
Within her coastal borders where they swell with pride.

Her enemies are filled with envy and her allies praise her fame;
Conspiracies are her secrets and her leaders have no shame.
But she offers a dream to strangers and a decree she gives to all;
Life, liberty and happiness to every man who calls.

TWELVE

Answering the call

When I was a young boy attending church with my mom and siblings there was this woman in the church name Sister White. She had predicted years ago that I would become a preacher. At that time in my life I paid it no mind and chalked it up to a senile old woman's babble. She seems to make it her profession to make sure everyone knew of her prediction. I would grin and bear her claim but never accepted it as a possibility. I didn't feel that becoming a minister was a responsibility I could fill, not to mention I thought that their lifestyle was rather insipid, this would no doubt clash with the things that held my interest. Years passed and yet I embraced the same notion of becoming a clergyman.

What bothered me the most was this gentleman name Kenneth who worked for the fire department. Every time he would see me he would call out "Hey Preacher"! This would give people the impression that I was actually a preacher. One day as we all gathered for a department function he called out to me once again "Hey Preacher"! I pulled him to one side and began to chew him out for making such accusations. "Look man don't be going around calling me that you've got other people calling me preacher, I'd appreciate it if you would stop," I scolded. "I'm sorry I didn't mean to upset you Doc I won't do it again," he apologized. In parting he left me with these words; "But that don't change the fact that you're still a preacher." I couldn't bring myself to continue my argument with him I just wanted to let him know that I was fed up with what I thought were embarrassing slurs.

So I continued my course running from the inevitable; I even went as far as to stop going to church. My idiotic belief was if I didn't go to His house and continued to keep on living immorally then He would see the vileness of character and lose interest. Boy was I in for a spiritual awakening. One day while in deep thought I began to have this vision; I was standing elevated before a group of people and they seem, for the most part, interested in what I was saying, they seem to be clinging to every word.

All at once a feeling of gratification filled me and I began to weep. This would be a series of visions I would have and they would all play out the same way I would be standing elevated before a group of people and suddenly I would began to weep. The crying stemmed from the unction of knowing that God had placed His hands on me. The overwhelming feeling of being called into a profession that the world would not receive made my tears even harder to contain.

For a period that seems like months I was withdrawn from any contact with family or friends. My mother would call and I could not bear talking to her, it was if though no one could possibly understand what I was going through. I wasn't upset with anyone it was all based on the fact that my every thought was being consumed with Him preparing me. Thoughts of me running gave way to the desires to stand and fight. My running brought to fruition a desire to please Him and the writing of these lines of thought called "Running".

> Beneath a rock or in a cave I tried to hide from Thee;
> But in those very places you would appear to me.
> So intrusive were the thoughts of You,
> Even in sleep I dared to escape;
> A perpetual, consuming forbearance of how patiently You
>   would wait.
> I went about my pleasure, forsaking Your pleading call;
> Only to seek Your mercies whenever I would fall.

Time after time You would lift me and mend me from the
    pain;
Only to see me indulge myself in promiscuity again.
The method of Your aid showed the promise of Your
    concern;
A lesson for a foolish lad that took some time to learn.
But with persistence and patience You allowed me to falter;
Never withdrawing your grace or Your love that never
    altered.
And when I had prepared myself to take upon Your yoke;
You didn't remind me of my past or of my ignorance in
    which I spoke.
You accepted me as I was and placed in me Your best;
Teaching me all that I had experienced was merely just a test,
So that I could endure the trials of life, prevail even though
    I fall;
And witness to the lost whenever they may call.

The bible tells us in 1Timothy 3:1 this *saying is true and irrefutable if any man eagerly seeks the office of bishop (superintendent, overseer), he desires an excellent task (work).* Receiving or accepting the task is out of love for God, so that the souls of men may be won unto Him. There is no reward except that which the Lord God will pay; neither is there any glory in its work because all glory belongs to God. Nevertheless, somewhere in the middle of this work man somehow forgets his purpose and mission. I have seen time after time the down- fall of many so called men of God, how they have exploited the minds, goods and will of people who were looking for something to believe. This was another reason why I ran from that service. I did not want to be associated with men of that caliber; men like Jim Jones or Marshall Applewhite to name a few. This category of clergymen still exist today, they operate in the name of God and prey on the weak, molest our young children and accept the trends of a secular society. They allow people to believe that Jesus is my homeboy, heaven is a ghetto or that hell is one hell of a party with malfunctioning air conditioning. In 1 Timothy 3: 1 Paul warns Timothy in the characteristics of a bishop that a bishop is not to be a lover of money among other things. Furthermore, he must have a good reputation and be well thought of by those outside the church, or he could become involved in slander and bring upon himself reproach and find himself in Satan's traps (vs. 7).These were also discouraging thoughts "What would others think of my calling and would they accept me as a man of God"? All of this added to the perplexity of my accepting my charge. Once again I would have to refer to the Word of God for an answer. Matthew 10:14 tells us *"And whoever will not receive, accept or welcome you nor listen to your message, as you leave that house or town, shake the dust [of it] from your feet.* With advice like this from Christ Himself it made the pilgrimage a lot more bearable.

As a maturing person in the gospel I'm less apt to be overly concerned about what someone thinks about me. I don't mean that in an arrogant way it's just that I value what God knows about me versus what man thinks of me. Timidity is not a trait of a persecuting world; God's people are more susceptible to it if anything, but Christ warned us of this very thing, He tells His disciples in John 15:20 *"Remember that I told you, A servant is not greater than his master [is not superior to him]. If they persecuted Me, they will also persecute you; if they kept My word and obeyed My teachings, they will also keep and obey yours."*

Again He gives me the tools and encouragement I need to grow in the ministry of reconciliation. The things that our Father wants us to know He prepares us for such an occasion. The training maybe demanding but it is never harsh.

Men in the last days will have a form of religion, its appearance will look impeccable but it will turn their backs to the power of the truth. This form of religion will cause many to become spiritually lost; the persecutors will become the persecuted and it will be a terrible thing to be in such a state. It will be worse than just being off the beaten path, man will look at his spiritual plight as one of life's common ruts in which he can pull himself out. He will wander in his life journey trying to apply physical therapy and psychotherapeutic solutions to a divine and spiritual crisis; that my friend is like placing a bandage on a dead man. It just doesn't make sense. In the climax of this religion men will forsake their own families. I know of a young man who has done just that, no phone calls to his children, no cards of concern on their birthday, not even a candy-cane for Christmas. Witnessing this saddened me so much. It was a thought that I could not get out of my head, so I sat and wrote from a child's perspective:

"A letter to Daddy,"

Talk to me daddy, I miss hearing your voice;
I try to think that leaving us wasn't an easy choice.
Mommy won't stop crying, she's still hurting inside;
Holidays are the worst this Christmas was denied.
Come play with us daddy I haven't laughed in a while;
Mommy won't stop crying and she hardly ever smiles.
Let's sit together and I'll read a book just like we use to do;
I'm reading one now entitled "Will my grey skies ever be blue?"
I try to understand why you wouldn't stay;
Maybe God will answer me tonight when I kneel to pray.
The other night I had a dream, it was weird but yet it seem;
That you were here again, but oh yeah it was only a dream.
I've grown pass the notches that we've placed upon the door;
I hope to see you soon before there're several more.
Well, I've got to go daddy call me or write me sometime;
Mommy finally stopped crying, God said she'd be fine.

My desire was to be a part of a ministry that would allow me to help in the efforts of saving the family charter or more importantly the souls of men. I trust that God will in all things establish his ministers for this work, and see those through whom He has called in times of inconveniences with consolation, and recompense our faithfulness with a just reward. Though our gifts may differ they are all for His glory. In some He has placed a song of hope, in others He may place a manuscript, but in all who are proclaimed preachers of the word of God He will plant a sermon. *Therefore, everyone who acknowledges Me before men and confesses Me* Matthew 10:32-33 says. *I will also acknowledge him before My Father Who is in heaven and confess that I am in him. But whoever denies and disowns Me before men, I also will deny and disown him before My Father Who is in heaven.*

In spite of what I've learned there was still a sentiment of apathy that needed to be dealt with; an inoculation of some sort to boost my spirit. Was it doubt? I'm sure it was but it had to be controlled. I gained it when a minister friend of my wife prayed for me one day. She had said to my wife that she noticed something different about me. She told me that she wanted to pray for us both. She instructed me to just receive what God had for me; she placed her hand on my abdomen and began to pray. A feeling of affirmation swept through me giving me the assurance I needed to employ God's plans for me. The Lord has many ways of affirming a person regardless of what their circumstances are (not that I could boast). He has called many men from many walks of life and refined them into the messengers He wants them to be. I was ashamed of where I had come from and the things that I had done. I did not want to dishonor the profession, but He revealed to me that if He could use a murderer or a drunk He could use someone who once lived a lascivious life. What we as humans see with our eyes leaves a lasting impression in our mind and hearts. Only God can change the hearts and minds of His people. We can't move past what we have seen; the drunk will remain the drunk, the murderer will remain the murderer until we look at things from a God's eye view.

To warn Israel of the possible judgment before them God employs a herdsman, a shepherd name Amos to reprove and warn the people of Israel. Whomever God gives abilities to for His services, they should not be blamed or reviled for their origin in which they come, or for their employment. I think it is important to reiterate a point made earlier.

"God has selected the foolish things of this world so that He might put the wise to shame; and He has chosen the feeble things of this world that He might put to shame the strong."

This was the case for both Amos and myself; Amos who was called by God to speak against Israel and its neighboring people said to Amaziah the priest of Bethel, *"I was no prophet, neither was I the son of a prophet; but I was a herdsman, and one who gathered fruit from the sycamore tree. And the Lord took me as I followed the flock, and the Lord said unto me, Go, prophesy unto my people Israel.* If God had not strengthened Amos to speak as he did he could not have faced the people with such boldness. They would have had him for breakfast; his ministry would have been over before it had begun. Being empowered by God gave him the boldness he needed to speak with conviction and authority. My fate was as the herdsman Amos; it took a compelling testament from God to give me that little push into obedience. Therefore, all I do is of Him and for Him. To God be the glory forever and ever.

What God has in store for us only He knows and yet Amos 3:7 tells us *"Surely the Lord God will do nothing without revealing His secret to His servants the prophets."*

God knows in dealing with people there must first be a warning, this warning is spoken by whomever the Lord calls. Romans 10:14 says *But how are people to call upon Him Whom they have not believe? And how are they to believe in Him of Whom they have never heard? And how are they to hear without a preacher?* There were times when I would not heed to such warnings and would be left dealing with consequences and the feelings of hopelessness. Secondly, reproof is spoken to those in question to get them to repent from their sins, and like anyone who is faced with chastisement only two conclusions are certain; they will either rebel or conform. If they continue to defy Him judgment and punishment is a certainty.

Rebellion is a demonic spirit that has to be broken. Jeremiah knew all to well about the hardships of Judah in their rebellion against God; after God showed him the two signs, one which pertained to the potter and of the broken flask it should have been well received by those in question, but as it would be they continued to do evil. God said through the prophet Jeremiah *"Behold, I will bring such a catastrophe on this place, that whoever hears of it, his ears will tingle."* Wow! What a warning. He warns them, he rebukes them and as the story goes they are led into captivity by the invading Babylonians for their disobedience.

In the midst of it all the prophet was suffering some issues of his own. He was jailed and constantly being mocked by those he was enlisted to help. In his protest before God he complained of being made a laughingstock and vowed to not make mention of the Lord nor would he speak anymore in His name. When we witness to people for God we find that many of them do not want to adhere to the Word of God, and some of them may try to intimidate you by making your witness meaningless by making scornful comments. The propensity of man is to be ashamed, which adds to the frustration and difficulty of witnessing to others. I too can relate to the prophet Jeremiah. There are times when you try to witness to people and they seem more concerned with things of this world rather than the things of the Kingdom.

Jeremiah was at a point where he was suffering trepidation from both sides; physical violence from his persecutors and judgment from the Lord for his disobedience. The Words that the Lord revealed to him has power, so much in fact that it was like a burning fire in his heart that was shut up in his bones. The desire to do as God had called him to do became so overwhelming that he could not hold back. He had heard his conspirators sitting around and whispering to do him evil; trying to persuade him to give up and give in to the immoral life- style as of the children of Judah in the hope of causing him to stumble. Jeremiah answers their ploy with this statement, *"But the Lord is with me as a mighty and terrible One; therefore my persecutors will stumble, and they will not overcome me."*

When adversity is before us even that which seeks to destroy us; it is not so formidable a thing to not trust in the Lord. After all I have suffered through in this life it is a blessing to be able to say that God has had His hands on me. He has proven Himself time after time, and when my back is against the wall or I'm faced with my own lion's den it is He, our Lord and our God, that has delivered me from life snares. Tried and tested He is the best thing that could have ever happened to me. He awaits being tried and tested by you as well.

Malachi 3: 10 tells us *Bring all the tithes (the whole tenth of your income) into the storehouse, that there may be food in My house, and* **prove** *(test) Me now by it, says the Lord of hosts, if I will not open the windows of heaven for you and pour you out a blessing, that there*

shall not be room enough to receive it. That tells me that a blessing from God is a conscience act because it is with purpose that He opens the closed windows of heaven to bless; not by accident or a mere whim. He thinks enough of those who are obedient to Him that it is in action that we are blessed. We do, then He does it is a reciprocating relationship, but God so loved us first that He gave his only Son, so that whoever has faith in Him may not come to destruction but have eternal life.

Something that prohibits our blessing from those windows is a grudging spirit. To hold a grudge would not be Christ like and it is a sure way to inhibit your spiritual growth. From that I have learned this, you know you have recovered from a crisis when your desire to strike out has been supplanted by your desire to reach out to those who may have caused or instigated the crisis. In past relationships I wanted nothing more than to see the person who had hurt me suffer, to feel the full extent of pain that had been my affliction, but with pain comes growth and with growth the understanding of life's circumstances and the knowledge of knowing that your suffering is not in vain. Agony can be a superb instructor if we are able to bear its sometimes harsh lessons that it teaches. No one has ever entered into a relationship with the intentions of being hurt, the Christian relationship is as such; no one becomes a Christian with the expectation of clashing with another but in God's word He reveals that it is bound to happen. We must remind ourselves that the Christian body is made up of imperfect people striving to obtain perfection. Christians will clash but it should not be to the point that their disagreement causes division.

When we answer the call to follow Christ we agree to operate to the best of our ability under a unique consonance. As harmonious as it is, it has its problems and without any deliberation it can be said that it is the people who make up the body. The doctrine is infallible and the Person of whom the doctrine speaks is also flawless, but again the members who are called to carry out its ordinance are subject to err. With no offense or disrespect to dwarfs

I refer to these people as having midget spirits. 1Thessalonians 4:9-12 gives us a perspective of how to conduct ourselves in the body of Christ.

"But concerning brotherly love (for all other Christians), you have no need to have anyone write you, for you yourselves have been taught by God (personally) to love one another. And indeed you already are [extending, displaying your love] to all the brethren throughout Macedonia. But we beseech and earnestly exhort you, brethren that you excel [in this matter] more and more. Make it your ambition and definitely endeavor to live quietly and peacefully, to mind your own affairs, and to work with your hands, as we charged you, So that you may bear yourselves becomingly and be correct and honorable and command the respect of the outside world, being dependent on nobody [self-supporting] and having need of nothing.

If there was a better illustration on how to conduct ourselves certainly it would have been divulged in the Word of God. So faith, hope, love continues to abide; and the greatest of these still remains to be love for one another. Paul commends the church at Thessaloniki and implores them to increase more and more. He understands the mentality of the midget spirit and does all he can to discourage it. Ambition to live a life of peace is greatly encouraged because Paul knows that the life of a Christian would be greatly scrutinized. We shouldn't concern ourselves with matters of the world and to be quite frank we are to mind your own business. A person with a midget spirit has a hard time with the principles of Christian living; they are filled with discontent and have no desire to increase. The unruly, feebleminded and weak, seeks to render evil for evil unto every man. The midget spirit boasts of yesterday, can't see pass today and has no hope in tomorrow. With no perspective of Christian living they seem all to eager to furnish your demise, but Christians whatever the situation we are called to rejoice always, pray without ceasing and in everything give thanks to our Lord and Savior Jesus Christ.

Any lifestyle outside of the kind that God has called us to live is hopeless. The purpose He has for you is not a passing impulse or an afterthought. I know and I feel that this novel would be my testament and I didn't want to get lost in a selfish mind-set of prosperity that clouds the thinking and distorts the vision that He has created. Nothing that He created has returned to Him void (that is without serving and completing its desired effect). The urgency to reap the benefits of this project became a fallacy, the distortion in a vision which was to become my own. With any gift from God it must be cared for, appreciated, shared and not thought of as a basis for selfish gain. I have found that the key to staying focused on any assignment is to have an explicit understanding of what the vision will accomplish.

If you are building a home, plan for a dwelling place and not business space. And by the same token if you are baking a pie plan for pastry and not entrees. With every vision there is a plan and a timeframe in which it will all happen short-cuts are a good way to ruin any vision. Planning, timing, obedience and patience are essential for the vision that God has prepared for you. The vision is for a purpose; it serves as a window into what is coming, giving you hope in the things that God has predestined for your life and all that shall come to pass.

"If you fail to plan your plan will fail." Sometimes the greatest idea goes astray because there was no plan implemented to support the dream. "Is planning easy?" No. "Is it necessary?" Yes, if it is to go forward and do what it was called to do. Not only that but timing is critical; everything has its season. To force something into happening is a sure way to have it fail, pressure burst pipes and consequently leaves you with a bigger mess to deal with. "Work the plan the plan will work." When the plan is given stick to it, there is a reason why they are called blue prints. Unless you are the engineer who developed the plan your deviation will cause a catastrophic end when inadvertent changes are made. You may not understand the plan in the beginning but in your patience clarity will be given. Remain obedient and faithful to the plan it is essential for the end results, and it is then when you can appreciate it in its entirety.

My job as a fireman is pretty simple; people for whatever reason call 911 and speak with a dispatcher; the dispatchers rings the appropriate station, gives all pertinent information and we scurry to our big red trucks to assist those in need. So often I am asked, "What makes you run into a burning building when everything inside is trying to get out or how can you stand to see such horrific scenes daily." What makes it possible is learning how not to become a part of the problem. If someone calls you for help then help and don't hinder. The thing that has helped me the most in coping with such chaos is a little phrase that I repeat to myself while in route to an incident is this; "I didn't create this situation, but I have been trained in an array of skills and techniques to help mitigate this situation, I have been called because no one there is able to help, they called me because they needed a professional." I'm not trying to sound arrogant but it's true people call us for everything and if you can think of it we have probably responded to it.

This is all relative for this reason; no matter what the situation is whether brought on by you or someone else, we all need help. People answer all sorts of calls daily, yet some of them fail to answer the most important question ever posed. "Do you believe that Jesus Christ is the Son of God; who died for our sins, was buried in a tomb and three days later rose from the grave?" The answer should be unequivocally YES!

What I've noticed about adults is that they are discriminate optimists on what they believe and what they compel their children to believe. We are more concerned with our children being nice and not naughty for a season in order to receive a few trinkets under a tree rather than making an impression on a Man that gave His life for our sins. I've instilled in my kids to put their hope and trust in Christ Jesus, not Santa Claus, the Tooth Fairy or the Easter Bunny. I've taught them this because neither one of these fictional characters have ever made such a profound proclamation about themselves. Christ declared in Matthew 28:20 Teach *them to observe all things whatsoever I have commanded you and lo; I am with you always, even unto the end of the world. Amen.* He also spoke to His followers these words in Luke 21:8 *Be on your guard and be careful that you are not led astray; for many will come in My name saying, I am He! and, The time is at hand! Do not go out after them.*

Contrary to popular belief Santa Claus is not coming to town, the Tooth Fairy is not visiting tonight and Peter Cotton Tail is not hopping down the bunny trail. Nevertheless Christ did tell His disciples in John 14: 2 & 3 In *my Father's house are many mansions if it were not so, I would have told you. I go to prepare a place for you. And if I go and prepare a place for you, I will come again and will receive you to Myself, that where I am you may be also.* How awesome is that? There is actually a place far greater than this place that is prepared for us. Not only has this Man given His life for the entire world but He has left to go to prepare a place for all of those who believe in Him. None of the aforementioned characters could even come close to the promises made by our Lord and Savior. Yet we encourage our children to believe in a figure that can neither redeem nor save.

THIRTEEN

No time like the present

So where do we go from here? Do we perpetuate the traditions and lies of our past or move forward? I vote to move forward because the past is complete and cannot be undone. You may even wish for the chance to do it all over again, but would you do better, would you be the same person, more importantly would you be the person that God wants you to be. Contrary to what people may say or think about you God is not through with you yet, that is if you have allowed Him to start the molding process.

The thing that gets me about change is the boisterous way in which we broadcast it to others through New Year's resolutions or some other pompous affair. I'm not saying that change isn't good but when we boast about what we want to change or how we are going to change, we rob God of all His due glory. Change is like a pregnancy it goes through different phases and once announced it becomes an event seen and witnessed by all.

So when you are going through and you are being molded by God what do you do?

"You stand and press." *Stand fast in the liberty wherewith Christ has made us free, and be not entangled again with the things that may entrap us* Galatians 5:1. *And we press toward the mark for the prize of the high calling of God in Christ,* Philippians 3:14. The means to stand and press must be done by faith. When situations look impossible and you can't even contemplate a way out stand

and press. The road may be difficult but it is not a unique one. Christ has already suffered the things that we have gone through or are going through.

So what are some of the things that we may encounter? What are some of the things we may have to endure because of the vindictiveness of others? Solomon warns us of the abominable acts that are done in the world; these are obstacles for believers if they choose to deal with them without divine help, and as stated in scripture they are detested by God: they are the counter balance for success, and they are: *a proud look, a lying tongue, hands that shed innocent blood, a heart that plots evil plans, feet hurrying to run to mischief, a false witness who breathes lies, and he who causes strife among brothers,* Proverbs 6:16.The afore- mentioned are provoking to God. He hates them and it would be wise for us to hate them as well, not just in others but also in ourselves if they may be present.

If we were to take the time to examine situations surrounding us we would notice at least one, if not all, of these repulsive acts taking place daily. God sees the actions and intention of every man, rewards those that are good and judges that which is evil. It would be fitting and good for our souls if we would embrace holiness and live to become sanctified in the eyes of the Lord. Find favor with God, do those things that are pleasing to Him. Surround yourself with a mentor/people that have found favor with God and you will find yourself being blessed and a blessing. It is also noteworthy to mention at this time a lesson I'd learned and that is that holiness begets holiness and corruption begets corruption. God in His infinite wisdom will allow one's heart to be changed before He changes your situation. How can you say that, you might ask? Have you ever seen a physically challenged person with a debilitating condition and yet their hearts are still filled with joy. Maybe you have seen someone imprisoned but they act as though they are free. My only reply that could explain their cheerful behavior, the Spirit of God was upon them.

The bible calls those things which are corruptible that we engage in or that engages us "Works". Galatians 5:18-21 tells us *But if you be led of the Spirit, you are not under the law. Now the works of the flesh are evident, which are these; adultery, fornication, uncleanness, lasciviousness (sexually unrestrained), idolatry, witchcraft, hatred, variance, emulations, wrath, strife, seditions, heresies, envying, murders, drunkenness, reveling, and the like of which I tell you before, as I have also told you in time past, that they which do such things shall not inherit the kingdom of God.*

Wisdom of the law is important it makes us conscious of forever present sin. We need not look far to see the corruptible acts. They are in every hamlet, street corner; they are transmitted into our homes and undoubtedly have made their way to the hearts and minds of our young people. This very country is in darkness. It has forsaken its first love, God. At the conception and birth of this nation God was foremost in the minds of its founders, but now they have allowed immoral acts and corruption to run rampant. It rewards evil acts and lessen the praises for honorable deeds. In contrast to this the Lord Jesus has called for us to be perfect, even as our Father which is in heaven is perfect.

This perfection is worked in us by the Holy Spirit because Galatians 5:22 & 23 tells us *but the fruit(the work or the accomplishments) of the Spirit is love, joy, peace, longsuffering, gentleness, goodness, faith, meekness, and temperance against such there is no law.* Please note that there is no law against (Godly) loving someone too much, but there is one against lasciviousness, adultery, and fornication. None against joy but Paul preaches that there is against hate. I think my point is validated. Christ continues to tell His believers to let their light shine so that those observing may see their good works and ultimately glorify God. When we present to those that seek Christ those works / fruits that the Holy Spirit accomplishes in us then God is truly glorified. As for light it does not have to be pointed out in the darkness and when light comes forth darkness and those acquainted with it are put to shame. This light and/or wisdom are of God and He would not allow it to be haphazardly found. It is a trait too powerful to possess and to not have an understanding of its dynamics. It is granted to those that are in the seasons of God that is when He sees fit. Yet Christ instructs us in Matthew 7:7, 8 to *Ask, and it shall be given to you; seek, and you shall find; knock, and it shall be opened unto you. For every one that ask receives; and he that seeks find; and to him that knock it shall be opened.*

There are attributes of the Spirit He shares with humanity and yet there are some He alone can only possess. After analyzing these attributes I can understand why we as humans cannot have them. The power within them is too great. We are not far from the works/acts mentioned in Galatians; they seem to be woven into the fabric that makes us a nation and a people. So in my disgust I sat and wrote "Of Thee I scream"

These are great and terrible times; we stand idle
And watch as others fall to wicked schemes.
The brave ones were killed because they gave birth to
    Dreams.
Together, but united we do not stand;
Within these broken borders we are a battered and burning
    land.
Masked as one nation, indivisible under God;
Our amber waves of grain have become fields of looted
    shame.
O' land where our fathers died, wet with tears our mothers
    cried.
Of thee I scream.
Our doors are wide open; enemies come and go as they
    please;

Stripping you of your beauty, bringing you slowly to your
    knees.
Your rulers are perverted, even in sleep they are depraved;
Wealth has become their god, sin has made them slaves.
The torch of Lady Liberty is extinguished; her wick has been
    removed;
She plays harlot for the highest bid, by many she is abused.
Selfishness is the disease that eats away at her heart;
Showing charity in the sun and nurturing evil in the dark.
Not honor but your disgrace from sea to shining sea;
Immoral nation repent and truly be set free.
O' land for which my Savior died, wet with tears His mother
    cried.
Of thee I scream. Of thee I do scream
My country it is of thee; no longer a true democracy,
An escalating hypocrisy, stagnated bureaucracy.
Greed is the sin that they try to hide; shrouded with
    stubborn pride.
Justifying lies within to gain praise of wealthy friends.
O' land where our fathers died, wet with tears our mothers
    cried;
Of thee I scream. Of thee I scream

It was difficult to start this chapter because I was baffled over
whether it was the end or whether it was the beginning of a new
ending. Yet again I say in all things "God is good."

I can say confidently that I do not resent or regret my life, but
rather I resent and regret some of the decisions I have made in
it. If only I had pursued wisdom instead of women the outcome
would have been different. If this novel gains me not one dime,
God will still be glorified; it will also serve as a testament to my
sons just as the words of Solomon did for his children.

Solomon tells his children that wisdom is the principal thing;
therefore, get wisdom and with all their getting get understanding.
Not only pursue it, but obtain it because all that you may ever
need or desire can be had when you obtain Godly wisdom. The
world tells us that we have the right to life, liberty and the pursuit

of happiness, but she only offers oppression, misery, and death. In nature only the strong survives, the weak are killed, but in the Kingdom of God the meek shall inherit the earth. In business it is said, "You have to step over a few people to get to the top," but in the Kingdom of God whosoever humbles himself as a little child, is greatest in the kingdom of heaven. Every true child of God believes what He says about our present situation, and that is that it is temporary. This world is not our home.

Heaven and earth shall pass away; but His word will not, in knowing that I am assured of this, that there is power in His words. "Let there be, peace be still, take up thy bed, only believe," are a few of the phrases spoken by Him and they all displayed His eternal power.

So how is this wisdom obtained? Proverbs 9: 10 declare that *the fear of the Lord is the beginning of wisdom and the knowledge of the Holy One is understanding.* Fear but not that kind that we associate with terror or terrorism. God doesn't want us afraid. Many times He has said to those he approached, "Be not afraid." So why fear? I offer this analogy- father and son.

As a father there is a certain amount of fear I want my kids to have of me. I am the authority figure in their life. I am not their best friend. I can't punish my best friend. So a line has to be drawn when it comes to our relationship. (God said to the children of Israel, "You will be my people and I will be your God). It is a respectful fear, a respectful fear of authority. It is knowing that if they do something wrong just punishment can be administered. As a father I cannot be separated from disciplinarian; it is who and what I am given charge to do, along with providing, educating, nurturing and loving. Do you see the symbolism? Fear produces obedience. Several of the psalms and proverbs list rewards that are revealed when a person fears the Lord.

Psalms 19:9 *The fear of the LORD is clean, enduring forever: the judgments of the LORD are true and righteous altogether.*

Psalms 111:10 *The fear of the LORD is the beginning of wisdom: a good understanding have all they that do his commandments: His praise endures forever.*

Proverbs 1:7 *The fear of the LORD is the beginning of knowledge but fools despise wisdom and instruction.*

Proverbs 8:13 *The fear of the LORD is to hate evil, pride and arrogance, and the evil way, and the perverted mouth, do I hate.*

Proverbs 9:10 *The fear of the LORD is the beginning of wisdom and the knowledge of the Holy One is understanding.*

Proverbs 10:27 *The fear of the LORD prolongs days but the years of the wicked shall be shortened.*

Proverbs 14:26 *In the fear of the LORD is strong confidence and his children shall have a place of refuge.*

Proverbs 14:27 *The fear of the LORD is a fountain of life, to depart from the snares of death.*

Proverbs 15:33 *The fear of the LORD is the instruction of wisdom and before honor is humility.*

Proverbs 19:23 *The fear of the LORD tends to life and he that hath it shall abide satisfied; he shall not be visited with evil.*

People spend their entire lives in the pursuit of happiness and may never find it. They chase the ideology of obtaining the perfect job, the perfect spouse, living in the perfect neighborhood and raising the perfect family and fail to see the importance of the perfect spiritual life. God gives us the key and it is found in Proverbs 3:13-16 *"Happy is the man who finds wisdom, and the man who gets understanding. For its profit is better than the gain from silver, and its increase more than fine gold. She is more precious than rubies, and all the things you can desire are not to be compared with her. Length of days is in her right hand, riches and honor in her left hand.*" Discovering the Wisdom of God brings happiness but it is hinged on three consistencies: Searching, Finding and Understanding. The one who searches for it must find it, not only that but they must understand its principles in order to benefit from her treasures. Remember "Ask, seek and knock."

There is no time like the present to search out Godly wisdom. Satan has entire generations busy with matters so irrelevant that they can't focus on the important issue at hand. I've noticed here in the past ten plus years that video games have captured the interest of not only our children, but a growing number of adult men. Fantasy has been masked to look far greater than reality, and therefore, many hours of the day are spent entrenched in activities that prevent them from obtaining the wisdom God wants them to have. You can't search, find and understand it all on Sunday morning in the pews of a watered down sermon and resume the games on Monday and expect the benefits of a blessing. A conscientious effort must be made and a desire for spiritual maturity is essential.

With spiritual maturity your discernment of super-natural hindrances are honed. What is moral versus what's immoral becomes a governing force. Your connection and awareness of the inner being takes precedence. Your interest is as those which can be found in Galatians.

Remember those fruits *love, joy, peace, patience, kindness, goodness, faithfulness, Gentleness (meekness, humility), self-control. Against such things there is no law.*

Paul goes on to admonish them by telling them. "If by the Holy Spirit we have our life in God, let us go forward walking circumspectly, with our actions and conduct controlled by the Holy

Spirit." Being controlled by the spirit is the noticeable difference between those in Christ and those in the world. Christians are governed by love; the world is governed by lust. The desire of love is to give, but the desire of lust is to get.

Contrary to most people's belief Satan doesn't necessarily have to have you addicted   although he wants to. If he can just keep you distracted; one more pull on the lever with a chance of winning big, one more drag on a cigarette to calm your nerves or one more drink to knock the edge off is how it is disguised. In knowing his tactics we become familiar with the tactician. His cruel deceptive tactic gives the impression that everything is fine and then from out of nowhere absolute chaos and mayhem is unleashed. It presents itself so swiftly that there is hardly, if any, time to respond. Therefore we react, our emotions take control and often we find ourselves in a more pressing situation, but if we had prepared, if we were walking in the spirit and being guided by Him our decisions would have been guided. The situation could be negated entirely.

1Peter 5:8 gives this warning as it pertains to Satan. *Be sober; be vigilant; because your adversary the devil walks about as a roaring lion, seeking whom he may devour.* If he is walking about looking to consume then I / we should be as observant and expecting his worst. Yet our connection to the Holy Spirit should be so firm that we are able to withstand his fiery darts. My investment for protection is in the whole armament of God. It is completely functional, it never goes out of style, nor can you wear it out, one size truly fits all and it has been tried and tested under some of the most arduous conditions known to man. Satan has a wicked arsenal and we as believers of the most high God are offered the best when it comes to combat.

Every soldier needs a belt (truth), a good belt needs no other support it is self-sufficient and just like the truth it will always bind. A sturdy breastplate (integrity) is essential because oftentimes the devil's attack is aimed directly at the heart where the integrity of man is stored and if you are without it you are susceptible to defeat. The proper shoes (the gospel of peace), are good for all, everyone needs to have the gospel employed upon them so that they may be dispatched at anytime with the Good News. Behind every strong shield (faith), is a soldier relying on its strength. Our faith in God should be as visible as the shield that protects them. A soldier in battle without a helmet (salvation) is a soldier without hope and is doomed from the beginning. Without an implement of war a soldier is worthless, for it is with the sword (the word of God) that wins the battle. A soldier who is completely dressed for battle knows the importance of having all of these tools in his ministry as well as his life.

As with all of my thoughts I felt that this one was most difficult to write, but I wanted to try and capture it poetically. I wanted it to convey the overlooked persona of the fallen angel. His beguilement and craftiness that has imprisoned so many for so long moved me to simply entitle this poem "Enemy".

O' formidable foe of mine indeed;
Peace of mind and progress he wishes to impede.
Devoid of truth and full of lies;
Deceptive and deceitful but pleasure is his disguise.
A tongue filled with emptiness;
Equal only to his heart.
A master of illusions;
Working delusions in the dark.
Infallible fabricator of twisted and broken dreams;
Proverbial persecutor of frantic dying screams.
Father of forbidden fruit, so easy to obtain;
Sweet is its nectar, which leaves a bitter stain.
Cunning and clever a tactician of calamity;
Wanting nothing more than to sow his own misery.
Antagonistic angel cast into Hades from on high;
Placed there by God, the Creator whom you would defy.
O' adversary of mine your deeds are not kind;
But my God holds the keys to death and hell to which you
    are confined.
Conquered and defeated; a foot stool for His heels;
I'm no longer a sheep for the slaughter or a lamb to be killed.

I have shared in Christ suffering and He has made me a son.
He has assured me of the outcome and through Him I have
won.

On the other hand if you have accepted Christ as your
Lord and Savior then what awaits you is a mansion (John 14:2).
Philippians 3:15 goes on to tell us *So let those [of us] who are spiritually
mature and full-grown have this mind and hold these convictions; and if in
any respect you have a different attitude of mind, God will make that clear
to you also.* The mind set is in reference to the previous scripture
in which Paul encourages the church of Philippi to persevere, to
press toward the goal of learning and believing in the wonders of
Christ; to strive for perfection and to forget those things which
are behind so that we can obtain those things which are ahead
of us.

Both Christ and Satan have a future; if you choose not to
repent then your future is as bleak as Satan's. Joy once confessed
to me that she couldn't understand a God that would not allow
her to love whomever she wanted to love. In defense, I told her
that God does not have a problem with you loving anyone, but
morally a man is given to a woman and a woman to a man. When
we abuse what God has given us then He is displeased. I would
have to insert that love is not as complex as we make it. Love is
simple. When love is spoken actions follow. "God so loved that He
gave". It doesn't matter if we don't understand it, the thing is that
we embrace it, understanding comes later. The process in which
understanding comes is sometimes lengthy, but when we began
to understand love, we are granted more insight to how great a
walk with the Lord can be.

Our past should not be the thing that causes us to falter. If
anything it should be a great catalyst for learning and a testament
of where God has brought us from. You cannot change your

past but what you see, hear and believe about Christ can help you in developing your future. Evil, corrupt men and women have repented and come to Christ, yet it is difficult for society to receive them. They are forever condemned and forever persecuted for their wrong- doing. It even took me some time to forgive Joy for what she put me through. I remember becoming a bitter and malicious person, wishing a house would fall on her or anything that would cause her harm. It's ironic that when someone hurts you emotionally that you want physical harm to come to them. Such a fleshy response to an emotional situation; so what is the remedy? I can only offer this analogy.

I started smoking in 1990 and I can remember the evening well. I was atop of an A-1 Abram tank on a shooting range in Ft. Hood, Texas. The day had been filled with great trepidation on whether our nation would be going to war or not. More so on whether our unit would be hitting the sands. The sun was going down and a buddy (Eric) had joined me. The two of us sat listening to a radio I kept with me to keep up with what was going on in the news while we were in the field. The commentator returned after a commercial and announced, "America is at war." I looked over at Eric and said, "Man give me one of those cigarettes, if I'm going to go and die for my country I'm going out trying everything I can." He laughed and passed me my first cig. I told you that to say this I quit smoking sixteen years later, but not before irreparable damage had been done. The cravings for the nicotine were so strong that I thought I would never quit. Then God gave me this revelation, "Deny your flesh." Be encouraged in knowing that, *"Therefore, there is now no condemnation for those who are in Christ Jesus, who live [and] walk not after the dictates of the flesh, but after the dictates of the Spirit.* Romans 8:1.

There comes a time when the inner spirit becomes mature and realizes that there is nothing good in our flesh. We are formed from the dust or dirt of the earth and shall return, and thus the very breath that was breathe into man has to return to its rightful owner, God.

The carnality of man is enmity with God; resentful, resisting and rebellious to the spirit. Remember the two are contrary to one another and are constantly warring. These earthen vessels are in bondage to sin, but we are liberated by Christ Jesus in our belief and His shed blood.

The process of walking in the spirit is a matter of choice, maturity, faith and not sight.

I am most certain that there are situations we would refuse to put ourselves in simply because it looks bad. Recalling the event when Christ was seen walking on water; Peter a fisherman had probably never thought about walking on water. His desire was to be with or walk with Christ, and with Christ all things are possible. Notice Christ didn't summon or demand him to come out of the ship. Our free will is not a thing He wishes to control, but rather Peter asked Lord if it is you allow me to come walk with you. Christ simply replied, "Come". Peter was perfectly safe in the ship, and more so as he walked with Him. He wants you to follow Him because you want to, not because He makes you.

When you think of some of the things you were made or forced to do and didn't understand them, they didn't settle so well with you did they? Yet when we believe in Him and He gives us a glimpse of Who He is the ability to trust is far better and therefore we walk without doubt. We are able to stand even when the winds are boisterous because He has proven to us that He will not allow us to go under.

Some people experience adverse ordeals in their lives that it brings them to a point of growth. They ultimately see the benefits of surrendering to Christ versus kicking against the pricks. Doing it their way for so long with no sight of accomplishment becomes apparent and the conclusive scenario for success seems stark in comparison. Consequently, their faith is activated and no matter what they are faced with they can't revert to the old mode of operation; it has proven not to work. They know this with all of their being they sense that the old way is not even an option, and therefore they began to walk by faith and not by sight. Take for instance Abraham and Sarah of the Old Testament. I won't go into detail you can read his story in the book of Genesis 13 chapter. It all started with a promise that God made to him. "*This one shall not be your heir, but one who come from your own body shall be your heir,*" Genesis 15:4. With a barren wife and them both being well advanced in age God took what seemed impossible by any standard and did the possible. Sarah birth a male child to Abraham who they named Isaac. But Sarah doubted the Lord God, she even laughed at the thought. In Genesis 18:14 God posed a unique question to Abraham, "Is anything too hard for the Lord?" Unequivocally the response should have been no, but as God would have it His will would be done to prove to Sarah and establish with Abraham an everlasting covenant.

"Serene" was a poem that came to me as I thought of how we were initially established as a people. The rise and fall of Adam and Eve, the preservation of Noah and his family and the promise to Abraham are events that God had a hand in. If given the chance He would love to manifest Himself in ways you could not even imagine. The greatest thing man could ever need can be found with God through His Son Jesus Christ. Imagine a problem you may have encountered in your life. Now imagine no hope of a solution. God is omniscient He knows all that we need, all we may desire, and most importantly what is best for us. We should never think our heavenly Father would ask us to pray, and then refuse to hear us, nor give to us what would be harmful. The relationship that God anticipates having with us is one of communion, one in which He shares His creation.

> Walk with me Lord because alone I do not stand a chance.
> Allow me to abide with You Lord despite my circumstance.
> Speak to me Lord because I need to hear Your voice;
> And when faced with opposition assist me in my choice.
> Bridle my thoughts and seize hold of my eager tongue;
> Replace them with praise and the words of my mouth with
>   a song.
> Listen to me Lord; hear me when I cry;
> And if I should fail, encourage me when I try.
> Wash me Lord Jesus; cleanse me from my sin;
> Do not let Hades become my soul's end.
> Touch me Lord God and relieve me from my iniquity;
> Restore unto me Your righteousness, peace and serenity.
> Give unto me thine Eden; as in the days of old.
> Commune with me again and ease my weary soul.

A man once told me, "Do what you can and if you can do more do it." I wish that I could take credit for what I'm about to share with you, but they were shared with me by an on-line friend. Besides the authors are anonymous; yet they still hold a great amount of truth.

"Many people want to serve God, But only as advisors."

"If the church wants a better pastor, it only needs to pray for the one it has."

"God Himself does not propose to judge A man until he is dead. So why should you?"

"We were called to be witnesses, not judges."

"Be ye fishers of men. You catch them, God will clean them."

"Never place a question mark where God has placed a period."

"God doesn't call the qualified, He qualifies the called."

"God loves everyone, but probably prefers fruit of the spirit over religious nuts."

How do I end this? When do I place the parchment and quill away? I think now. All that I have done, all I have witnessed has been disclosed. I know nothing else to share with you but this.

For God so loved the world, that he gave his only begotten Son, that whosoever believeth in him should not perish, but have everlasting life. For God send not his Son into the world to condemn the world; but that the world through him might be saved. He that believeth on him is not condemned: but he that believeth not is condemned already, because he hath not believed in the name of the only begotten Son of God. John 3:16-18.

Lord God, I pray right now that You will bless those who call on your holy name. And simply do as Your word says You would do. Save those who believe in Your Son. Let Your word alone be the only word that governs the hearts of men and women and allow this to be testament of what You have done for me and what You can and will do for others. May this novel, I pray, not become a hindrance to anyone trying to have a relationship with You. I pray that You are glorified with every letter, word, phrase, sentence, paragraph and chapter written. Thank You God for choosing me to touch the hearts of individuals I may never meet. To You God be the glory forever and ever. And again I say let the words of my mouth, and the meditation of my heart, be acceptable in Your sight.

SCRIPTURE INDEX

AS THEY APPEAR BY CHAPTERS

ORIGINAL POEMS FROM THE WRITER

AS THEY APPEAR BY CHAPTERS

Chapter One
"A Rose Petal's Confession" "Reminiscence"

Chapter Two
"How Much"

Chapter Three
"The Kiss" "Certain As the Sun"

Chapter Five
"Uncertainty" "Chaotic Asylum"

Chapter Six
"Love No More"

Chapter Seven
"Hope" "The Sweetest Dream" "Duality"

Chapter 8
"If and When" "Unwinding Roads"

Chapter 9
"A Priceless Portrait" "Epistle to Mary" "Brother"

ADDITIONAL ORIGINAL
POEMS FROM THE WRITER

"My Err"
On Valentine's Day I fail to express that I truly care
The feelings were present and so was the time;
But the words just were not there.
Words unspoken,
Promises were broken,
Neither a kiss nor hug did we share
I'm sorry seemed so insufficient;
But forgive me for my err

Our anniversary came and passed;
It's been a trying three full years
And many times I've watched you,
Your face flowing with tears
Thoughts unspoken
Vows were broken,
Neither a word nor sound that I care
I'm sorry seemed so inadequate;
But forgive me for my err.

I can't change that of yesterday,
And tomorrow is but a distant dream,
So let me tell you today precisely what I mean
I love you. I need you.
Only kisses and hugs I will sway,
And if I must I'll tell you for life,
Each and every day.

ADDITIONAL ORIGINAL POEMS FROM THE WRITER

"Vice versa"
What I hide is on the inside;
But my eyes make known what I feel.
What I suffer I can't shield;
Because my heart is open wide.

What's inside I can't hide;
Because the eyes are the windows to my soul.
What I grasp I can't control;
Because my mind is filled with pride.

What I reveal I can't conceal;
But my mouth expresses what I pray.
What I speak I can't betray;
Because my soul is at ease with zeal.

What I conceal I can't reveal;
Because my word is my bond.
What I've done it can't be undone;
Because my body no longer has the will.

ADDITIONAL ORIGINAL POEMS FROM THE WRITER

"I will sleep"
What great fortune or misfortune will this day bring?
Will I find joy in a song that the bluebird sings?
Will I be warmed by the sun,
Will clouds linger like thoughts in my mind
Dark and ominous ones.
Are the winds contrary; do they stir autumn leaves?
Or do they blow like kisses on a beautiful summer's eve
Will the day be as pleasant, as pleasant as a first Love;
Reminiscent of those you could not see enough of
I pray that she's not atrocious, brutal, bitter or cold;
But calming, relaxing and comforting to my soul.
If she has no promise of peace and all appears to be somber;
Then I shall slumber, I shall slumber.

And of that great day will doves fly or will ravens cry;
Will the sun or clouds dominate the sky?
Will I be acclaimed by my sons,
Will memories remain like bellowing flames;
Bright and illuminating ones.
Will the winds be contrary for no man knows at all;
Be it summer, spring, winter or fall.
The day will be dismal for some nevertheless;
Reminiscent of those that you came to detest.
I pray that she's not atrocious, brutal, bitter or cold;
But calming, relaxing and comforting to my soul.
If she has no promise of peace and all appears to be bleak;
Then I will sleep, I will sleep.

ADDITIONAL ORIGINAL
POEMS FROM THE WRITER

"Un-caged"
Love or hate to what degree;
The intensity can be the same.
Emotions totally different?
But when unleashed they can
Hardly be contained.
I love you, I hate you;
Spoken in the same breath.
I can love you for life or
Hate you till death.
Compassion seeks to build up,
Rage looks to destroy;
With only a situation governing
Which to deploy.
Filled with blissful love or
Consumed by a burning rage;
Both are characteristics that can
Never be caged.
Suppress them if you will
The end results are sole;
Love can't be cage and rage
Can't be controlled.
But man has the canny ability
To administer them as he please;
To love a little, to hate a little
And to give them in unvarying
degrees.

ABOUT THE WRITER

I have been both son and father, student and teacher, as well as follower and leader, congregant and preacher, friend and foe and now reader and writer. Unquestionably the latter of these have been the most difficult. In my present occupation as a fire suppression captain I try to lead by example; drawing from those great leaders before me. As a father not having the best earthly role model to draw from I gathered the majority of parental skills from my heavenly Father. Mom played a large part as well. Thanks Mom.

So from the stand point of not wanting to sound arrogant in my meager and modest accomplishments I felt it only appropriate for those who have known me to write as such. The assignment was given to the people I truly, truly love. I ask God to bless them continually and I thank them from the depth of my heart.

My husband is my friend and he has been since grade school. Even then I had a crush on him. We remained good friends over the years; we saw each other go through other relationships and two awful marriages between the both of us. Through it all I've seen Tommy grow into a very good and intelligent man. We dated for about seven years and have been married presently for four. I think that I'm very blessed to have him as my husband. I'm glad he overlooked his doubts and some of the advice he received giving our love a chance. He is great with his three boys and he puts them before everything. - Le

My son is a man that I greatly admire. As a young man he has been through so much but his passion has pushed him to achieve much. He is very thoughtful and places the needs of others first.

I have seen him brought to tears, with hurt and anger due to the issues of life, but he has managed to internalize his heartache and use it for the glory of God. I am blessed by God with a great gift to have a son who is as compassionate and giving as Tommy.

When I think of what I would miss the most about my son if he were not in my life, it would have to be the sweet kiss that he places on my forehead every time he greets me. - Mom

My daddy is …..Well I say he is the best father any three boys could have. He tries to give us things he never had when he was our age, and if you ask me he is very good at it. My dad lets me get away with a little bit of stuff, but at the same time he shows me and my two little brothers right from wrong. If it was not for my dad I might have been one of those thugs you see on the corner everyday. I thank him for getting onto me about stuff like that. - Trey

My daddy is a great father. He got me an Xbox for Christmas and I really thank him. I brag about how he is a great dad. He is there for me when I need help with anything. He might fuss, he might get mad but in his heart and mine we still love each other. - Michael

My dad is very cool. He gives me presents. He teaches me things I need to know. He teaches me reading, math and social studies. He lends me money. He raised me to. Thank you so much daddy. – Tyrek

My brother is an innovative spirit. His worth to those who are blessed to know him is immeasurable. He is a humble man who has achieved great things in the midst of adversities that some

ABOUT THE WRITER continued

would say challenged his whole being. He is a man that is deeply in love with God and shows his profound gratefulness through love for his family and friends. He speaks encouragement that shows his concern for all who encounters his friendship. I am elated to know such a man that I have the pleasure of calling "my brother". - Tina

My brother Tommy is an excellent example of a brother, father, husband, son and friend. He is smart, innovative and a progressive thinker. He is one who lives with the future in mind. His credibility as a father has been proven through the years by the examples he set for his sons. His sons have inherited a lifetime of knowledge from the standards he has already set. His wife and family are proud to say he is a vital part of their lives. - Leeneen

My friend is a tactfully opinionated man toward people and life. I've known him to be that way since childhood and he does it with respect. Life situations have bent Tommy to the limit, but he always finds a way to spring straight up through faith, slapping life's challenges back in its face. You can't break him. For a young man Tommy has acquired some wisdom and is not shy about admitting his mistakes. Being a detailed listener helps when he offers common sense and positive advice to anyone that hears him. I'm proud to say he's my only real life friend, he is more than a friend he's more like a brother. I know when T.A. asks for anything I try my best to accommodate him and many times he has called just to ask what's up with his "old road dog." With that being said I can honestly say that he has helped me and many others, and he has done it without being judgmental. - Derek

My friend Tommy has been my friend for about 12 years. This was the best accident that has happened to me. We did not start out trying to be friends. I met him in 1997 through his cousin. I had a huge crush on him for a long time. Nevertheless being more than friends was not our fate. Over the years we have talked on just about every imaginable life situation. Even though we have not figured out why I am still single, his voice in my life has been astounding. There have been times when I did not agree with some of the decisions he had made or just did not agree with what he was saying about a situation that I was going through, but we never let our opinions get in the way of our respect for each other. I could not and would not ask for anything more than what I get from Tommy. I have a friendship with this man that has lasted longer than everything else in my life. - Lynn

My brother is one of the funniest people I know. He does a number of character impersonations that are hilarious. On one occasion we were going to see my sister in Texas; he started in with his impersonations. I was laughing so hard that I began to get sick; we had to pull over. I've had a rare opportunity to ride with him on the fire truck and it was amazing.

I love my brother to death and I really enjoy being around him in spite of our differences. Laughter is a big part of our relationship it's like good medicine, (Tylenol Extra Strength).

My brother has a deep serious side that is rarely seen. What I like about it is that it's balanced between- serious as a heart attack and funny as hell. He is an outstanding steward, captain, teacher among many other things. He understands that life is not always so serious and he balances it well; that's what I like and admire about my brother. - Ronald

Printed in the United States
by Baker & Taylor Publisher Services